A MASTER MARINER'S TALE

(Third Edition)

by FRED COOPER

ABOUT THIS BOOK

This is County Durham on the wild, rugged north-east coast of England. It is the year of our Lord 1881.

Europe is a boiling cauldron of warring states, fledgling nations, political scheming and meddling in the internal affairs of neighbouring nations. Five major powers hold the fragile peace together. Great Britain, Russia, France, Austria and Germany all watch and wait for the tinderbox to spark and ignite hostilities one nation against another. The German Chancellor, Prince Otto von Bismarck is at the centre of all of the political manoeuvring and meddling in the affairs of other nations and always to the advantage of Germany.

Richard Raine is an experienced master mariner and the captain of the collier brigantine, "The William Thrift" that ships coal from the colliery districts in County Durham to the fuel hungry industrial towns along the east coast. Richard is an honourable man who believes strongly in his principles and is more concerned about his family, the working conditions of his crew, the weather and loyalty to his employer and shipowner Mrs Anderson. He has never shown any interest in the delicate diplomatic issues that plague international affairs and relationships between countries.

The maritime town of Seaham Harbour provides the stage for his story. It was here that the aristocrat, the Marquess of Londonderry, invested a small fortune in 1828, to develop a new harbour that would prove to be the stimulus for the building of a new town. In less than ten years Seaham had become a bustling harbour town bringing in up to fifty sailing collier ships daily and supplying London with coal for their gas supply and power for their business and industry.

The town prospered and grew from the opening of the harbour in 1831. The Marquess of Londonderry provided land for public buildings, churches, and public utilities and as patron of the town he sponsored and financed industrial ventures. It is now 1881, fifty years later. His grandson the 6th Marquess portrays the typical flamboyant and fantastically wealthy playboy born into a privileged world but what secrets were lurking behind this façade? How could the covert activities of this party loving nobleman have any bearing on the security of the nation?

Richard Raine could never have imagined the adventure that was to unfold when he sailed out of Seaham Harbour in April 1881 and the crucial part he would play in maintaining the fragile peace that existed in Queen Victoria's empire. More than a century after these events took place the real story of this reluctant secret agent, "A Master Mariner's Tale", is finally told.

Fred Cooper BSc ACMA CGMA

COPYRIGHT

ISBN 978-1-9160174-2-9

TABLE OF CONTENTS

CHAPTER 1

The brigantine "William Thrift"

Looking out of the cabin window at the blue sky and the gentle, light green rolling waves I think to myself "what a crisp, fresh and bright spring morning". It's going to be a fine day. The sky is clear, the sea is calm and the mercury in the barometer in my cabin is steadily rising. I feel quite optimistic that this voyage from Dundee to Seaham Harbour on the north-east coast of England will be without incident, productive and profitable. I am the master of the "William Thrift" a wooden brigantine built at Perth, Scotland in the year 1852. My ship is designed and engineered to survive a hard life in the coal trade and is 112 feet from bow to stern with a beam of 25 feet and built of English elm and oak with 3-½ inch pitch pine for deck planking. Like most collier sailing ships, she does not have a figurehead and is flat bottomed so that she can settle on the harbour bed if necessary. She is a seaworthy, watertight and trim vessel which displaces 151 tons gross and she is the property of Mrs Elizabeth Anderson of 28 Marlborough Street, Seaham Harbour. Mrs Anderson is a demanding but fair owner and a good businesswoman who can always find a cargo from one port to next on the east coast of England and Scotland. My pay as "Master" is sufficient to provide me with a comfortable life style and allows me to provide savings for my pension; eight pounds ten shillings per voyage while the crew sail for a 30-day month at five pounds ten shillings for the Mate and three pounds ten shillings for an Able-Bodied Seaman.

All the crew eat at the table in my cabin and enjoy the same meals and portions as myself prepared by Bob Mustard our self-taught cook who can serve wholesome but simple and tasty meals. The master's accommodation is not unusual for a vessel of this type. My cabin is set in the aft triangle of the ship and is entered down a companionway that makes a 90-degree turn in about 9 feet of fall. It is cramped but comfortable and the two cabin sides are fitted with narrow hard upholstered seats. In the centre of the room is a large oak table with six upholstered chairs and my bunk is neatly fitted against one wall.

The Master's cabin in the brigantine "William Thrift"

A skylight occupies part of the deck head and below it swings two large oil lamps with a compass fixed at the aft end of the skylight. I can hear the helmsman at his station above and the creak of the steering gear aft. I carry very few personal possessions because of the cramped accommodation I have to endure. All of my clothing is kept dry and secure in a traditional oak sailor's chest at the foot of my bed and my sextant, tide charts and maps are stored in a narrow chest of drawers underneath the table in the centre of the cabin.

Dividing the master and crew accommodation is 70 feet of cargo hold in three separate hatches. Each hatch has a separate cover that is made waterproof and airtight with oil tarpaulins. My crew understand the importance of making the hold airtight after they witnessed the hold of the schooner "Lagonna" spontaneously ignite with the combination of friction from movement of coals and a plentiful oxygen supply from badly fitted hatch covers. Forward of the hold is the galley and built into the forward bulkhead is a cast iron stove and fireplace which is used for cooking and heating. Next-door to the galley is the mate's cabin – with his bedhead backing on to the stove wall – the warmest place on the ship. Next door are the crew quarters which are sparse and cramped but that is not unusual as ship-owners design ships to carry cargo not crew. Nevertheless, the space available accords with Mercantile Law requirements so the crew don't complain and in any case with watch duties there are only ever two crew members in there at any one time.

The Crew Quarters

I have been promised a new maritime water closet by the owner but apparently this newly patented toilet is in such demand it may be some months before it is delivered and fitted. All in all, in my experience of sailing ships and crew, this is as comfortable as any ship I have sailed and the crew seem to be happy enough with their conditions and my command.

Bob Mustard the ship's cook and steward has just taken away my breakfast dish – hot steaming porridge and a mug of tea –standard fare to start a working day whilst at sea depending of course on whether the cook is able to light the cast iron stove. This is not always possible in heavy seas and an unappetising alternative when the stove cannot be lit is sea biscuits, twice baked so they do not go mouldy, and water or perhaps yesterday's bread with a portion of cheese. The ship's complement is a crew of five, including myself, and they have all breakfasted and are about their duties. George Marwick, ship's mate, an Orcadian from Stromness has already briefed me on the provisions we need when we make harbour. George is thirteen years older than me but an old, experienced hand of fifty-two who has been mate on board sailing vessels for over twenty-five years. A ship is more than just a vessel with masts, sails and cargo to George. It is a lifelong companion. For more than ten years he worked on a square-rigged, ocean-going barquentine carrying supplies and workers from London and the eastern counties to Orkney where they re-provisioned before setting off for the Hudson Bay Company and Nova Scotia in Canada. He has a handsome blue anchor tattooed on his left forearm – the mariner's insignia that he has sailed the Atlantic Ocean. We have been discussing the future of Tom Colling, one of my two Able Bodied seamen, who has asked George what he needs to do to get his "mates' tickets". It has been quite a while since I visited these regulations so I have written them down for Tom to study. The regulations read: -

"Under the provisions of the "Merchant Shipping Act 1856 no home trade ship can obtain clearance to legally proceed to sea from any port in the United

Kingdom unless the master and mate have obtained a valid certificate of competency.

An "only" mate must be nineteen years of age and have been five years at sea. He must be able to write in a legible hand and understand the first five rules of arithmetic and the use of logarithms. He must be able to work a day's work complete, including bearings and distance of the port he is bound to, by Mercator's method; to correct the sun's declination for longitude, and find his latitude by meridian altitude of the sun and to work such other easy problems of a like nature as may be put to him. He must understand the use of the sextant. In seamanship he must know how to moor and unmoor, and to keep a clear anchor, to carry out an anchor, to stow a hold and to make requisite entries in the ships log. He will also be questioned as to his knowledge of the mortar and rocket lines in the case of the stranding of a vessel."

Tom Colling is twenty years old - a Seaham lad who has only been at sea for two years – so he needs to have at least another three years' service in a sailing ship. It will probably take that time for Tom to brush up on his arithmetic, learn to use logarithms and master the compass and sextant. As master I had to be twenty-one years old, six years at sea, of which one year was as mate and at least one years' experience in a square-rigged ship. I needed to be able to navigate by the stars and was examined in the laws of the tides, soundings and depths, navigating lights and management of crew including health and safety issues. Tom is hard working and much more intelligent than everyday sailors of his age but he has a long way to go before he will be ready to sit a first mate's examination. However, he has no other pastime to occupy himself with when he is not on watch so if he perseveres with his studies, I am sure he could become a good first mate in time.

Climbing up the companionway I step on deck and draw up the collar on my reefer jacket as a fresh, chilly breeze brushes my face. The time is 7:35 am and the dawn is just breaking over the horizon to the east. To the west I can make out the harbour and town lights of Seaham. The town stands in a break in the coastal cliffs that rise to heights of 45 to 55 feet. A light is shining from a prominent structure, about 30 feet high, standing on the head of the north breakwater. About one mile north-west of the harbour entrance stands a conspicuous chimney and along the coast on the south side of the harbour the sky is red from the several blast furnace ovens and chemical works at Watson Town, an area on the periphery of Dawdon. This harbour is affectionately known by ship captains as "The Hole-in-the-Wall" because of the nature of its construction. Unlike most harbours which lie in a bluff or a bay Seaham Harbour was cut out of the limestone cliffs and ships ride into the dock with their topgallant mast-heads just below the cliff top.

South East view of Seaham Harbour in 1881

A harbour is the scene of the business end in the life of a ship. But there are good docks, bad docks, pretty docks and inhospitable and dangerous docks. One common feature of all docks is the timber like structures, scaffold like beams engrained with gritty coal dust whose sole purpose is to drop coals into the heart of a ship as quickly as possible so it can sail out on the next tide. I have always thought of Seaham Harbour as a good dock which has a fine history. This town was built as a result of the docks; they rely one on the other for their very existence.

"Good morning, Captain, I love these spring mornings when you can feel the ship rising and falling with the gently swell, don't you?" Billy Booth chirps without looking up from splicing the rope he is repairing.

Billy is just seventeen years old and a few years younger than Tom Colling. Although they went to the same school, he is clearly not the academic sort and has shown no interest in the technical aspects of seamanship although he is responding well to the day-to-day work of an ordinary seaman. His blonde hair, fair complexion and wiry build make him look younger than his years but surprisingly he is quite strong and agile. Unlike the Royal Navy the merchant marine has no formal dress or uniform and sailors wear what is practical, comfortable, hard-wearing and warm. Course serge trousers cover his legs to just below the knee and a white rough cotton shirt is tied at the waist with a faded yellow scarf. Like most sailors he favours white canvas shoes but his are fraying around the toes and have seen better days. "Aye Billy" I replied "That feeling of floating on a moving deck attracted me to a life at sea when I was even younger than you. The favourite part of any voyage when I was your age was when there was a rough swell and the jib boom dipped into tumbling frothy waves but I have mellowed since then. Give me a calm, flat sea with a following southerly breeze any day." Billy smiled as he gazed at the newly repaired rope with satisfaction and furled it tidily.

"Go and see if Bob has any more tea" I asked acknowledging his repair with a nod" I will be in my cabin" and before I had turned to climb down the companionway, he was half way along the ship heading for the galley.

It is time to make an entry in the ships log and to look up my "harbour notes" on the particular aspects of entering this harbour. Although I have done it many times in the past this part of the coast and in particular the fairway channel into harbour has a number of hazards and requires great care. My entry in the log reads: -

Sunday 3rd April 1881. Time 0735 hours. Lying at anchor off Seaham Harbour (54deg 50min North, 1deg 19min West). Wind, south-westerly, light. Cargo - timber for Lord Londonderry's collieries and silver sand for the Bottle works. Return cargo – coal to be shipped to the port of Colchester, Essex.

With half an hour spare before the full tide I turn my attention to the books of account which will need to be brought up to date before I go ashore. Every master mariner knows that it is important to requisition the appropriate amount of beef, bread, vegetables and rum for the next voyage, as specified by the Mercantile Marine Acts, otherwise the crew become demotivated and prone to insubordination. Many a mutiny has been prompted simply by serving the crew with eight ounces of beef per man per day instead of twelve ounces. In my view there are enough opportunities for the crew to become unhappy with their lot without creating further dissent over something as simple as the amount of meat they are served with their main meal. Yes – my crew are as content with their work and conditions as any other sailors serving the coastal trade along the east coast of England.

CHAPTER 2

The brave sea pilots of Seaham Harbour

Through my cabin window I can see approximately twenty vessels anchored to the lee waiting for the tide and the Harbourmasters instructions to enter port. The "Ytham", the "Mary", the "Summerside" and the "Matchless" are preparing to take on their pilots. With a bit of luck, I will be able to join Jacob Porritt, master of the Ytham and a fellow Yorkshire man hailing from Whitby, tonight in the Londonderry Arms – the first public house to be built in Seaham. The Londonderry Arms is a favourite of foreign sailors in port.

Glancing at my "harbour notes" I read in bold, underlined writing "Caution, *during southeast gales the gates at the wet dock cannot be opened due to the scend caused in the dock. Gales from the east-southeast cause the heaviest seas in the approach and entry to harbour should not be attempted. A detached shoal and rocky outcrop with a least depth of 4 fathoms called Louis Rocky Patch lies about a half mile east of the harbour entrance and shallow ledges and banks extend seaward from the shores on the north and south sides of the outer breakwaters. North Scar, a rocky shoal patch with a least depth of 1 fathom lies 400 yards south -southeast of the harbour. The outer harbour entrance has a depth of 3 fathoms and the fairway channel leading to the wet dock has a least depth of 2 fathoms. A rocky patch with a least depth of 1 fathom 3 feet lies east of the harbour entrance and should be passed to the south. Vessels cannot enter at low water.*

On each occasion I read the harbour notes for this port and I think to myself "Seaham owes a great debt to its many pilots who safely bring in our ships through such difficult waters in all weathers". I wonder who will be my pilot today – probably one of the Marshall, Scott or Miller boys whose family have been pilots at this harbour for over fifty years. At that moment Billy Booth knocks and puts his head around the cabin door. "Pilot Tom Scott is coming alongside in the coble "George & Francis". Are you coming on deck Captain Raine or I shall I bring him below?" The use of a pilot for this harbour is not optional. Ships may only enter Seaham Harbour with a pilot licenced to operate in these waters otherwise the Harbourmaster will report that ship's captain to the local Marine Board. Tom Scott and his brothers are skilled and experienced in their trade and I am always confident when under their guidance. Grabbing my coat, I climb back on deck just as Tom Scott throws his tow line to Billy Booth before skilfully leaping onto the Jacob's ladder slung over the side of the ship.

Tom greets me with a cheery smile "Morning Richard" he chirps. His ruddy complexion and muscular body is testament to his fitness and typical of the class of men who spend every day and many nights rowing through strong currents to be first aboard ships entering Seaham roads and needing a pilot into harbour. At that point I think again about my harbour notes and the perils awaiting the ship entering this harbour. Piloting is a risky and dangerous occupation. Little did I know then that Tom Scott was to be hit in the darkness and drown while trying to run alongside the Garron Tower in the dark just ten years later in 1891.

In a Board of Trade inquiry, held on 12th May 1891, it was determined that the Garron Tower collided with the pilot boat in the dark primarily because of lack of a light on the pilot boat – contrary to article 9 for pilot boats - and because of the inability of Tom Scott to manage the pilot boat single handed as the other pilot had just been put aboard the SS Wynyard Park. Tom Scott was the second of the "Scott pilots" to drown in just four years and his two other brothers also had collisions although they were safely picked up.

Tom casts his eye to the North and points out the Mary Ann, a schooner collier, about ¼ mile off our starboard bow. "Henry Bedwell is casting ballast – he will be fined £2 if the Harbourmaster sees his ship casting ballast at that anchor point. There are less than ten fathoms of water under his keel." We both return our gaze to the harbour. The Harbourmaster brings each vessel into port in turn and every master knows they will be in trouble if they try to come in without instruction. "There it is", Tom exclaims, "the Harbourmaster is signalling for us to enter". Sure enough, a blue pendant above a red flag is flying over the Harbourmasters Office signalling vessels drawing six feet or under may enter the harbour. Without an instruction the Mate bellows to the crew to raise anchor and away aloft to set the top gallants and royals on the fore and main masts. Soon the William Thrift is approaching the harbour entrance and Tom Scott throws a line to the paddle tug "Harry Vane" who takes us in tow. "Better get your topsail yards hoisted, sails furled and jib-boom hauled close in" says Tom "the Harbour will be full to overflowing and there will be little room to manoeuvre around the moorings." George Marwick, the Mate, shouts out to Tom Collings to stow the anchor on deck otherwise I, as Master, will be answerable for any damage to other vessels while hauling the ship between the loading moorings. The "Harry Vane" adeptly manoeuvres us into the North Dock in a berth close to the coal drops and as usual the agile Tom Colling throws a mooring line off the foredeck onto the dockside which is slipped around a mooring post by a dockworker. Billy Booth throws the aft mooring line.as the Dock Berthing Master looks on. All along the dock chain cables and stout ropes keep ships firmly bound to the quayside. I wait in anticipation to see if the Dock Berthing Master is going to suggest that another mooring line should be cast. There are never enough chains and ropes binding ships to the dockside to satisfy even the most affable of Berthing Masters.

Billy Booth and Tom Colling furling sails on topsail yards

As soon as we are securely tied up the crew set about unloosening the hatches to make way for unloading the timber and silver sand and I make my way to the Harbourmasters office to have my "turn for loading" decided. The Harbourmaster is William Sheridan; he is in his mid-sixties and a ship owner himself who has been Harbourmaster here for the last thirty years. A stout man with red flushed cheeks he clearly likes good food and although he takes his duties very seriously, he is always jocular and light-hearted when meeting ships masters. I had reason to call at his private residence a few years ago in Sebastopol Place – opposite Bath Terrace - where he lives with his wife, six children and three servants – a much respected and wealthy man indeed. On every occasion when the town organises a civic event or there are visiting dignitaries that require to be dined and entertained the Sheridan's are amongst the first on the guest list. William is giving instructions to his clerk and has a queue of three Ships Masters waiting to agree their turn so I idly peruse the current harbour dues list posted on the notice board.

1.Light and Harbour dues – vessels of 50 tons and under 3 shillings, above 50 tons halfpenny per ton additional

2.Moving vessels in the dock – vessels of 8 keels and under 5 shillings, above 8 keels 4 pence per each additional keel

3.Ballast – Taking out, 1 shilling per ton

4.Night Watch – 8 keels and under 6 pence, above 8 keels 1 shilling

5.Cooking – 8 keels and under 1 shilling, above 8 keels 1 shilling and 6 pence

6.Fresh water - 8 keels and under 9 pence, above 8 keels 1 shilling, steamers 2 shillings and 6 pence

7.Pier rope – 7 keels and under 9pence, above 7 keels 1 shilling

8.Gas – 6 keels and under 3 pence, above 6 keels 6 pence

9.Hospital - 8 keels and under 1 shilling, above 8 keels 1 shilling and 6 pence

10.Lifeboat – 1 penny per voyage on every vessel

11.Trinity dues – Under 100 tons 11 pence, above 100 tons 1 shilling and 2 pence for every additional 100 tons

12.Steam boat towage – 7 keels and under 7 shillings, and 1 shilling per keel for each extra keel

My thoughts linger on harbour dues number nine; *Hospital 1 shilling,* and I recall the accident young Bob Mustard had a few months ago. While slackening sheets on the foremast to enter harbour in a blustery gale he was caught a glancing blow from a loose shackle and he took a nasty knock at the back of his head. He was knocked unconscious and was losing a lot of blood and as soon as we berthed, I called for a stretcher to get him ashore. At that time there were no horse drawn ambulances and two dock workers ran him to the infirmary laid out on a fisherman's cart. Lady Frances Anne, the wife of the Marquess, had built an impressive infirmary in 1844 at the corner of North Terrace and Tempest Place for all workers in the coalmines, railway and engine works or docks. Each ship entering harbour paid one shilling per voyage and this entitled all crew to the benefits of the infirmary free of charge. Luckily Bob Mustard came around due to the efforts of the matron and had the gash in his head repaired by the house surgeon. He was back to his normal self within a couple of days although he has now got a fine scar to boast about in the pubs.

"Richard Raine, how are you?" bellows William. "I've just had Jacob Porritt in from the Ytham and he asked me to tell you to get along to the Londonderry Arms after you have seen Mrs Anderson with your account books. He will be there about 7 o'clock tonight". William is a cheerful character but woe betides anyone who contravenes the Harbour regulations – he won't hesitate to impose the appropriate fines. "By the way – its Census Day today and you will be required to complete this form with details of your ship and the names of all on board at midnight tonight. These are normally handed out and returned to the Customs Officer but he is laid up in his bed with influenza so you can return it to me tomorrow before you sail" and he handed me a pre-printed blank census document. "I've slotted you in to the coals staithes for 2 o'clock this afternoon but make sure you have sufficient men to move your ship in dock otherwise I will have to pass your turn over and you will be charged a double shifting fee." The crew should be quite happy with that I thought, as they will have the coals loaded and hatches battened by 5 o'clock and into the Noah's Ark, Golden Lion or the Lord Seaham to spend their pay.

At last, our turn has come and the crew manhandle the William Thrift under the coal staithes. Tom Scott was right to advise us to haul in our jib booms and topsails as there is barely enough room to swing her alongside the staithes with so many vessels in port all impatiently waiting their turn. As the coal drops down the chutes blowing clouds of black dust that permanently colours the sails and deck in black and grey, I ponder on the lot of the trimmers down in the hold. They have one of the dirtiest jobs in the harbour – scrambling around the hold, levelling off the coals and balancing the weight in the ship – with only a great big 18-inch candle to throw light in the hatches. Many of these men have pneumoconiosis- a killer lung disease caused by inhaling the coal dust - and have probably all been momentarily buried under tons of coal at some stage in their lives. Their biggest problem is in shifting coal from the main hatchway to the ends of the vessel, which is a backbreaking job although they do charge at double the price of trimming for this work. Another danger they face manifested itself at Hartlepool six months ago. On loading the brig "Sunrise" the teamers jammed the chutes at the top of the coal staithes and they suspended loading for that day. The crew of the "Sunrise" covered the hatches in case it rained that night and the next morning the trimmers took off the covers and went into the hatches with their lit candles. The build-up of methane gas from the coals, known as fire-damp in the mines, immediately ignited and the explosion broke the back of the brig and mortally injured the trimmers. Every harbourmaster will have warned their workers by now so that type of accident should never happen again.

"The William Thrift" in the South Dock

As soon as the trimmers finish, my crew set about fastening up the hatches and I descend to my cabin for the cash to pay the trimmers mindful that "*all trimming accounts are to be paid as soon as the cargo is on board."* I am quite pleased with the trim of the vessel but it has not always been so – I did remonstrate with the head trimmer a few months ago who decided his men had done a good enough job. Off I went to the Staithes Master to complain – the ship becomes very difficult to manoeuvre at sea if she has not been trimmed correctly – and he upheld my complaint and got the trimmers to finish the job correctly.

CHAPTER 3

Into the town

Time now to go below, get washed and changed out of my working garb and oilskins and into clean shore clothes. Before I visit Mrs Anderson to go over the books of account, I will call into the popular sea front traders on North Terrace to order food provisions, ropes, studs to repair the sails and galley equipment. They need to be delivered before we leave port tomorrow morning. Perhaps I will have time for a glass of rum or two and a chat with Nicholas Hunter, the Manager of the Lord Seaham and a game of billiards with John Embleton, the "billiards master" although it will probably cost me the price of a drink as he always wins! John preys on sailors who think they are good at the game – they don't call him the master for nothing. The town magistrates, chaired by the Reverend Angus Bethune JP, presided in the upstairs rooms of The Lord Seaham Inn from 1846 until a courthouse was built about twenty years ago. Catholic services were also held there in an upstairs room until Lady Francis Anne, the Marchioness of Londonderry, finally relented and gave her approval to have a Catholic church built in 1869. The Lord Seaham is not just a public house; it is a conduit for social and civic functions and activities in the town.

As I climb the steps built into the side of the north dock wall the Customs House, in Hunters Building, stands guard at the exit from the Harbour. John Davison, the Customs Officer, is not on duty today because of influenza. To the right of the Customs House and over the railway line is North Terrace. In the Terrace area are shops of many kinds and it is a popular meeting place where English and foreign sailors mingle and exchange stories. A few years ago, while sitting on a bench at the north end of the Terrace Green – to the right of me, the

Infirmary on the corner, and Bath Terrace just behind me - I counted the wide array of businesses in North Terrace. There are two grocers, two shoe smiths, five drapers and tailors, a chemist and dentist, a carpenter, an engineer, a baker, two butchers, a blacksmith, a potato merchant, two public houses and a beer house. This Terrace provides me with everything my mate, George Marwick, has listed for our next voyage.

Map of the harbour area at Seaham

In the centre of the green stands the Russian cannon captured at Sebastopol in the Crimea and presented to the town by Queen Victoria in 1840 and further beyond stands the imposing and commanding "Londonderry Offices" – the administrative hub of the Londonderry family. The building was erected about twenty years ago and is designed in the French style. I wonder how many local industrialists and ship-owners fortunes have been made and lost in that building.

North Terrace and the Londonderry Offices

On my last visit to this harbour, I witnessed a fine spectacle on the Terrace Green. Early in 1860 Marchioness Frances Anne had formed the Seaham Volunteer Artillery Brigade in response to a national call from the Government concerned at the aggressive attitude of Napoleon III of France. The Brigade has over 800 enlisted volunteers from Seaham which must constitute more than twenty per cent of the adult population of the town. Perhaps the incentive to join the Brigade is a combination of national pride and the opportunity to wear a smart uniform at least once a week and proudly parade in front of your relatives and friends of your home town. Recently returned from the national artillery and shooting competition at Shoeburyness, winning many medals, cups and prize-money, the Volunteers smartly paraded for the town on the Terrace Green. The men wore blue uniforms with red facings and the officers' uniforms were braided with silver and gold. His Royal Highness, The Duke of Edinburgh on an official tour of the northern Volunteer brigades made the official inspection accompanied, in an open carriage driven by four horses with two outriders, by Major Eminson the officer commanding the battalion. The leading tradesmen and inhabitants of the town gave His Royal Highness a fitting reception and he could not fail to be impressed by the extensive display of flags and streamers throughout the length of North Terrace to the Londonderry Offices and North Railway Street. The ships in the harbour were all gaily decorated with bunting in an unbroken line from one side of the dock to the other. Apparently, arrangements had been made by the officers of the 2nd Durham Artillery Volunteers to fire a Royal salute of 21 guns but in asking permission of the War Office, the request was refused. Instead, a saluting party of 180 members of the various batteries was formed. The crowd cheered as the duke drove past the saluting party, the horses going at walking pace, and the regimental band struck up the National Anthem. The men were then exercised in rifle, cutlass and heavy gun drill after which His Royal Highness expressed himself to be very impressed with the drill. It was quite a stirring sight to witness.

With a few tots of rum, two games of billiards lost and provisions duly ordered I quickly strolled up Church Street passing number 51 where Tom Scott lives with his wife and I soon arrive at Marlborough Street, built for the new "middle classes" of the town. At one time Seaham Harbour had over sixty ship owners and many of them lived in this street. The ship-owners I know and see regularly in the harbour area are James Snell, number 8; Robert Lonsdale, number 18; James Ellemore, number 27; Elizabeth Henderson, number 30; and William Watson, number 51. Passing by number four I recall my previous employer,

James Scott, no relation to the pilot Scott's but a ship owner and greengrocer. It was reported in the London Gazette in January 1868 he had been declared bankrupt by the County Court at Durham. That was the first I knew about his problems and it took many months for the crew and I to recover from the loss of our berth on his ship. How lucky I was to be recommended by a number of close friends, all master mariners, to my new employer.

Elizabeth Anderson is a widow in her early fifties. She lives with her aged father, a retired Customs Officer, her spinster sister and two daughters; Mary aged twenty-one, Emma aged nineteen and her son Mark aged fifteen at 28 Marlborough Street. As I knock on the front door, I can hear Mary playing the piano in the parlour – Mary is a schoolmistress. Mrs Anderson opens the door and warmly welcomes me. "Good afternoon, Richard. Please come in. You are just in time for tea." Following her through the hall she leads me to the front room where she is entertaining a visitor – Mr Harry Slade – a Minister of the Church and her neighbour Mrs Elizabeth Henderson from Number 30.

"Richard, you know my neighbour Mrs Henderson and this is an old friend from Scotland, Harry Slade who is staying for a few days before travelling on to York. Mr Slade this is Richard the master of my ship "The William Thrift" who has just returned from Dundee with a cargo for Lord Londonderry". I have always been impressed with Mrs Anderson's front room which is well lit with the latest electric lights; lavish draperies hang from the windows and the mantelpiece above the fireplace and the polished mahogany display cabinet are filled with expensive ornaments. This room compliments Mrs Anderson's style, colour and bearing. Her dark red hair, brushed up and pinned, contrasts with a jade green tea dress, wide pagoda sleeves and a high lace neckline. For the next hour Mr Slade and I exchanged views on the ships and masters of the whaling fleet he is acquainted with in Dundee while Mrs Anderson and Mrs Henderson looked through a large pile of knitting patterns. After tea and biscuits Mrs

Anderson excused us and we retired to the Parlour to discuss business matters. After a cursory glance over the books Mrs Anderson briefed me on the next three cargos she has arranged, none of which should prove to be a problem. Glancing again at the expenses listed in the books she counted out the harbour fees due to the Harbourmasters office tomorrow. She is now quite knowledgeable about harbour procedure and knows that no vessel is allowed to leave the harbour unless her dues and fines have been paid. Handing over the harbour fees and the books of account I once again become aware of her hazel flashing eyes. For a woman she has a very unusual mannerism of looking at me straight in the eyes when we are talking or should I say deep into my eyes which is very pleasant but at the same time slightly embarrassing to a married man. Re-joining her guests in the front room I say goodbye to Mrs Henderson and wish Mr Slade a pleasant visit to York and walk out into the hall accompanied by Mrs Anderson. Opening the front door, she turns to face me. Wishing me a safe passage and once again looking at me intently with her dark brown eyes she warmly shakes my hand and bids me farewell.

As I stroll past St Johns Church I can hear the Minister, the Reverend Angus Bethune, bellowing out his sermon to his eager and silent congregation. Although he is now in his 70th year he still delivers two services every Sunday as well as presiding weekly on the bench of Magistrates.

Further down Church Street I pass by the imposing National School built by the Marchioness of Londonderry where I recall that Billy Booth and Tom Colling were taught to read, write and learn arithmetic. I linger for a moment and peruse the school noticeboard. It reads: -

"Built in 1844 by Lady Frances Anne, Marchioness of Londonderry, Headmistress – Miss Doherty (Certificated)".

The National School and St Johns Church

I am suddenly conscious that it is now nearly 8 o'clock and I am late for my appointment with Jacob Porritt so I quicken my pace and soon arrive at the Londonderry Arms, the first building to be built in Seaham Harbour in 1828. The area behind this public house is a popular place for itinerant exhibitions such as Wombwell's Wild Animals. The Great Billy Purvis's Show Booth regularly put on entertainment for the locals and a horse drawn omnibus service leaves from here each day to Sunderland. Although it is still relatively early in the evening the public house is already heaving – mostly with sailors and most of them already worse the wear for drink. At any day in the year the town can have as many as three hundred seamen in harbour, a welcome trade to the many public houses too numerous to be supported by the townsfolk alone. I was listening to Billy Booth and Tom Colling on the second watch a few weeks ago passing their time by recounting the names of all the public houses in Seaham Harbour. They had recalled that in this year, 1881, there were over thirty public houses and thirty-seven beer houses, which brew their own ale. The names of twenty-nine of these public houses were later included in a clever ditty "The Tale of Seaham Licensing Signs" which reads: –

"The fellows of the ***Royal Navy Reserve*** *entered the* ***Ship*** *built of* ***Royal Oak*** *and sailed up to the* ***Adam and Eve Gardens*** *where they met with some* ***Foresters*** *who informed them that the* ***Duke of Wellington****, on leaving the* ***Edinburgh Castle****, had got into a* ***Dray Cart****. He was escorted by some noble* ***Volunteers*** *all loyal to the* ***Rose and Crown*** *and headed by a* ***Highlander*** *playing on his pipes. He passed through* ***Northumberland****. On arriving at the* ***Bridge*** *they were met by* ***Marlborough****,* ***Zetland*** *and* ***Bradyll*** *who had just returned from* ***Canterbury****. The assembled company here set down to discuss various subjects, the merits of* ***Shakespeare,*** *the latest achievements of the* ***Engineers*** *and the industry of the* ***Bottlemakers****. But they were repeatedly interrupted by the chattering of the* ***Parrot****. Then a party of* ***Oddfellows*** *suddenly entered the room and informed them that a* ***Golden Lion*** *had escaped from the* ***Noah's Ark*** *and was speeding by the* ***Colliery*** *to the* ***Times Inn*** *hotly pursued by* ***Lord Seaham*** *wearing a* ***Hat and Feather*** *and mounted on a* ***Kicking Cuddy****.*

As I enter the bar Jacob catches my attention through the throng of noisy sailors and bids me to sit down at his table. A group of miners are angrily discussing events at Seaham Colliery where a terrifying explosion last September caused the death of 164 men and boys and 180 pit ponies. Owing to the fire that followed the explosion a decision was made by the best mining engineers in the region that the maudlin seam should be sealed until the fire had subsided. Resentment was still running high amongst the miners who were aggrieved that they were expected to work whilst many of their fellow workmates were still entombed in the maudlin seam. All Durham miners followed the tradition that they would down tools and walk out of the pit if a fellow worker was killed underground and they would not return to work until the body of their workmate was recovered and brought out of the pit. It would be a further three months before the seam was finally re-opened and the bodies exhumed. Eight miners had been evicted from their colliery houses because they were regarded by the colliery management as troublemakers. Everyone in the town knew they were actually the officials of the local Seaham Colliery Union Lodge.

The group of miners in the bar were becoming further incensed by a report that morning from Dr Luke Dillon, Chief Medical Officer for Seaham that at the time of the explosion there were no splints or bandages down the mine and no one knew how to apply them. There were no ambulances and injured survivors of the explosion were jolted home on scavenger carts. As I gladly take my seat near the welcome open hearth glowing red with coals Jacob orders me a pint of the local ale and a noggin of rum – the first of many that night. Whether it was the warmth of the fire; the convivial company of Jacob Porritt or the nostalgic reminiscences we both exuded about our family lives in Whitby and Sandsend I do not know but I do not recall walking back to the William Thrift. Abruptly I am awoken from my sleep by a knock on the cabin door. "Breakfast is up Captain," bellows Bob Mustard.

After a second cup of refreshing tea, I wash and dress. Looking at the Census form I thought how wise I was to leave it until this morning to complete – what a mess I would have made of it last night. Simple enough I thought as I listed the crew names, ages, marital status, where born and occupations. For the younger crewmembers I was able to verify their birth dates and birthplace from the Registration of Birth Certificate, which they produced when they signed on to this ship. However, civil registration of births (and deaths and marriages) only applied from 1837 and George Marwick, my Mate, was born in Stromness in 1829 – or so he tells me.

LIST of OFFICERS, CREW, and OTHERS on BOARD the SHIP or VESSEL named the *William Thrift*

on the NIGHT of SUNDAY, APRIL 3rd, 1881.

	NAME and SURNAME	CONDITION as to Marriage	AGE last Birthday		RANK, PROFESSION, or OCCUPATION	WHERE BORN	If (1) Deaf-and-Dumb (2) Blind (3) Imbecile or Idiot (4) Lunatic
	Write, after the Name of the Master, the Names of the Officers and Crew; and then the Names of Passengers and of all other Persons.	Write "Married" or "Unmarried," "Widower" or "Widow," opposite the Names of all Persons except Young Children.	Males	Females	State here the rank of the Officers, and the rating of the Men and Boys of the Crew. The rank or occupation of Passengers and of all other Persons should be stated as fully and clearly as possible.	Opposite the Names of those born in England, write the County and Town, or Parish. If born in Scotland, Ireland, the British Colonies, or the East Indies, state the Country or Colony. If born in Foreign parts, write the particular State or Country; and if also a British Subject, add "British Subject," or "Naturalised British Subject," as the case may be.	Write the respective Infirmities against the name of the afflicted Person; and if so from Birth, add "from Birth."
1	Richard Raine	Married	39		Master	Sandsend Yorkshire	
2	George Marwick	Widower	52		Mate	Stromness Orkney	
3	Thomas Colling	Single	20		AB	Seaham Durham	
4	Robert Mustard	Single	20		Cook & Steward	Seaham Durham	
5	William Booth	Single	17		O D	Seaham Durham	
6							
7							
8			5				
9							
10							
11							
12							
13							
14							
15							

Actual enumeration document completed by Richard Raine on Monday morning 4th April 1881

Duly completed I fold the census form, slip it into my coat pocket, and I climb up on deck. It is a fine morning and we have about an hour to prepare to get underway to catch the tide. First, I must pay the ship's harbour dues and deliver a dock office pass to the Harbourmasters office so he can put me in turn to leave harbour. Passing the cookhouse and bake house cabins on the south side of the docks I linger at the smell of fresh bread, bacon frying in large pans and smile at the hungry crews eagerly waiting for their ships cook to make their breakfast. A cardinal rule in port, strictly observed by the harbourmaster, is that no cooking is permitted on board moored ships. A fire would undoubtedly spread in minutes with wooden hulls and masts touching from bow to stern and tarred planking from one side of the harbour to the other.

As I enter the Harbourmasters office, William Sheridan is showing John Garnham, the master of "The Septimus", a letter he received many years ago regarding my ship, the William Thrift, which he shows to every captain who graces his port for the first time. It was written by Captain James Knill of the Annandale in 1870. I know it by memory now. It reads as follows: -

To the Harbourmaster at Seaham Harbour,

January 2nd, 1870

Sir, With due respect I write to you,

Not to inform, as know you do

That my ship the Annandale

Has broken the Will Thrift's martingale.

Her master looks to me for pay,

Which must be paid without delay;

And which I think is very hard,

As my ship was securely moored

Till by your orders cast adrift;

She went foul of the Wm Thrift;

My owner might think it rather queer

That I should do such damage here.

I think the estate of Londonderry

Should pay the cost to Bill and Jerry

William chuckled and told John Garnham that on receipt of Captain Knill's letter it amused him so much that he replied to ask him to order a martingale from the workshop for the William Thrift and at the harbour expense. William spins around and slaps me on the back introducing me as the very master who had her jib-boom stay broken because he had authorised the harbour workers to move the Annandale without the knowledge of Captain Knill. Every ships master on the East Coast routes must know that story by now but he still gets great pleasure from re-telling it. After settling my harbour dues with his clerk, I return to William Sheridan's office and hand him the completed Census form and dock pass. Keen to hear where every ship is bound for next I joke with the Harbourmaster that we are bound for Australia and he roars with laughter. I bid him farewell and leave his crowded office to return to the ship.

I stride briskly past the schooner "George & Mary" from Jersey stepping over her untidy mooring lines on the harbour side and make my way to the bridge over the dock gates to cross to the North side of the harbour. We need to be underway within the next hour in order to make the tide. The dock gateman, Jeremiah Hall, is preparing to open the sluice gates to equalise the pressure in the dock now that the tide is in full run. Jeremiah is a jolly fellow who was born in Rothbury, Northumberland in 1828, the very year that this harbour and town was founded. His family have followed an unusual but charming tradition of naming the first-born son in each generation "Jeremiah".

Jeremiah Hall, Ship-owner and Dock Gateman

He is well known by all the visiting captains; their crews; the local shipping fraternity and the townsfolk and has been dock gateman at this harbour for the last thirty years. Speculation amongst Seaham folk is that his ownership of two houses in Blandford Place and Marlborough Street, both impressive residences, is due to a legacy or from a wealthy relative but no-one has ever had a straight answer from him. I recall he once told me that his father had a flourishing tailor's business in Rothbury but he died only months after Jeremiah was born. He always takes the opportunity to say hello and enquire about the crew and to ask how the "William Thrift" is responding to the helm. Until twelve years ago Jeremiah was the owner of my ship the "William Thrift" until he sold it to his close neighbour and friend Mrs Anderson.

"Richard, are you sailing today?" he chants in his Northumberland drawl which he has never lost even after thirty years living amongst County Durham folk. After updating him on my last voyage and exchanging a few pleasantries I make my apologies that I can't talk for longer and hurry back to my ship.

With his usual efficiency George Marwick has everything shipshape and has readied the vessel to leave harbour and as soon as I climb on-board, he bellows to Tom Colling to hail the tug master of the waiting paddle tug "Harry Vane "to throw a towline and to untie the lines fore and aft. With a surge of power from its steam engines the tug pulls and the towrope on the "William Thrift" becomes tort and slowly draws us away from the harbour side. As we weave our way past the "Beta" and "Abeona" clouds of coal dust rush down from the staithes above spreading coal into their waiting holds and momentarily creating a black and grey cloud that obscures the tug ahead of us.

"The William Thrift" leaving Seaham Harbour

Soon we are approaching the harbour gates where Jeremiah is waving enthusiastically and wishing us good luck. George Marwick prepares to release the towrope. The "Harry Vanes" paddles slow down as the tug master throws his engines into slow-ahead and he pulls his wheel around hard starboard. Like the true professional, George slips the towrope at the precise moment the line slackens and signals to the "Harry Vane" that we are free and away and they haul the line back on board the tug.

It has been a pleasant visit – one thankfully without incident – and a profitable trip for the owner. As the crew fully dress the sails as we clear the harbour gates and a strong breeze drives us on our course to Colchester, I left Seaham behind us with a good heart and a good spirit.

I had no idea then that this ship, The "William Thrift" would shortly be involved in an adventure of mystery, intrigue and danger.

CHAPTER 4

A Schooner adrift and abandoned

There is no greater feeling than standing on the deck of a sailing ship on a bright, warm morning with the sails in full spread and the bow rising and falling up and over through the waves. The crew are all working independently but in harmony – not one of them needs instruction – they all know their roles and are cheerfully going about their duties. Each one of my crew are strong and muscly, in particular my mate George Marwick who has the height as well as the physique and commands respect from mariners aboard any vessel including sailors from Royal Navy ships of the line. The crews' duties require a lot of body strength for raising the sails, hoisting the anchor and manning the winches that load cargo on board. One skill that comes with practice is furling and unfurling the sails. This has to be carried out with speed and agility and requires a head for heights and precision balance to shin along the yards of the foremast tying or untying the sail even in a rolling, turbulent sea with a force eight gale blowing. If the sails are left flying loose in those conditions the wind will tear them to shreds and it is too dangerous to run before a heavy gale with full sails aloft. Torn mainsheets can be repaired but only up to a point and owners have a right to ask why new sails are needed and the circumstances leading to their damage. This part of my work is never seen by the crew. I have to justify every cost to the owner and balance my judgement between safety to the crew and working the crew harder to overcome difficulties and day-to-day maintenance problems. For this reason, I make sure the crew turn their attention to ships maintenance when at sea and each watch takes their turn in those thankless menial jobs that can make a difference between a dangerous, leaky death-trap and a safe and reliable sea-going ship. But this has got to be complemented with regular investment from the owners in major repairs and refurbishment. So many ships leave harbour in an unseaworthy condition that local north-east mariners have recently formed a "union" to pressure both ship-owners and the government to improve the safety record of sailing ships and the lives of mariners. Numerous complaints had been received by the Board of Trade sufficient to warrant a new Inspectorate of Shipping to be established to investigate complaints and to recommend legislation to eradicate sharp practice by greedy ship-owners and improve safety at sea. Billy Booth, Tom Colling and Bob Mustard have joined this sailor's union and there is growing support in most of the ports we visit along the north-east coast. I have no real objection to this labour collective, in fact, I can see some good aspects to membership which includes as part of their subscriptions a "Mariners Mutual Insurance" that guarantees a small annual pension to widows or mothers on death of the member. In an industry that has an annual mortality rate through drowning and accidents at sea of two out of every one hundred sailors any pension to dependants is clearly welcome. Thankfully, our owner Mrs Anderson is a benevolent employer and generally takes my recommendations as concerns refurbishment and repairs to the "William Thrift" and the crew and I have had little cause for complaint regarding her attitude to our safety. Having fulfilled her responsibilities it now falls upon the crew to make sure the "William Thrift" is shipshape and maintained to the high standard that I consider appropriate.

Bob is aloft inspecting the rigging and I can hear him calling off the condition of the stirrups to George Marwick who is co-ordinating every job being carried out on the ship from his station at the helm of the ship. Bob is in a safety harness that is tethered to jack lines that allow him to lean out to look at the rigging with both hands free.

Bob Mustard aloft checking the lubricant on the foremast

There is a temptation to overlook any defect or worn part of the rigging but I can assure you it is an emotion that is quickly forgotten as the crew know that if any injury occurs to them or to others through faulty rigging the outcome from those heights could be fatal.

"Make sure the foremast is well oiled or you will have more trouble hoisting the yards" shouts George and Bob responds with the expected "aye, aye" as he begins running his arms around the mast testing the lubrication and at the same time covering his hands with dirty grease that makes working aloft quite tricky. Tom is engrossed in his work on the main deck oblivious to everyone else on board ship. He has the spare sails stretched over the central cargo hatch and is pouring oil over them and vigorously rubbing it in to prevent the flax sails from becoming dry and porous. When that is done to the mate's satisfaction, he will begin to replace the worn sail studs with the new studs I bought yesterday in Seaham Harbour. We can all expect to hear shouts, groans and curses for the remainder of his watch as he pricks and nips his fingers with the boltrope needle trying to penetrate the tough oiled flaxen sail.

Billy Booth is caulking the seams of the main deck to make them watertight. He is forcing oakum in between the planking which is a material made of tarred hemp or manila rope fibres after which he will apply hot pitch to prevent it from rotting. One area of the ship no crew member will skimp on when caulking is the decking above the crew quarters. There is nothing worse than lying in a hammock whilst not on watch and the sea breaching the deck and seeping through into the crew area soaking bedding, clothes and anything not wrapped in oilcloths. The hot pitch is essential but an occupational trade mark of mariners. Consider, for example, a sailor's salute, whether from an ordinary seaman or from a ship's master, is different from a salute used in the British Army. A naval person salutes with a cupped, closed hand so as not to expose the tar and pitch on the palm of the hand which is impossible to remove whereas an army or artillery volunteer's salute has a flat open palm.

Tom Colling calls over from the main hatch "Can I have a word Captain Raine". Tom is often quizzing me about various aspects of seamanship and I enjoy passing on tales of my experiences in the hope he will remember them in years to come when he is a first mate or even a ship's master. "I've heard tell that there are some ships' masters that don't use the sextant and ships' charts to navigate voyages along this coast – Can that be right Captain Raine?"

"Yes Tom, it is possible to sail these waters without a sextant and charts but that's not to say you don't need to learn how to navigate by dead reckoning. If you want to attain competency as a first mate you will be examined in all of those aspects so they must be learnt." Tom looked a little puzzled so I continued "The older ships' captains use rhymes or songs to list the natural hazards, sandbanks, cliffs and rocks and they help to point out the safe passage route. For instance, if we were sailing from Norfolk, passing Lincolnshire and then on to Yorkshire and then Durham we would closely hug the north-east coast keeping land hazards in view. Those old master mariners pinpoint their location and their heading using the rhyme: -

First the Dudgeon, then the Spurn,

Flamborough Head is next in turn,

Filey Brigg is drawing nigh,

Scarboro' Castle stands on high,

Whitby Rock lies out to sea,

So, steer two points more northerly,

Huntscliff Foot is very high land,

Twenty-five miles from Sunderland.

Hartlepool lies in the bight,

Seaham Harbour is now in sight.

The 'Old Man' says: "if the weather's right

We'll be in the Tyne tomorrow night".

"Now Tom, look at the layout of the east coast and the hazards you will find along that route" and I quickly drew a sketch showing the notorious Dudgeon Shoal and the landmarks en route to Seaham Harbour and Tynemouth.

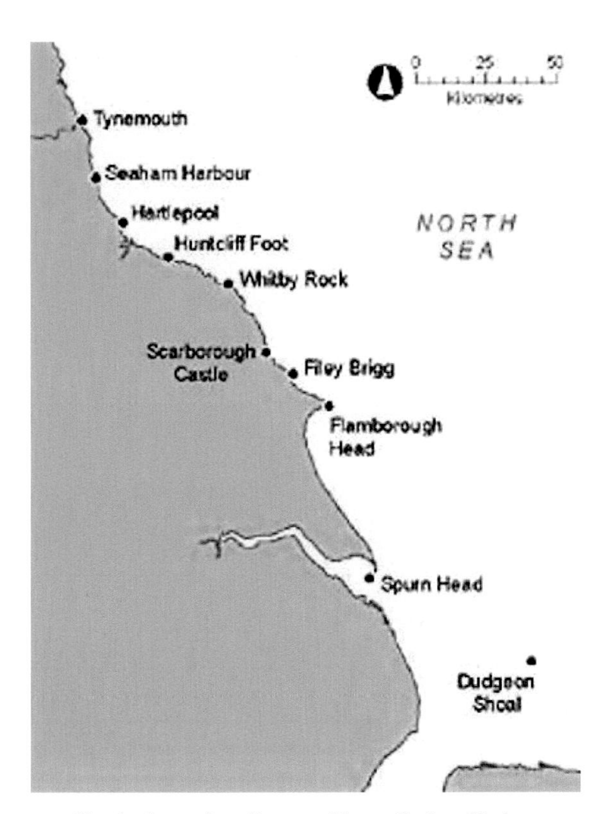

Sketch of coast from Dungeon Ness to Seaham Harbour

"So, it is possible for a master mariner to sail by-the-cuff and take a vessel from port to port without error with the lights from the coast his only guide and his one and only intellectual exercise to calculate the set of the ebb and the flood tides. But what would you do if the owner had arranged a cargo to Memel in the Baltics? Once you are out of sight of land and crossing the German Ocean then rhymes and songs are of no use, are they?" Tom smiled and with a simple "aye, aye captain" I could see he had learnt another lesson.

Of course, many of the master mariners that Richard knew were more accomplished than the droll legendary ships' captains that Tom had asked about but it was still true that valuable cargoes and sailors' lives were sometimes entrusted in such men who sailed by rule of thumb. With clumsy old craft that sailed in heavy weather as though they were dragging an anchor along the sea bed it was no wonder, Richard thought, that the newspapers were kept busy reporting accidents and collisions at sea, or on entering ports and even in the harbours.

That afternoon passed without any notable incident with the exception of a fifteen-minute spell where Bob Mustard and Billy Booth entertained us all with funny walks along the deck impersonating a pirate with a peg leg and an exaggerated pirate drawl which had us all holding our sides with the best belly-laugh we have had in weeks. Watching Bob and Billy going through their antics I could not help but feel a little apprehensive as I cast my eye to the south, on our very heading, and noticing that the wind was beginning to blow stronger and the ship was starting to roll with the increasing swell of the waves. It was clear from the darkening skies that we were heading into a squall.

"George – make sure everything is secured on deck before the lads come down to eat"

George Marwick immediately bellowed orders to Tom and Billy "Batten down the hatches, tie down all deck equipment lads and double check the jolly boat is secured for foul weather".

Looking ahead at the storm brewing up I felt a little uneasy. "Who is on first dog-watch while we eat George?"

I could tell my first mate was also feeling apprehensive. "I am at the helm and Billy is on watch Captain" replied George.

"Billy, keep a sharp eye out; it's going to be an uncomfortable watch for you" I shouted. The night watches are taxing on the crew who often have trouble staying awake although it is clear that will not be a problem through this night. The main hazard on a moonless, wild night, apart from following the wrong compass bearing and running aground, is the numerous colliers following this identical route both on a southerly and a northerly course and collisions are inevitable and frequent. From 1848 all vessels are required by the Mercantile Marine Acts to carry red and green sidelights and a white masthead light but in poor visibility there is very little time to avoid another vessel once these are sighted. With his usual inquisitiveness I heard Tom asking George how he knew we were heading into a squall. “The signals are all there in the change in wind direction, clouds and the motion of the sea lad” replies George. “You know the well-known saying “Red sky at night, sailors delight, red sky in the morning, sailors take warning” well there are many more that mariners use to predict the weather ahead” and one-by-one George reeled off the old sailors’ proverbs.

Mackerel skies and mares’ tails
Make tall ships carry short sails

Rainbow in the morning, sailors take warning,
Rainbow towards night, sailors delight

A backing wind says storms are nigh,
But a veering wind will clear the sky

Seagull, seagull, sit on the sand,
It’s never good weather when you’re on the land

When a halo rings the moon or sun,

The rain will come upon the run

If woolly fleeces deck the heavenly way,
Be sure no rain will mar a summer's day

With the rain before the wind,
Stays and topsails you must mind,
But with the wind before the rain,
Your topsails you may set again

When the boat horns sound hollow,
Rain will surely follow

"Over time lad you will just stick your head out of your bunk and you will instinctively know how the weather will fair without thinking about these old proverbs but until then you would do well to learn them," said George. With a nod Tom agrees and makes his way to the galley for the evening meal.

Retiring to my bunk that night I reluctantly fall into a sleep despite the heavy movement of the "William Thrift" in the water, the howling of the wind and the crashing of the waves against the prow of the ship. I have had many nights on board ship in such weather and find little cause to lose sleep unnecessarily – nothing I can do will ease the storm. Early next morning I thankfully realise that we are clear of bad weather and the ship has stopped rolling but in my half-conscious state, I hear a voice hailing "Ahoy there, Ahoy there". Tom Colling bursts into my cabin and excitedly reports "Schooner dead ahead Captain. Mr Marwick asks if you can join him on deck".

Dressing quickly and pulling on my sea boots, I climbed up the companionway two by two. George Marwick was five rungs up the rigging cupping his hand over his brow and squinting through the low sun which was streaming from the port side. One solitary sail could be seen about half a mile ahead. Clearly a collier schooner her head was turned in a like direction to our own but she did not show the quantity of sail that you would expect in open water. Perhaps her captain felt no pressing inducements to urge her home but whatever the motive it is unusual and it made me curious.

Mysterious schooner dead ahead

George jumped back on deck "There's no-one on watch or at the helm Captain Raine" and he stared at the vessel sitting almost dead in the water now only four hundred yards away.

"We had better check this out George" I said knowing full well that he was thinking the same thought. Immediately George responded "Lower foretop mast, royals and sky sails lads" and as quick as a flash Tom and Billy were scampering up the rigging. As we drew closer to the mysterious vessel the more intriguing it became. It was without doubt loaded with cargo but it was sitting very low in the water – very low indeed.

“George, take the helm and draw the “William Thrift” alongside. I intend to board her and see what’s amiss. Billy, you come along with me and keep your wits about you.” Both responded with an uneasy “Aye, aye Captain”

As we slowly passed the heel of the topmast of the schooner, I leapt down onto her deck followed a split second later by Billy Booth. There was not a soul in sight and with the main sheets running free and rattling against the masts it gave me an eerie feeling but I tried to hide my doubts from Billy.

“Ahoy there” I shouted at the top of my voice. Not a sound was heard other than the gentle lapping of the waves against the prow as we slowly moved through the water at about two knots with my ship running a parallel course at the same speed.

I grabbed two belay pins from the rack on the bulwarks and threw one to Billy and intimated with a nod that he should use it if necessary “Billy, go forward and check out the crews’ quarters and the galley. I’m going aft to search the bridge house and the aft cabin.

Slowly we worked through the ship looking into every corner. The bridge house had charts out of their cases and the wheel was running free. The aft cabin was empty but all of the usual ship’s equipment was lying around the cabin; compass, tide tables, ship’s log, charts, sextant. Picking up the ship’s log I could tell what sort of master commanded this vessel. It was tattered and torn with loose pages that fell out because he had torn pages out presumably to use for writing paper. The writing was not much better than a scribble with ink blots and runs on every line. Clearly the master took no pride in his work and I wondered if his seamanship was any better. The front page indicated that this was the schooner “Neptun”; the master, Hans Engel from Wismar, Germany and his last log entry was the day before yesterday berthed at Hartlepool. The entry then read “Kapitan Ernst Sturm with passenger boarded 10.00 am. Raised anchor and left harbour 10.15am”. Odd entry I thought as it may be normal to call the master of a vessel “Captain” but it is usual in the merchant marine to use the term “Master” when writing his name.

Climbing back on deck I looked aloft as a puzzled Billy Booth ran over to me “Not a soul on board Captain and the lifeboat has gone”. Checking over the condition of the sails fluttering in the light breeze I nodded “Whoever was on board left quickly” I replied “A captain doesn’t leave his tools of trade unless he has no other option”.

My attention now turned to the trim of the ship. “Billy, why is this vessel sitting so low in the water?” I wasn’t asking Billy a question – I was thinking out aloud but Billy knew that as he made no reply. “Let’s look at this cargo”

Starting at the forward hold Billy and I worked at each end of the hatch loosening the tarpaulin and lifting the hatch covers to one side. The hold was filled to about seven feet from the hatch with a cargo of coal as I would have expected but lapping around the side of the hold was water. The ship was taking on water and that was why her trim was so low. Every ship no matter how well built and maintained takes on water and has to be pumped every day but this amount of water will eventually sink her. I can only guess that the crew had tried to clear the water with the bilge pumps and realising that it was a forlorn hope had abandoned ship in the squall last night.

“Let’s look at the condition of the main hatch Billy” and soon we had the covers off. She was full of coal but surprisingly, apart from the normal level of bilge water she was as dry as could be expected. Well, there’s a stroke of luck I thought as the possibility began to grow on me that there could be a chance, if we take her in tow, or put her under sail, and the swell remains the way it is that we may get her the seven miles to Whitby.

“Billy, swing that bilge pump into the forward hatch and see if you can pump out any of that sea water while I inspect the rear hold for damage.” The tarpaulin on the rear hatch was partly loose so in no time I was throwing the hatch covers to one side.

“The rubbers on this bilge pump have rotted Captain and it’s not creating enough vacuum to draw off the water” Billy exclaimed.

“It would be easier to run down a ladder with a bucket than use this useless thing”

Staring through the rope netting into the aft hold I could see it was also filled with coal to about eight feet off the hatch. Listening and looking for sea water in the blackness below I detected just the usual level of bilge water and my hopes rose that this could result in a good salvage price for the crew and I if only we could keep the schooner afloat and get her into port. At that moment I recoiled with surprise as a figure scrambled out of the shadows and stood looking up at me protecting his eyes from the bright sun above him.

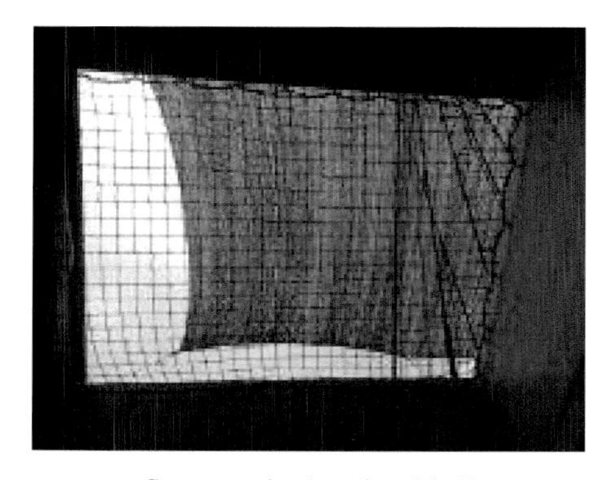

Sun streaming into the aft hold

CHAPTER 5

Lying at anchor off Whitby

Quickly recovering from the shock of the sudden appearance of the strange apparition from the shadows I steadied my voice and leaned over the hatch so he could see me "Do you understand English?"

"Of course, I understand English – I am bloody English" he snapped. "I heard someone hailing but I thought it might have been the German crew coming back on board. Can you get me out of here; I am cold, hungry and I've been rolling around these wet coals for more than ten hours."

Tethered over the guardrail was a rope ladder which the crew had obviously used to alight into their lifeboat. "Billy lend a hand to drop this Jacob's ladder into the hold" and no sooner had we rolled it down than the apparition adeptly climbed up and pulled himself on deck.

Standing wet and shivering the spectre should have been in shock and subdued after suffering the ordeal of near drowning in the closed cargo hold of a ship but this man stood tall and proud. Reaching about 5 feet 10 inches in height; light brown shoulder length hair and wearing a dark blue coat, white waistcoat with a fine white linen shirt fastened at the neck with criss-cross laces. Although his face, hands and clothes were dirty with coal dust and grime I could tell from their cut that this was a gentleman – not only that – I had often seen gentlemen like him, dressed in that particular naval style, around Greenwich village on the River Thames.

"If you are not one of the crew and you are not the German, Kapitan Sturm, then who are you and what happened here" I asked.

"What do you know of Sturm retorted the stranger?"

"Absolutely nothing" I replied "The master of this vessel has logged a German called Sturm boarding the Neptun at Hartlepool. I am Captain Richard Raine, master of the collier brigantine "William Thrift" which you can see off the starboard bow. Now who are you and what happened here"

The stranger visibly relaxed and his manner and disposition softened. "I do apologise Captain Raine. I have been through an ordeal but should not have spoken in such a manner to the man who has certainly saved me from certain death. I am First Lieutenant Jack Edward Smith, Naval Intelligence Officer at the Admiralty". Gesturing at his sad appearance he asked "Do you mind if I clean myself up a little. In due course I will gladly tell you what I am doing here and what I am permitted to reveal about my presence here"

I nodded in agreement. Standing on the guardrail I steadied myself by holding on to the rigging and hailed George Marwick. "Bring the "William Thrift" alongside George and sling our spare bilge pump over onto this deck. We have a guest coming aboard. Make him welcome and as comfortable as you can. Within minutes George and Bob Mustard had slung the bilge pump onto a spar with block and tackle and carefully manipulated it onto the deck of the Neptun. With the agility you would expect of a naval officer Jack Smith leapt aboard the William Thrift and was led to the galley by Bob Mustard.

Two hours later an exhausted Billy Booth, Tom Colling and I relaxed from the exertion of our continuous efforts on the bilge pump. The water level had visibly fallen by at least four feet in the forward hold, sufficient in my view to safely make sail and head for the fairway channel of Whitby roads. The weather was still in our favour and the wind and the swell of the waves would cause no problem if it stayed the same. Returning on board the William Thrift I could see a puzzled look on George's face. "What's going on Captain? Who is our passenger?"

"George, all I know is that he is a Royal Navy officer working for Naval Intelligence and his name is Lieutenant Jack Smith". Bearing a puzzled look George retorted "Does that mean he is a spy?

"No, I don't think so George. From what I know the Admiralty don't employ spies as we would think of them. I heard that after the Franco-Prussian war the stunning success of the Prussian army was attributed to accurate intelligence and it prompted the War Office to form an "Intelligence Branch". Junior officers of the Army and Royal Navy go on fishing and sporting trips or undertake travel into interesting areas and to produce reports on their return. To a young naval officer, it is an exciting although dangerous business. They need to learn about every conceivable intelligence skill such as signals, semaphore, foreign guns, gun mountings, ammunition, armour, coastal defences and port deployments. Our Lieutenant Smith must be a very resourceful officer"

"Now then George. What shall we do about our prize, the Neptun? In maritime law when a master abandons his ship for whatever reason he cedes all rights to the vessel and its cargo. If we can get her into harbour at Whitby, we will all take a share of the salvage fee. Do you think you could handle her at the helm with the help of Tom Colling manning the sails and rigging for the next seven miles? The "William Thrift" will stay on a broad tack following you in although we will not berth in harbour. We will drop anchor in Whitby roads about a half mile to the south of the harbour entrance so we do not foul any ship entering or leaving port." With a simple "Aye, aye Captain" it was agreed and George beckoned Tom Colling over. "Come on Tom, you are about to take up your first mates' position" and an unmistakable air of pride came over Tom.

“George, before you set off, search around the aft cabin of the Neptun. I am sure I saw the regulation signal flags in a trunk. Run up the flags for “damaged and in distress” and the Harbour Master will bring you straight in without having to wait your turn.” When the paddle tug comes out to tow you, instruct the tug master to take you in to the dry harbour and she will settle on the mud bottom. When the tide turns and goes out, we can inspect the damage to her hull. The schooner will need to undergo repairs before she can be sold but I will leave the “William Thrift” in the jolly boat and join you to sort that out. With no further delay George and Tom Colling boarded the schooner and Billy Booth returned on board our ship.

“Take the wheel Bob and where is our passenger? I need to find out what has been going on aboard that schooner”. Firmly taking a hold of the wheel Bob replies “he’s in the galley. I have cleaned his clothes as best I can; he has washed and devoured a bowl of my hot broth which he reckons is the best he has tasted.” I smiled because I knew no one could make our visitor more welcome than Bob Mustard.

Entering the galley, the heat from the stove was overpowering. Bob had really banked up the coal and it was glowing red and our guest was dressing into his dry, clean clothes and looking much healthier than the spectre that stared up at me two hours ago.

“Now then Lieutenant Smith. What’s been going on? I’ll need a full report for the harbour authorities”.

“Please call me Jack, Captain Raine. In my business it does not pay to acknowledge my rank or that I am a naval officer. I must ask that you do not mention me in your report to the authorities. My assignment is of a secret and diplomatically sensitive nature that cannot be subject to sensationalist newspaper reports or public scrutiny. Can I ask if you are a true Englishman who would fight for the security of his country and hold true to that ideal no matter what the cost?"

Pricked into a sudden sense of pride and nationalism I promptly replied "Jack, when the call came for members of the merchant marine to step forward and sign up for the newly formed Royal Navy Reserve to defend this country in the event of a national emergency, I was the first to march into Lieutenant Usher's office in Seaham Harbour to join the Reserve Force."

"I knew you would be a patriot, Captain Raine. Can we talk confidentially in your cabin?" and as we both descended the companionway, I mused to myself what tales of daring do I might have become entangled in.

Sitting down at the table I poured two glasses of rum. "Now Captain Raine" he began "What I am about to relay to you must be kept secret for the sake of the security of your country. Do you understand? No-one must hear about this venture. My superiors may confide more information to you but that is their prerogative. I am only at liberty to tell you about the events leading to the situation in which you found me and not to the facts of the special assignment I was undertaking."

I simply nodded and said "I understand Jack. You have my word that I will not speak of this."

Jack continued "Two days ago I was at Wynyard Hall in County Durham attending a meeting, a special briefing, of national importance. There should have been no particular risk involved in this meeting but somehow an alien power had gained intelligence which directed their agents to Wynyard Hall."

"I know about Wynyard Hall" I interrupted "That is the residence of the 6th Marquess of Londonderry who owns Seaham Hall and most of the land and local businesses including Seaham Colliery, the docks, railway and engine works. What has an aristocratic landowner got to do with national security?"

Jack seemed surprised that I knew of Lord Londonderry but if he had ever visited Seaham Harbour, he would have realised that his stamp was on every financial investment opportunity in the town and he must have directly employed at least half of the townsfolk and indirectly another quarter. Jack carried on. "Well – did you know his grandfather; the 3rd Marquess was one of the greatest diplomats this country had seen for many generations. He was Under-Secretary of State for War and the Colonies for two years, fought in the Napoleonic Wars and was Ambassador to Austria and then Prussia. He was without doubt one of the most important politicians and diplomats of his time. The current Lord Londonderry is his grandson. Despite the appearance he may make to the public of an over indulged rich aristocrat who has been cossetted with a privileged education and upbringing he works tirelessly for the naval intelligence service. The social circles in which he moves include most of the senior royals and nobility of Europe who also have high ranking military appointments in their armies and navy. Two weeks ago, Lord Londonderry was invited to a shooting weekend by the Earl of Warwick. Also invited were about thirty other guests including the Russian Ambassador; the Portuguese Ambassador; the Turkish Ambassador and in particular the new head of the Imperial German Navy, General von Caprivi. Lord Londonderry was able to have long and revealing conversations with each of these guests at times when they were not in full control of their faculties and he was able to put together some critical pieces of intelligence about their collective joint interests. Of particular importance were the foreign policy conversations von Caprivi inadvertently let slip between himself and Prince Otto von Bismarck, the German Chancellor."

The young naval officer took a long sip of his rum and waited to see if I had any comments to make. I was intrigued but had no questions to ask. Jack took another sip and continued "I suspect that General von Caprivi awoke the next morning and realising he had been compromised and had let slip some very important information that could embarrass himself; his employer von Bismarck and the German government he determined that he would assign Kapitan Ernst Sturm of the German naval intelligence the task of correcting the situation. Sturm is a ruthless and determined foe whom I have met on two or three occasions before when travelling around Europe. He knows what my role is in the Royal Navy and he knows I am aware of his position in the Imperial German Navy. Sturm and his men must have had Wynyard Hall under observation for the last week and seeing my arrival two days ago assumed correctly that I had received the intelligence from Lord Londonderry that he had been entreated by von Caprivi to erase. After making my leave of Lord Londonderry I rode out of the grounds of Wynyard Hall and was immediately set upon by Sturm and his men; bundled into a carriage and carried to Hartlepool docks"

"Ah ha" I exclaimed "the entry in Hans Engel's ship log referred to Sturm and a passenger embarking on the Neptun at Hartlepool".

"Correct" said Jack "I was trussed up like a hog and left in the aft cabin while they set sail. I got the impression Sturms' orders were not to kill me but to pass me over to General von Caprivi and his naval intelligence for interrogation. However, the master, Hans Engel, must have misread his charts and he ran into a sand bar twenty miles south of Hartlepool. From the sounds I heard from the bow, when the schooner eventually managed to float free, the copper skin covering the prow must have torn away."

"And the caulking between the bow planking would have dried out underneath the copper skin so she began leaking like a sieve when she was exposed" I exclaimed.

"Correct again" said Jack "Only it would appear that the master believed he had been holed and finding that the bilges pump was not making any difference and with the sea level in the forward hold becoming perilously close to capsizing her he decided the schooner could not possibly ride the storm that was brewing up. The master, crew and Kapitan Sturm therefore launched the lifeboat but not before Sturm had me thrown into the aft hold and replaced the hatch covers. No doubt he assumed I would go down with the Neptun and that would be an end to General von Caprivi's problem."

"Well, what will you do now" I said "Surely you must pass on Lord Londonderry's information to naval intelligence as soon as you can?"

Standing up and finishing off his glass of rum Jack Smith agreed "If you can land me at Whitby, I will telegraph the Admiralty and await instructions. How long before we reach port Captain Raine?"

Thinking out aloud I looked at my pocket watch and estimated "If we continue to have this following wind behind us, we should be dropping anchor about mid-afternoon. I'm going on deck to check on my crew and prepare our story for the harbour authorities. Of course, there will be no mention of you in my report."

A quarter of a mile ahead of us George Marwick and Tom Colling were making excellent progress and seemed to be handling the Neptun well enough. Just as I had requested, George had raised the regulation signal flag for a ship in distress and as soon as she was in Whitby roads the Harbour Master hoisted the tide flag on a staff on the west cliff and sent out a paddle tug to bring her in to the dry harbour. I thought it wise, in the circumstances; to raise our signal flags to identify my ship otherwise the Harbour Master will have cause for suspicion and contact the coastguard. The commercial code of signals used by masters of ships at sea and at signal stations on shore identifies a unique flag code for each ship. The Harbour Master will look to the Maritime Directory and Shipping Register, an annual publication, and seeing my flag signals "J.S.B.P." on the flying jib will identify us as the "William Thrift". Approaching my intended anchorage, I shouted to Bob and Billy "Aloft lads, and reef the mainsails and topsails" and within seconds of slipping the wind out of the sails the "William Thrift" ground to a stop and I knocked the ratchet on the windlass dropping the anchor".

Whitby Harbour

Looking over to Whitby Harbour just under half a mile away I could see two whaling ships coming around the bottle shaped estuary of the River Esk and putting on full canvas as they passed the west pier. The harbour is sheltered by an east and west pier with a lighthouse at the end of the east pier and a beacon on the west pier. On the outskirts of the town to the west rises Sneaton Castle – a new property- recently built to look like a medieval castle by James Wilson who is said to have made his money in the slavery trade. The arms of the entrance piers extend out to sea in a northerly direction leaving the entrance exposed to strong winds from the north but sheltered when blowing from other directions. As I expected most of the waiting vessels are anchored north of the harbour so that when their turn is signalled, they will sail into harbour directly without having to tack around the piers. Within sight are at least four schooners, six brigs, an unusual looking barquentine, two or three ketches all at anchor with another four or five sail approaching from the east.

"Now look Jack" I said catching our passenger's attention "I've been thinking about your Kapitan Sturm and the crew of the Neptun. They abandoned ship about nine or ten miles north of here. I would not be surprised if they made for Whitby – in the same situation that is the heading I would make as Whitby is the only natural harbour along the 100 mile stretch between Hartlepool and the Humber. If they are in the town then I think it is too dangerous for you to go ashore. The information you have, whatever it is, must be protected."

"You are quite right Captain Raine" Jack replied nodding in agreement. "It would be foolish to jeopardise my assignment unnecessarily. Would you be able to send a telegraphic message to the Admiralty when you go ashore? It is unlikely that the staff in the Admiralty will be able to contact my superiors and reply with orders before the Post Office in Whitby closes at 5.00 pm. so I will not expect a reply until tomorrow morning."

Leaving Lieutenant Smith on board I climbed down into the waiting jolly boat. Bob Mustard fended off and then effortlessly rowed for the harbour. High on the cliff top overlooking the town stands the lofty ruins of Whitby Abbey. I first climbed the 199 steps from the town to Whitby Abbey when I was just a youngster visiting from my hometown of Sandsend. Once past the east pier lighthouse the current carried us into the River Esk passing the three Ropery

Works so necessary in a sea going port, several large shipbuilding yards and then as we approached the dry dock, I could see the Neptun moored alongside the quay. The tide was ebbing and she had settled on her flat hull on the mud riverbed. With the agility of a young man Bob leapt from the jollyboat as we approached the pontoon and tied our mooring line around a post. Climbing from the quayside onto the Neptun I was helped over the guardrail by George Marwick and Tom Colling.

"Welcome aboard, Captain," said George. Acknowledging his welcome, I asked "everything in order George? You seem to have brought her in without any problem." Replying with a broad grin George chirped "I must commend the way Tom ably assisted me as first mate, Captain" which had Tom clearly bursting with pride. "It looks like you were right about the copper skin below the prow. It has been torn away when the schooner hit the sand bar so it should be easy enough to have the forward hull timbers caulked, tarred and then have the copper skin replaced".

"Right then, let's go and see Robert Gibson, the Harbour Master and tell him what we are doing here" I said "but remember lads, no mention of our naval friend". Nodding in agreement they alighted onto the quay and walked towards the Harbour Masters office. Ten minutes later I gave Robert Gibson my verbal report about the abandoned schooner which we had come across after the storm and how we brought the leaky vessel into harbour.

"What puzzles me, Captain Raine" the Harbour Master said scratching his head with his pipe "No-one has reported abandoning a ship at those map co-ordinates and I have heard no reports of a crew being landed along the coast". Thinking to myself I was not surprised as it is unlikely that Kapitan Sturm or the master Hans Engel would come forward to claim the Neptun in case they were accused of espionage and kidnapping but I gave no reply to Robert Gibson.

"Where is the Receiver of Wreck's office, Mr Gibson" I asked "I will be lodging a claim for salvage" and I was given directions to the Customs Office at the head of the port. Relaying the same information to the Customs Officer I handed over a written testimony which I had completed on board the "William Thrift" and after inspecting the schooner and cargo the Receiver of Wrecks confirmed my position. "We will advertise in the national press that the schooner Neptun has been found abandoned and brought into harbour at Whitby. The cargo of coals will be sold by auction to pay for your costs as the salvager and if no claim is made by the owners of the vessel after twelve months, then we will auction the Neptun off. After deduction of repair costs, harbour dues and our commission you will be entitled to the proceeds." I could feel a smile growing inside of me which I tried to suppress. This was the news I had hoped for but had not dared to think about. The Receiver of Wrecks had estimated the value of the cargo at about £320 after deduction of unloading costs and the net proceeds from the sale of the schooner would be about £450. All in all, the crew and I were in line for a windfall of about four years pay.

Making our way out of the harbour and into town George, Tom and I joined the crowds of people walking through the streets on their way to and from the market place. Passing through narrow streets, alleyways, court yards and the many fine houses built by prosperous ship owners we made our way up the steeply sloping bank to the main Post Office. Inside I gave Jack Smith's message to the Telegrapher.

It read: -

"Temporarily delayed by Sturm.
I am now in friendly hands.
On board the collier brigantine William Thrift.
Anchored off Whitby.

Await your instructions."

Lieut Commander Jack Edward Smith.

"Where is this to be delivered" asked the official behind the counter. Speaking as quietly as I could amidst the noisy, day-to-day hustle and bustle of the busy Post Office I softly replied "The Admiralty, Ripley Building, Horse Guards Parade, Whitehall, London." I paid the one shilling fee, informed the telegrapher that I would return first thing tomorrow morning for the reply and left the Post Office.

Walking down through the winding streets I felt that we had need to celebrate our good fortune. It would be good for the crew to relax and enjoy the good news that I was bringing to them. Calling into the bakers I bought freshly baked white bread, still hot out of the oven, a large pork pie; smoked kippers from the fishmonger; beef sausages and bacon from the butcher. To make the feast complete George Marwick carried back two bottles of port, three bottles of brandy and Tom lifted a keg of ale on his shoulder and we all headed back to the ship. But one last thought was lingering on my mind. I needed to buy something for my lovely wife Isabella. I didn't need to but I wanted to give her something as soon as I returned to Seaham Harbour. Passing by a jeweller's shop there was just the thing on display in the window. A beautiful brooch made from Whitby jet – a black gemstone made from the fossilised remains of monkey puzzle trees. Isabella would be delighted with that I thought as the jeweller neatly wrapped and tied the box. Our very own Queen Victoria favoured Whitby jet whilst in her state of perpetual mourning for Prince Albert making this gemstone all the fashion in society.

That evening we all had a feast to remember on board the "William Thrift". After a meal of contrasting flavours but very welcome all the same George and the crew left my cabin taking the keg of ale and a bottle of brandy up on deck and Lieutenant Smith and I enjoyed listening to their songs and banter until it was clear they had either retired to their bunks or been put to bed by the first mate. I had never known George incapable through drink and I guessed he would probably be watching out for his crewmates. Jack and I sat talking until midnight enjoying two very good bottles of port and nibbling portions of mature cheese. After a very eventful day we both retired to our bunks and drifted into a deep sleep.

CHAPTER 6

The sea chase

The joyful group that partied last night were all on deck when I stepped up from the companionway at first light but none were singing or in the same boisterous mood. I suspect there are a few sore heads this morning I thought - including mine. Everything was back to an orderly routine and the crew were about their chores as if nothing had happened although I suspect they were all daydreaming about what they would do with their forthcoming windfall. Lieutenant Smith looked particularly smart and dapper this morning as he met me by the foredeck. Looking over to the harbour he turned to me "Captain Raine, I think I will come ashore with you to the telegraphy office. I am thinking that their Lordship's at the Admiralty may need a reply so I had better be at hand when we collect their communication". I didn't argue – Jack knew the dangers of going ashore but he was right that a reply might be needed.

"Well just in case Jack I am going to take George with us – he can be useful if we get in a corner." Stepping back down into my cabin I searched amongst my shore possessions and returned after a few moments. "Here, wear this Jack" and I passed him the sword and belt I use when on Royal Navy Reserve drill." It's not a particularly fancy sword and not the quality of blade that you would normally choose but I will feel happier if you wore it."

Boarding the jollyboat George rowed us towards the harbour entrance, passing the shipyards and bonded warehouses we eventually moored up at the steps below the Customs Office. Just behind the wall to the harbour gate five or six sailors were playing pitch and toss for halfpennies. My crew know that I do not approve of this game. Although it may seem harmless fun, it can and often does, lead to heavy gambling. Soon we arrived at the Post Office and Jack stood at the telegrapher's window impatiently waiting for him to open the hatch and begin his work for the day. After what seemed like an hour but would only have been five minutes the incessant chatter of the telegraph equipment could be heard through the hatch and then it went quiet. Knocking on the hatch door Jack impatiently shouted "Any messages for me" and a post office official poked his head through the opening. "Name?" and Jack replied in a quiet voice "Lieutenant Commander Jack Edward Smith expecting a communication from the Admiralty". "Yes, here it is. It's just come through" said the official.

Finding a quiet corner in the Post Office Jack quietly read out the telegraph.

"Imperative you pass intelligence to VIP and accompany him to his destination.

We will rendezvous with the William Thrift by midday at 54° 6′ 59.13″ N, 0° 4′ 56.14″ W,

The Earl of Northbrook, First Lord of the Admiralty".

My immediate thought was that this intelligence that Jack was in possession of, whatever it is, must be of real importance if the First Lord of the Admiralty was personally communicating instructions. "Jack, I know I shouldn't ask, but who is the VIP and what destination are you headed for" I asked hopefully but with a shake of the head Jack made it clear that he couldn't answer.

Briskly walking down the narrow, winding streets towards the harbour we looked down upon the many red pantile roofs which are typical of Yorkshire coastal towns. I could clearly see the ships in harbour busily loading and unloading cargo and carrying out their daily business. Then as we rounded a corner, I had a full view of the dry dock where the Neptun was moored.

“Jack, look at the deck of the Neptun. There are four men crawling all over it and two of them are shining a lantern into the aft hold.”

Jack Smith replied “I can see them, Captain Raine. They don’t look like dockworkers to me!” Then as we approached the schooner Jack shouted “It’s the master of the Neptun, Hans Engel and his crew. They must have got a shock seeing their ship in dock and are checking out whether I am dead in the hold”. At that moment one of the German sailors looked over the guardrail and spotted Jack. Leaping over the ship side and onto the quayside he threw himself at Jack Smith but unfortunately for him George had caught him in full flight and using the sailor’s own momentum and his own mighty strength threw him into the mud and water in the dock. Without hesitation I shouted to our naval friend to get back to the jollyboat and we all ran to the landing steps. Hearing the shouts from his crewman in the mud, Hans Engel dashed to the ship side, to see what was going on.

With only fifty yards to the landing steps the air was pierced by a shrill shout from Hans Engel” bhören Sie sie auf” which brought six burly, foreign sailors rushing up the steps towards us.

“Follow me” I screamed to Jack and George as we quickly turned on our heels and sprinted for our lives out of the dry dock and heading towards the steps leading up to the Abbey. “We can lose ourselves in the Abbey ruins and slip out and back down to the harbour when the coast is clear.”

Although I had climbed up to the Benedictine Abbey many times as a young lad, I had never sprinted up all 199 steps. After the first 40 steps were taken three at a time, I decided that two at a time was more sensible particularly when it felt like the height of each step was increasing the further up we climbed. Soon the three of us reached the top, breathless, and with so much adrenaline pumping through our veins we could have taken on the entire German navy –

except that these six German sailors were hard on our heels and armed to the teeth with knives, cudgels and cutlasses. One thing puzzled me as I looked back at our pursuers. These were clearly German sailors from the unmistakeable way they dressed but where did they come from? The crew of the Neptun and the master Hans Engel were back in the dry dock.

Entering the west front of the Abbey it occurred to me that the stone structures had very much deteriorated since I was last here. Built of two types of stone; white and brown Whitby sandstone the former had weathered much better. It was originally erected in the 7th century as a monastery dedicated to St Hilda overlooking the German Ocean on the east cliff and towering over Whitby and the River Esk. Later it was elevated to a Priory and then an Abbey and finally disestablished during the reign of Henry VIII.

Whitby Abbey ruins

"Split up and hide amongst the ruins" shouted Jack as we entered the Abbey building and without a word George and I threw ourselves behind a stone buttress only seconds before our pursuers reached the top of the steps giving them a full view of the Abbey ruins. Just as I was about to shout to Jack to take cover one of the German sailors spotted him and all six took off in pursuit. Passing by our hiding place I could not help but wonder if they could hear our lungs bursting and our hearts pounding. Unsurprisingly as they ran past our hiding place they were as breathless as we were and panting just as loud and on they ran chasing after Jack.

Grimacing, I whispered to George "The direction that Jack has taken will lead him into trouble. Once he gets through the ruins and across that open ground, he will be at the top of the cliff with his back to a vertical drop of more than 150 feet. Our young Lieutenant has a very important rendezvous to keep. If we do nothing he is done for."

"George, this may be the most important thing we may ever do for our country. I think we only have one road to take. Are you with me?"

Without hesitation George nodded "We can take all six Captain – let's show them how Englishmen fight when they get angry" and we made our way quickly and stealthily towards the open ground beyond the Abbey.

Silently sprinting over the open ground, we approached a small bushy outcrop bordering the lawn of the Abbey with the cliff top only twenty yards beyond. Crouching low behind a blackthorn bush I strained my neck to one side. There, as I feared with his back to the cliff edge was Jack with the six menacing sailors slowly approaching him and cutting off all routes of escape – except one. With his sword drawn Jack began to fend off two assailants armed with cutlasses. The other four had cudgels raised but were clearly not eager to move forward against the sharp gleaming sword being used with such confidence by the young navy officer. Thrusting, lunging and parrying like a sword master Jack was giving an excellent account of himself with sparks flying from all angles as sword and cutlass crossed. Blood began to stream down the arm of one of the sailors who moved back with the shock of being struck. Without warning the largest of the six leapt forward swinging his cudgel. All sailors become involved in a fight when drunk and on shore leave but clearly from the scars on his forehead and his broken nose this six-footer was a regular brawler.

Picking up two fallen tree branches about three feet long I passed one to George. "You take the big guy and the one with the silk scarf around his waist. I will go for the other two. With a bit of luck, we may be able to open up an opportunity for Jack to escape and get back to the ship. Let's see if we can give those six a fight they will never forget."

Standing up to his full height George took off at full speed and was soon in the fray swinging his makeshift weapon. He connected with pin point accuracy on the back of the tall German sailor's head knocking him to the ground and momentarily stunning him. Following straight in behind him I caught one of the other sailors on the forearm knocking the cudgel flying and then swung wildly at another connecting with the side of his head. Clearly, they were shocked at our sudden appearance and re-grouped together facing us.

"Jack" I screamed "Get back to the ship. We will hold them off and join you later" and without a word Jack took to his heels and sprinted towards the Abbey ruins.

By now George had one of the sailors in a headlock and was fending off the tall sailor who had by now recovered his senses. I was exchanging blow to blow with two of the others and giving a good account of myself when I lost my footing and slipped onto my back. Seizing their opportunity, I was immediately set upon and blows began to rain down on my head and boots began to kick relentlessly at my ribs and legs.

To my surprise the onslaught abruptly stopped as three of my assailants hit the ground. Jack had seen my predicament and had turned immediately and ran back to us launching himself feet first at the sailors knocking them down. Quickly recovering they resumed their attack. Although the odds were against us I could see that we were holding our own until, to my dismay, I could see Hans Engel and the crew of the Neptun running through the clearing. Joining their countrymen, they soon overwhelmed all three of us. Jack and I were pinned to the ground while poor George was held down and rendered senseless by blow after blow with a cudgel swung by the big brute that he had tackled first.

Dragging Jack and I kicking and struggling and carrying my unconscious first mate we were taken to a ramshackle building about half a mile away. I guessed that these German sailors had been using this building to avoid the attention of the harbour authorities in the town. Once inside Hans Engel unlocked a back-room door and threw all three of us to the floor locking the door behind him.

My first thought was to see how badly George had been beaten. Quickly looking around the room I grabbed hold of some loose sacking, propped it behind George's head and I began to wipe the blood away from his brow and face. Looking up to Jack whose eyes were darting around the room I asked "Why did you come back? You could have got clean away and safely back to the ship and then on to your rendezvous."

"Without looking at me Jack replied "Well, you seemed to be having such fun I thought I should join in again. What is this place?"

"It's an old signal station. A new one was built further along the cliff about five years ago and this has been unused ever since". Signal stations are placed at strategic points along the coast to enable coastguard officers on shore and Masters of ships at sea to signal and report passing ships but I didn't need to tell Jack what a signal station is used for.

"How is George. Is he still unconscious" Jack asked while rummaging through a jumble of chandlery and maritime bits and pieces lying against the wall of the room? On the adjacent wall light was streaming through a window. The window was about six feet off the ground with vertical bars four inches apart.

Back wall of the signal station

"He's starting to come around Jack. I'm sure he will be alright although he will have a sore head for a day or two. George, can you hear me" I anxiously asked while gently patting his cheeks. "Yes Captain, I can hear you" George mumbled and opened his eyes. "What's happening. Where are we?"

At that moment Jack knelt down at the locked door and whispered "Quiet; I can hear them talking in the next room". Listening intently for a few minutes Jack slowly walked towards us and knelt on the floor beside us.

"What's up Jack" I asked as it was clear he was in deep thought.

"I could hear Hans Engel talking - Only short murmurs and some indistinct words – but what I could make out was "Warten Sie bis es dunkel……. Tragen Sie ihn durch die Stadt…. Die anderen beiden zu töten" which roughly translated means "Wait until dark… Carry him through the town…. Kill the other two. Gentlemen, I think we need to get out of here as quickly as possible"

Jack leapt up and started sorting through the maritime equipment lying against the wall as I tried to stem the bleeding on George's brow with strips of linen torn from a faded curtain. By now George was fully conscious and staggered to his feet insisting that he was fully recovered. Turning around I could see Jack had been busy. He had coupled up a light mooring iron to one end of a rope and threaded the other end through a block and tackle which he had anchored to an iron ring cemented into the floor in the middle of the room. Pushing the mooring iron through the iron bars on the window he asked George if he was well enough to heave. Without hesitation George grabbed the rope leading from the block and tackle, slung it over his shoulder and under his arm and heaved on the block and tackle.

"Pull with everything you've got George" I urged "Our lives depend on you" and the rope began to pull on the mooring iron. The bars creaked as the masonry began to crumble. Every muscle in his body strained as this giant of a man heaved with all his might; heaved for our very lives; heaved as though he were Atlas himself with the mountains of the world on his shoulders. One by one the bars broke away leaving a wide-open window.

"Well done, George, I knew you could do it" Jack exclaimed as he stood an old box on end and climbed up to the window. After a few seconds staring through the window Jack looked down at us. "Bad luck, lads. There is a sheer drop on the other side; this signal station is built right on the side of the cliff"

"Let me see Jack" and I pulled myself up onto the box and looked out. Looking around at the surrounding cliffs I exclaimed "Hang on – I used to play around these cliffs when I was a boy and I remember a narrow footpath allegedly used by smugglers from the beach threaded its way up the side of the cliff to the top and I'm sure the path passed about thirty feet below this signal station. It was known locally as the "nanny goat's path". Hitch that rope to the ring on the floor and bring it over here."

"Hang on Richard" Jack exclaimed "Tie a knot every two feet in the rope. If the path has crumbled away below us you will need to climb back up. The knots will help. Put this other hawser-laid rope over your shoulder just in case you need to secure yourself when you reach the end of the rope."

"Good luck Captain" George exclaimed "Don't take any unnecessary risks; the cliffs around this part of the coast are limestone and look as though they can crumble with the least bit of weight."

Standing on the box and then onto the shoulder offered up by George I grabbed hold of the rope and slipped out of the window. The first ten feet overhung the window and I thought to myself how glad I was that we had put knots in the rope as it swung and twisted violently. Then the cliff face became closer as I descended further until after about thirty-feet I stepped onto a narrow ledge about two-feet wide hugging the cliff side and clearly leading down to the beach.

"Come on you two" I shouted "The path is still here although it has crumbled a little". Soon Jack and George had joined me on the ledge and we gingerly made our way down the path. By the time we had descended another fifty feet the path had widened out to about three feet. At that point I noticed loose stones and bits of limestone tumbling down from above and the sound of foreign voices. Hans Engel and his crew must have come back into the room; discovered us gone and climbed out onto the rope in pursuit.

Quickly making our way we rounded a bend in the path and then we stopped in our tracks. There, just twenty yards further on was a breach in the path about ten feet wide where the path had collapsed revealing a shear drop of about ninety feet onto the rocks below.

The collapsed "nanny goat's path"

Without hesitating George eyed up the gap and the drop below. "I can jump that Captain. Give me that rope over your shoulder and stand back so I can get a good run up." Walking back to get a decent run-up he turned and sprinted at top speed towards the gap and took a mighty leap. There was no doubt that George had the longest legs and the widest gait between the three of us but he was risking his life to prove his statement. Landing in a crouched position on the other side with one foot on the ledge his momentum carried him forward tumbling over and over.

"Catch this rope Jack and tie it around your waist. Take a fast run up; I will try and pull the slack in as you approach the gap and don't worry if you don't make the ledge on this side".

With his usual chuckle Jack replied "Don't worry if I don't reach the ledge. Why, what is there to worry about?" and with that he began his run up and leapt over the breach. This is the craziest example of having blind faith in your comrades I thought as Jack disappeared into the chasm. George was dragged forward with the initial dead weight on the end of the rope but then he took the strain of the rope around his huge shoulders and pulled, arm over arm, until at last Jack's hand appeared and grabbed the ledge followed by his head and then his shoulders.

My relief at seeing Jack safely on the other side was cut short by the sound of footsteps just around the bend behind me. "George, move back from the edge. I don't have time for your rope. I'm coming over now" and I dashed back toward the bend in the track to get a long run up. Only yards in front of me appeared the scar-faced big brute with Hans Engel and the rest of his crew just behind. No time for exchanging pleasantries I thought as I quickly turned and set off at full speed. Reaching the gap, I pushed off with my leading leg and pulled my other leg forward searching for the ledge on the other side. Although both legs missed the ledge my forearms stretched out and momentarily held me until I could feel my weight dragging me down. With no handhold to halt my slide I slowly started to slip back to what I knew was certain death. Only a second before my left forearm disappeared over the ledge to join the rest of my body George's giant hand grabbed me by the wrist and his other hand grabbed the belt around my waist and hauled me up as though I was a sack of flour.

All three of us looked back at the puzzled German sailors on the other side of the gap. Staring into the chasm they began shaking their heads. I knew there was no way they would follow us. They weren't crazy enough to attempt to leap that gap.

"Come on you two. Let's get down to the beach as quickly as possible. Hans Engel will have to climb back up to the top of the cliff; go through the Abbey ruins and down through the town. We only have to walk along this cove and the harbour is around that bluff.in front of us. We have at least a fifteen-minute start on them.

Cove leading to Whitby Harbour

The sight of the Harbour as we rounded the bluff lifted our spirits and with no sign of any danger we ran to the landing jetty, untied the mooring lines and launched our boat. Taking an oar each George and I pulled for the "William Thrift" as hard as we could. Climbing on board I called all hands to make ready for sailing immediately and with precision and speed the crew were shinning up the rigging, climbing out over the yards, loosening the reef lines and unfurling the sails. Turning to face the harbour I could see someone running to the end of the East pier. "Look, over there Jack, at the end of the pier" I shouted.

"It's Hans Engel" replied Jack "He has yellow and black flags in his hands and he's using semaphore signals to one of those ships anchored to the north of the harbour. Captain, write this down - use the back of this telegram" and he started reeling off letters as he watched the German agent relaying his message.

"jmnc eaib orct olbk hrlr sadi iges semn etna sgoj ciip shen pumn s--j p--- er-- -de- --oi ---

"There, end of message" blurted Jack. "But it doesn't make any sense at all Jack" I replied.

"That's because it's in code. German naval signals are always relayed in a simple code. They use a five-by-five cypher. Now look, putting these letters in five rows at a time from left to right and the message is read down and along each of the five columns column in each block. So, we have,

J	M	N	C	E
A	I	B	O	R
C	T	O	L	B
K	H	R	L	R
S	A	D	I	I

G	E	S	S	E
M	N	E	T	N
A	S	G	O	J
C	I	I	P	S
H	E	N	P	U

M	N	S	-	-
J	P	-	-	-
E	R	-	-	-
D	E	-	-	-
E	I	-	-	-

It reads "Jack Smith an bord collier brig. Machen sie segin. Stoppen JS um jeden preis" which roughly translates as" Jack Smith on board collier brig. Make Sail, Stop JS at all cost" and with a wry smile Jack said "They'll have to catch me first"

The gravity of the situation dawned on me. These villains were prepared to stop at nothing, even murder, to achieve their objective and yet this young naval officer at my side was quite undaunted by the events unfolding before us. By now George was hauling the anchor with Bob Mustard and with the sails now unfurled the "William Thrift" was starting to run with the wind behind us. Jack

Smith had my telescope raised and was scanning the ships anchored to the north.

"Captain Raine. Do you remember that merchantman – the odd-looking barquentine - that was lying off yesterday afternoon? Well, she is making sail and raising her anchor. I'm trying to see the name on her bow. Ah there it is, The Ernst Friedrick. I bet that's the ship that Hans Engel was supposed to transfer me onto from the Neptun and wait a minute – who do you think is on deck looking down a telescope at us? None other than that despicable Kapitan Ernst Sturm of the German naval intelligence. She's now showing full canvass. Do you think we can outrun her?"

All sort of thoughts were going through my head. A ship chasing another should have the advantage in point of sailing if all other things were equal. Of course, things at sea are often unequal. The skills of the master; the cut of the ship and how well each ship manoeuvres make the general principle of chasers advantage an uncertain one and for a time at least the master of the ship being pursued can frustrate attempts to be caught. Sometimes it is only a matter of time. Fully laden colliers and merchantmen differ only slightly in the speed they move though the sea. The amount of canvas the crew can get aloft and the way the master manoeuvres the ship into the wind can temporarily give an advantage in a sea chase. I knew that I must keep on a straight course without tacking or I would lose time in the manoeuvre of coming about and the Ernst Friedrick would gain ground. Of course, Kapitan Sturm would be equally aware of this and would be seeking to keep the wind in his sails and keeping a straight course behind the "William Thrift". If he had to tack to keep the wind he would only prolong the chase and so Sturm's strategy would be to keep the same heading and eventually the ships would come together where the two courses intersect.

“Well Jack” I said “If there were banks of fog that we could run into or a small cove that we could duck into and hide then I would say we had an even chance of making your rendezvous south of Flamborough Head. As it is with clear weather ahead and shallow rocky waters along the coast the advantage is with the German barquentine. Flamborough Head is nine miles ahead of us and we do not know how far around the point we have to go to reach your destination and safety. Kapitan Sturm will do his best to close on us but what he does not realise is that our draft, even with a full cargo of coals, is much less than the Ernst Friedrick, and we can sail into much shallower water. I have no doubt that the German ship will do what it can to pull alongside and then use grappling irons to board us. If she does then I will make sure she has to come into much shallower waters to come alongside of us and there is every chance she may run aground.”

Over the course of the next two hours both ships exchanged similar tactics. Main, royals and sky sail set. Foretop studding sails braced so far forward so as to be cleverly full in the prevailing wind. However, the Ernst Friedrick had packed every stitch of sail that could be set and the three-masted barquentine carried more sail than the “William Thrifts” two masts. Slowly the stranger’s hull drew closer to our stern and I knew it would only be a matter of minutes before she would be running a parallel course at which point, they would try to board us.

“Jack, I have an idea” I shouted. “George, tell the crew to be ready to slab reef the sails. When Kapitan Sturm tries to draw alongside I will draw away into shallower water forcing him closer to the coast. We are just off the point of Flamborough Head and if I can tempt him under the lee of the cliffs he will lose the wind and give us the chance to make for the point. To avoid us becoming becalmed as well tell the lads I will wait until the very last minute, we will slab reef the mainsail which will slow us down quickly and tack on the port side and slip behind the stern of our German friend. George, as soon as we come about get Tom to hoist the spanker sail on the mizzen mast so we keep the wind until the mainsail is fully hoisted again and we make for the point. Does everyone understand what we are doing?" A ring of "Aye, aye Captain" rang from all quarters.

Just as I anticipated the Ernst Friedrick slowly drew alongside and we could see the German crew readied for action. Kapitan Sturm was bellowing orders to the sailors standing on the lower rigging, grappling irons and ropes in hand swinging them around and waiting for the right moment to launch their assault. Nudging the helm to starboard, bit by bit, I maintained enough distance between us to avoid the boarders. Without realising how close we were sailing to the shore Kapitan Sturm continued urging his helmsman to draw closer to us until we were almost in the lea of the cliffs now towering above us. "Now George" I screamed and without even a seconds delay the lads had slab reefed the mainsail, the sail dropped half down the mast and immediately the "William Thrift" dragged in the water as the wind was lost from the sail. The Ernst Friedrick continued forward in full sail and before Sturm had realised what we were up to I shouted "Coming about" to warn the crew of my manoeuvre and threw the wheel hard to port just missing the stern of the chasing barquentine as we tacked behind crossing the Neptun's wake and pulled away from the cliffs. Simultaneously Tom and Billy hauled the spanker sail up the mizzen mast with so much adrenaline that within seconds we had regained the speed we had lost and were pulling away for the point of Flamborough Head. Looking back at the Ernst Friedrick I could see the anger on Sturm's face as he ordered his helmsman to come about and continue the pursuit. Although we had gained a short-term advantage I began to wonder if we were running out of alternatives. It may only be just a matter of time – the German ship was four hundred yards behind us and closing the distance minute by minute. At that moment my concentration was broken by a crack and the ricochet of a bullet off the stern anchor only feet away from Jack Smith. Seconds later a bullet shattered the binnacle housing showering him with splinters.

“Jack, get behind the windlass” I screamed, but Jack must have read my thoughts as he threw himself behind it before the words were out of my mouth. Crouched low on the wheel I looked back to see the Ernst Friedrick only fifty yards behind us with Ernst Sturm half way up the rigging. His arm was looped around a halyard to steady him as he took aim with a rifle and he began reigning shot after shot at the windlass. It was clear that he was determined to finish off our young naval officer once and for all. Keeping my head down I desperately tried to think what I could do but my mind was blank – I could think of no solution. Then the crack from the rifle stopped and I looked back to see the Ernst Friedrick bearing off to port and heading due east into open sea. What on earth was Sturm up to now? With a cheer Jack jumped up from behind the windlass waving with both arms over our prow. There coming around the point was a Royal Navy man-of-war fully rigged and drawing up to us with speed.

“It’s my old ship the frigate HMS Galatea,” shouted Jack. “Thank god, she’s saved our bacon”. Joining Jack on the prow I could not avoid showing my sense of relief. “Will your ship sink the Ernst Friedrick Jack” I hopefully asked.

“Probably not Captain Raine, it would raise too many political questions”. At that precise moment an almighty boom, smoke and a flash of fire could be seen from one of the guns on board HMS Galatea and the topmast of the Ernst Friedrick shattered and fell with rigging and sail littered on her decks. Laughing with glee Jack shouted “There – she’s given Otto a bloody nose” as the German merchantman limped away into the distance.

HMS Galatea

“Heave to and drop anchor Captain” said Jack “I’ll get on-board the Galatea and make my report and I’d like you to come with me if you would be so kind”. With great delight I replied “I would be honoured to have the privilege of boarding such a majestic ship-of-the-line”. Turning to my first mate I shouted “Turn us into the wind George and prepare to drop anchor” and the crew were soon hauling and tying up the sails. Around the prow of the frigate a cutter pulled past the Galatea’s anchor and the four sailors, all rowing in unison, soon reached the “William Thrift”. “Are you ready Captain” Jack chirped eagerly and without any further ado we were on board the cutter and pulling towards the man-of-war. Climbing the boarding ladder behind this young naval officer I felt a wave of pride and emotion at this magnificent ship and the men that wear the uniform of our Royal Navy. On reaching the top of the ladder Jack stepped on deck, straightened his coat and spoke out loud and confidently “Permission to come aboard Captain". With a smile the captain in full naval uniform, gold braid and sword glistening in the sunshine replied "Permission granted Lieutenant Commander Smith" and he stepped forward and gleefully grasped Jack's hand. "Good to see you fit and well Jack. You had us worried for a time but his Lordship kept saying he had every confidence that you would be joining him. He is in my cabin and is eager to receive your report. I will catch up with events as soon as you are free."

Turning to me Jack politely said "Captain Armstrong, may I introduce Captain Raine, Master of the William Thrift and to whom I owe my life. The part he has played in safely bringing me to this rendezvous is immeasurable". Once again Captain Armstrong eagerly stepped forward vigorously shaking my hand. "Captain Raine – we are in your debt. The assignment that Jack Smith is involved in is of national importance and we are also pleased that he is safely back with us. Can I give you a tour of my ship while Lieutenant Smith gives his report to his Lordship" and he led me down onto the main gun deck? The Galatea, an Ariadne class, 26 guns, sixth rate ship-of-the-line took my breath away at her size and fighting capability. With a keel length of 245 feet; a beam of 50 feet; a complement of 450 officers and men; 24 x 10-inch guns on the middle deck and 2 x 68-pounder pivot-mounted guns on the upper deck she could not fail to impress with spotless decks cleared, ropes tidily curled, brasses shining in the sun and not a belay pin out of position. With great pride Captain Armstrong asked "What do you think of our master gunner's marksmanship today? At 1,000 yards he un-masted that German merchantman with the pivot-mounted 68-pounder on the upper deck". Before I had the chance to answer Jack had returned and politely saluted his captain and said "Excuse me sir, His Lordship has asked if you and Captain Raine could join him at your earliest convenience." With a nod Captain Armstrong turned to me "Come along Captain Raine and meet our VIP" and he led me to his aft cabin below the quarterdeck. Entering the "great cabin" which spanned the width of the stern with large windows allowing the room to be illuminated with natural light and sunshine I was overawed by the luxury of so much dark, polished wood panelling. Below the large window was the captain's desk and chart table and in the centre of the room a number of deep leather padded chairs surrounded a large oval dining table that could comfortably seat twenty diners.

Rising from a sofa next to the chart table an elderly gentleman purposefully strode towards us as we entered the room. "Your Lordship, May I present Captain Richard Raine, Master of the brigantine William Thrift" announced Captain Armstrong. Turning to me he continued "Captain Raine, May I present Lord Salisbury, Foreign Secretary of Great Britain and Ireland."

Lord Salisbury. Foreign Secretary of Great Britain and Ireland

"Captain Raine" his Lordship politely bowed his head whilst at the same time shaking my hand with a firm grip. "We meet in unusual circumstances and in the strangest of places but I can tell you that it is a long time since I was so pleased to meet someone. Jack has relayed to me the events of the last two days."

Lord Salisbury was impeccably dressed as you would expect for a peer of the realm and a senior politician and widely admired statesman in Her Majesty's government. Despite his lofty position his deep blue eyes and his warm smile dispelled any reservations I would normally have in meeting someone of his rank and I felt very much at ease in his presence. I was aware of his reputation as the best orator and diplomat in government and now I understood how he had made such a success in his political career. His whole aura and demeanour was warm, friendly and dignified.

Responding to his welcome I replied "I am very pleased to meet your Lordship. It has indeed been an unexpected adventure. When I left Seaham Harbour bound for Colchester three days ago, I could not have anticipated the series of events that were to unfold but I am relieved that we are all out of danger now and that Jack has been able to deliver his intelligence to you".

"Jack has told me of the risks you have taken to help him to complete his mission" continued Lord Salisbury "Not only has he brought invaluable information to me but Jack is also highly valued by me and the Royal Navy and I am sure Captain Armstrong and their Lordships at the Admiralty are watching Jack's progress and career with great interest." Beckoning us all to sit on the sofa and easy chairs Lord Salisbury asked "Glass of madeira everyone?" and before anyone replied he was passing a large crystal glass filled to the brim to the three of us and then he added "Please excuse me but I will not join you – I prefer tea"

“Now Captain Raine, I think you deserve an explanation from me but first” Lord Salisbury hesitated “I must stress that what I am about to tell you is of national importance. If the facts were to become known to the press or to foreign powers the implications for Great Britain and many European countries could be catastrophic and destroy the peace that has recently existed between so many sovereign states in Europe. Do you understand the importance of my request that you keep this conversation to yourself and do not repeat what I am about to tell you to anyone my dear sir?”

It was clear to me that, somehow, I had become entangled in political events that someone from my station could never have conceived. To me the four corners of the globe were Memel in the Baltics, Seaham Harbour, London and Rotterdam and the only risks were the weather and the sea. The world of Lord Salisbury was infinitely greater, geographically boundless and socially and politically so different to mine. Without hesitation I proudly and confidently spoke out “You have made my part in this matter very clear your Lordship. I give you my word that I will not speak of this to anyone”. I looked at Jack and Captain Armstrong and they gave Lord Salisbury a reassuring smile and a nod.

“Excellent, my dear sir. I knew I could rely on you!” continued his Lordship “First, you are now aware of the clandestine nature of the work of the Marquess of Londonderry. I used to work with his grandfather, the 3rd Marquess, many years ago in the diplomatic corps at the British Embassy in Austria and we were the best of friends. Lord Londonderry approached me several years ago to ask if he could be of service to his country as he, like his grandfather, is extremely patriotic. Together we developed this façade that he acts out with great skill of a nobleman who has no interest in life but self-interest and gracious living. In fact Lord Londonderry feeds back intelligence to me through our young Lieutenant Smith that is invaluable in diplomatic circles and which has far reaching implications. I need not tell you, then, how this guise must continue otherwise his work would be compromised."

"Let me appraise you of the sorry state of events in Europe. Politically it is like watching and waiting for a tinderbox to spark which will ignite nations one against the other. There are five major powers in Europe; Great Britain, Russia, France, Austria and Germany. You will know that recently Germany annexed Alsace-Lorraine and provoked the hostility of France. Unfortunately, France is still recovering economically from the Franco-Prussian war of ten years ago and cannot respond militarily to this action by Germany. Then we have the demise of the Ottoman Empire casting a shadow over international relations in Europe. The reparations demanded by Russia after the Russo-Turkish War have bankrupted Turkey and internally pressures are building up within the now weakened Ottoman Empire to have a separate Bulgarian state and for many of the Balkan states to declare independence. Lord Londonderry has detected political aspirations by the Austria-Hungary Empire to acquire the state of Bosnia and other Slavic speaking states. In the centre of this entire web of political manoeuvring stands Prince Otto von Bismarck, Chancellor of Germany. The German Empire has been built largely upon his devious political scheming and his meddling in the affairs of other nations always to the advantage of Germany."

Re-filling our glasses Lord Salisbury continued "We have detected from indiscreet conversations revealed by his Head of Navy, General von Caprivi, that the German Chancellor has three main objectives in his foreign policy. On the one hand he means to isolate France politically which will leave them vulnerable to more aggressive actions. Then he seeks to foster greater links and an alliance with Russia to strengthen his bargaining and bullying tactics of other countries. Finally, he is seeking to unite the Germanic speaking people of Austria-Hungary into one super state of Germany." Looking out of the large master cabin window Lord Salisbury shook his head and sat down again. "von Bismarck now intends to draw Italy into his web of intrigue. Lord Londonderry has learned that the German Chancellor is to use his characteristic technique of secretly encouraging French ambitions in North Africa, mainly to divert her from recovering Alsace-Lorraine but also to bring her into conflict with Italy who also have ambitions, and 20,000 settlers, in the Tunis area. This would throw Italy into the arms of Germany and further isolate France even further in European diplomatic affairs."

"Captain Raine" his Lordship exclaimed "the only thing that holds von Bismarck in check is the might of the Royal Navy. At this point in time he has no intention of becoming involved in a war with Great Britain because his navy cannot match the firepower and number of capital ships of Her Majesty's Royal Navy. It is Great Britain alone that has the power and influence to intervene and put a stop to the German Chancellor's scheming plans. I have called together an international convention of the five major powers to be held in Berlin in five days' time. You may think that this would be like putting our heads in the lion's mouth but Germany and, Ernst Sturm in particular, would not dare to compromise myself, Lieutenant Smith or this ships company whilst we are engaged on a diplomatic mission. You may, by now, have guessed my objective at the Berlin conference. I intend to convince the Russian delegation that they would be falling into the hands of Germany if they allow the balance of power in Europe to be completely upset by the annihilation or further weakening of France. The argument of the unification of the Germanic speaking people is merely a smokescreen and I will convince the Austria-Hungary delegation that Germany will simply seek to be the dominant partner in such unification. Although our country has been at war for the best part of eight hundred years with France we must, for the sake of peace in Europe, reach an alliance; an entente cordiale between Great Britain and France and together with an Anglo-

Russian alliance we may hope that peace might continue for a further generation at least."

All of this diplomatic manoeuvring and intrigue had my head in a spin but I could see the gravity of the situation between these politically diverse nations in Europe. "I had no idea that relations were so tense and sensitive between European nations" I finally exclaimed. "I can only hope that your plans succeed for the sake of Great Britain and that peace in Europe is a legacy that you will be remembered for. Thank you, sir, for sharing your confidences with me and let me take your hand and wish you well for a speedy and safe return home from Berlin." With a warm smile Lord Salisbury politely bowed and shook my hand. "We will remember the part you have played in making these events possible Captain Raine" he said "I wish you good luck on the remainder of your voyage and a safe return to Seaham Harbour".

Jack and Captain Armstrong accompanied me on deck and they could quite clearly see that I was lost for words. "Jack" I said "if ever you need a friend or a ship, you know where you can find me, and do not hesitate to ask.

"Richard" Jack replied "Words cannot express how glad I am that you came across me in the hold of the Neptun. We have had such an adventure together and I couldn't wish for a better friend to have at my side in a tight spot. With luck I will be back and forth to Wynyard Hall to be briefed by Lord Londonderry so don't be surprised if one day I come knocking on your cabin door."

Hugging each other tightly we shook hands and reluctantly said our goodbyes. I climbed down the boarding ladder into the cutter and returned to the "William Thrift".

Within the hour we weighed anchor, hauled up a full set of canvas and took our heading for Colchester. Three uneventful days of plain sailing later we entered the estuary of the River Colne. It is always an anxious time entering a river course which requires a different style of sailing. The crew instinctively focus on our heading and the hidden hazards in the river as we grope our way around sandbanks. Every hundred yards throws up an array of beacons and buoys. On each occasion I make this voyage the natural features of channels and sandbanks change. Sailing upstream we moored alongside the quay at Wivenhoe which is about five miles downstream from Colchester. The river is tidal and not navigable by sea going vessels from this point and I arranged for our cargo to be loaded onto lighters; flat bottom barges for the last five miles upstream to the coal merchant's wharf in Colchester. For those three days sailing to Wivenhoe the crew continued to press me to tell them what transpired on board the frigate HMS Galatea but all I would reveal was a description of that magnificent ship-of-the-line. By the time we had returned from Wivenhoe to Seaham Harbour a week later with a cargo of gravel and silver sand the crew had stopped asking questions and had returned to the day-to-day chatter of sailors. It would seem to a third party as though our voyage had been totally uneventful. However, that did not apply to me. I was full of a sense of personal satisfaction as I steered the "William Thrift" through the dock gates at Seaham Harbour where a welcoming Jeremiah Hall stood waving from the same place as when we had left two weeks earlier. I had been of service to my country on a stage that I could never have imagined and my involvement in the proceedings had such far-reaching implications. I was enjoying the utter exhilaration that true patriots like Lieutenant Jack Smith and Lord Salisbury must feel when they successfully achieve diplomatic gains for their country.

It has been an eventful and memorable voyage and one that I shall never forget. In addition, it has been a profitable trip for the owner – Mrs Anderson – and for myself and the crew. We should expect the proceeds from the sale of the cargo of coals from the Neptun within the next month and the schooner itself will be auctioned off by the Receiver of Wrecks at Whitby after twelve months. All in all my spirits were high for a number of reasons not least because I was back in my home port again and soon I would be reunited with my lovely wife and adorable children.

CHAPTER 7

An intriguing plot is uncovered

Three weeks later and I was still in a state of disbelief and shock at the incredible events that had slipped into my life without warning. Every moment whilst my attention was not occupied with affairs of the ship my mind recalled the events of that voyage to Colchester and, on each occasion, I felt near to bursting with pride. It had been a long time since I looked forward to evenings in my cabin. For many years I had viewed the end of a working day as the time to put my head on the pillow and rest my body for the trials of the next day at sea – nothing more. Now I looked forward to closing the door in my cabin; lying in my bunk, recounting the characters I had met and the adventure I had experienced and that wonderful feeling would come flooding back.

The William Thrift had sailed to the port of Memel in the Baltics. The demand for timber and wooden props for the coal mines in the Northumberland and Durham coalfields directed ship-owners to seek cargoes in this ample spruce and Norwegian fir tree growing area of Scandinavia. The high custom duties imposed by neighbouring Riga had blighted their timber trade but the free-trade attitude by Memel civic officials encouraged the establishment of industrial sawmills in the town. This specialisation in wood manufacturing guaranteed income and stability for the town and undoubtedly underpinned the building of the finest harbour in the Baltic. Mrs Anderson had bought for shipment four hundred barrels of salted herring in Newcastle from the herring fleet as they followed the "silver darlings" on their migration from the North East of Scotland down the east coast of England. The local traders in Memel would have no problem in selling this cargo on as it is a delicacy that graces every table in East Prussia.

When visiting this port, I always remind the crew to take extra care about what they eat and drink whilst on-shore. Thirty years ago, a world-wide epidemic of cholera was carried to England on ships from the Baltics. It had started on the banks of the Ganges River in India, spread to China, Russia and then to the Baltic ports where numerous ships carried the infection to their home ports in England. I understand the short sea going routes from this part of Europe to north-east ports was not long enough to act as a sufficient quarantine period and ships arrived with full on-board infection. Two outbreaks of cholera in Seaham Harbour had prompted the fitting out of an "Isolation Hospital" to treat all sailors arriving in port with fever or sea-borne cholera-like symptoms. The British Port Sanitation Authority however had inspected this facility and were so unimpressed that they put the word "Hospital" in inverted commas throughout their report; it was in fact the upper floor of a rope store and blacksmith's shop.

Our return journey this time was not to Seaham Harbour but to the Port of Sunderland just six miles further north of our home port. Our hold was filled to capacity with timber for Lord Lambton whose fourteen collieries in Durham together with Lord Londonderry's' collieries dominate the coal trade in the north of England. During the course of the last three weeks, I have recorded twelve sightings of north-east colliers in the ships log that have all been hailed and reported as "all's well" by their master. Ship-owners are making the most of the fair-weather window to the Baltic States keen to profit from the new season's timber crop.

The Baltic Sea is a large inland sea about 900 miles long and 150 miles wide that joins the German Ocean with Northern Europe. Sailing through these waters requires extra vigilance from all hands due to the numerous islands and shallow waters and I follow tried and tested navigation routes marked on my charts to sail the safe passage back into the German Ocean. The tides are scarcely perceptible as we pass through the Gulf of Gdansk and we weave our way through the islands between Malmo and Copenhagen into the dangerous waters of Kattegat Bay. Favourable westerly winds drive us into the Skagerrak Strait north of Denmark where the Baltic Sea finally merges with the German Ocean.

"How far before we see the north-east coast, Captain?" asks Tom Colling as he hauls up the spanker sail and we leave the Skagerrak Strait behind us.

"We're crossing the widest part of the German Ocean, Tom. That's about 360 miles before we strike land again. We are taking a heading of 55 degrees North which will take us to Newcastle and our cargo is to be landed at Sunderland which, as you know, is about ten miles further south."

"Is it plain sailing from here on Captain?" Tom continues. This was the first voyage Tom had made to the Baltic Sea. He was clearly absorbing as much information as possible aware that this route to The Baltic States and back is a frequent destination for merchant shipping.

"Well, it appears so but looks can be deceptive. The German Ocean is traversed by immense sand banks. In particular Dogger Bank and The Long Forties are constantly shifting with depths as little as ten fathoms but the main hazard to be aware of in this sea is the weather. Strong gales and currents can easily blow a ship off course and allowance must be made when working out compass headings. We should make Sunderland in three days if we can keep this following easterly breeze".

Three days of plain sailing later and Billy Booth is aloft at almost the highest point of the main mast. George Marwick has asked him to check the shackles on the gaff; the spar securing the head of the fore and aft sail.

“Land ho!” shouts Billy excitedly “over the prow Captain” and he shins down the rigging eagerly pointing out the landfall to Tom who strains his eyes to see.

“Where do you think that is Mr Marwick” quizzes Tom.

George looks at me with a smile and replies “Well – the captain has continued on a heading of 55 degrees north; he has allowed for the wind and currents so you can bet that is Newcastle on the River Tyne straight ahead. The captain always works on dead reckoning and I have never known him to get it wrong. Once we are close enough to confirm we are off the River Tyne we will change course and follow the coast south until we reach Sunderland roads off the mouth of the River Wear.”

Just one hour later we were approaching the two outer piers at Sunderland harbour. A lighthouse stands to attention at the end of the north pier and I am told that a subway was built into the concrete blocks used to build the pier so that access to the lighthouse is possible in stormy weather.

George steadies his arm on the binnacle and extends and focuses the telescope. “We’re in luck Captain. The harbourmaster is flying the tide flag and the South outlet gates are open so we are all clear to enter harbour. The pilot boat is just passing the north pier and will be with us in about ten minutes.”

Last year a lock was constructed at this new South outlet to connect to the three South docks. This has proved to be a great convenience and an aid to trade as vessels can enter and leave the docks by sea without entering the river and shipping using this outlet are totally independent of ordinary tides. It also makes life easier for pilots who do not have to dodge and weave around ships entering and leaving the narrow river mouth.

Soon we are moored up to the satisfaction of the Berthing Master and I make my way to the Harbour Masters Office. George and the crew remove the hatch covers to allow the impatient dock workers to begin unloading the timber onto the dockside.

“Well hello Richard” exclaims Bob Purvis the Harbour Master. “I haven’t seen you for some time. How are you?”

Quickly briefing Bob on our voyage from Memel with the shipment of timber I provide his clerk with details of ships passed on route with “all’s well” reported in case they are subsequently lost in storms or are leaky and sink. Insurance companies highly value this maritime intelligence when settling or disputing claims for losses from ship-owners.

Keen to reach Seaham harbour before nightfall I pay my harbour dues to the clerk and receive a dock office pass so that the Harbourmaster can put me in turn to leave port. Bob Purvis wishes me “bon voyage” and tells me that a paddle tug should be available within the next half hour if my ship is ready to set sail. With a spring in my step that I should be spending tonight in my home port I stride briskly back to the dockside.

George greets me with the news “Cargo unloaded Captain and Lord Lambton’s representative, Mr Watson, has checked off the quantities. He is waiting for you on the dockside next to that ketch from London which is unloading a second-hand steam engine for the colliery at Houghton.

“Mr Watson - nice to see you again. It has been quite a while since we have met. I trust everything is in order with Lord Lambton’s timber” I asked hoping that he had no problem with the inventory that may delay my departure.

“None at all Captain Raine. I hope your voyage was pleasant and the weather in the Baltics was not too bad. If you have the bill of lading to hand, I will sign it off and take possession of the cargo. I can see Mr Marwick has readied your ship to sail. You must be keen to get back to Seaham tonight and find your slippers warming by the fireside".

Laughing at his comments I wondered if he could read my mind. That was just what I wanted. After a five week voyage it was the only thing I could think of and with luck I was only three hours away from opening my front door and holding my wife and family in my arms. Isabella would be smiling, kissing me and blurting out all of the news in the town since I was last home. Then she would be fussing around asking what I would like to eat. Elizabeth Ann has her tenth birthday next month and she would be dropping hints about the latest toys in Rutherford's Store whilst her younger brother Richard Henry would be asking me to tell him a story about my last voyage.

Just as the Harbourmaster had promised the paddle tug shunted over to our moorings within the half hour and cast a tow rope. Soon we were passing through the south outlet lock gates and out into open water. "Take over George and let's head for home" I eagerly asked. For the short hop down the coast to Seaham my first mate took entire charge of the ship allowing me time in my cabin to bring the ships' records up-to-date. Shortly afterwards our pilot was on-board and we were heading for the South Dock. As I would have expected Jeremiah Hall was on duty and waving to us as we passed the dock gates.

Unusually there were very few ships in the South Dock and we berthed more than three ship lengths from the nearest vessel. "Mr Marwick" I shouted as George was giving instructions to Bob Mustard and Billy Booth. "I will call into the Harbourmaster's office and arrange for a night watchman to sit on board tonight so that we can all have a night ashore". A cheer from the whole crew rang out bringing a broad smile to my face.

The time was now three o'clock in the afternoon. The sky was clear and a warm sun bathed my face as I walked towards William Sheridan's office. Stepping inside I went straight to the clerk's office and knocking twice on the open door was called inside.

"Ah, good afternoon, Captain Raine. How are you today?" exclaimed William's clerk and before I had time to set out my request for a night watchman he continued. "We have been asked that as soon as you moor up you should present yourself at the Londonderry Offices on North Terrace"

"Whatever for" I asked "Why does the Londonderry Estates want to talk to me?"

"Don't know Captain Raine but I am told that it is extremely important so it would be wise to do as they ask."

Climbing up the steps cut into the side of the docks I pondered on the reason for this request. Lord Londonderry's Chief Financial Agent, Mr Eminson is a Justice of the Peace presiding on the bench of Seaham Magistrates; a Major in the Seaham Artillery Volunteers and a prominent member of Seaham society. What would he want with me? Day-to-day operational matters affecting Londonderry docks, railways, collieries and estates are dealt with by the appropriate Manager – not by Mr Eminson. Perhaps he is looking for a captain to join his new fleet of steam collier ships or had he some objection to Seaham ship-owners carrying cargoes for Lord Lambton. If that was the case he would be better to speak to Mrs Anderson. Whatever the reason I would soon find out I thought as I walked through the main gates and across the gravel driveway towards the main entrance to the Londonderry Offices.

The Londonderry Offices

I opened the outer door, walked through the porch turning the shining brass door handle of the inner door and entered the grand and imposing building designed in the Italian style but with French ornamentation and an impressive central tower. Corridors ran off the main reception hall to the left, to the right and a wide carpeted staircase wound its way up to the next floor but no signs were visible to guide me to Mr Eminson's office. However, sitting at a desk only ten yards away was a gentleman with a high winged collar and tie and brown suit who was sorting through the recently delivered post. My shoes clicked loudly on the marble mosaic floor as I strode across to his desk.

"I have been asked to report to Mr Eminson" I declared as the clerk peered up at me through round wire rimmed spectacles "My name is Captain Richard Raine, Master of The William Thrift"

Standing immediately to his feet the short wiry clerk replied "Please take a seat over there Captain. I will speak to Mr Eminson's chief clerk and return in a few moments and he slowly shuffled down the corridor to the right.

After a few minutes I could hear his footsteps echoing along the passage as he returned to the main entrance hall.

“I am sorry Captain Raine but Mr Eminson’s chief clerk has confirmed that Mr Eminson has made no appointment with you”.

Thank goodness for that I thought with a sense of relief but why on earth did the Harbourmaster ask me to report here then?

“However,” the clerk continued “I have checked in the appointments book and it is his Lordship, the Marquess of Londonderry who has asked to see you”.

My mind went into a spin; for a few seconds I froze and eventually I recovered my senses and asked “Can you tell me what his Lordship wishes to discuss with me - Is he available to see me today?”

“I am sorry Captain but no-one knows why his Lordship wishes to see you but he is upstairs in the board room. I shall take you up and see if he is available to speak with you.”

Following him up the grand staircase I glanced at the portraits of the Londonderry heirs from the 1st Marquess to the 6th and current Marquess which were each surrounded with pictures of their wives and children. On the first floor the clerk stopped at a door just off the main staircase, knocked and went inside. A minute later the door opened and he peered around the door beckoning me towards him. “His Lordship will see you now” he whispered and he ushered me into the room and then quietly left closing the door behind him.

I looked around the room. It was a spectacular sight to see for someone who was used to living in a cramped, poorly lit ship’s cabin. I was conscious that I was standing on a luxurious red and gold carpet with pile so thick my feet could feel the warmth through my shoes. The walls and ceiling were brightly decorated and beautiful paintings of Italian landscapes adorned the walls. A polished mahogany table with leather studded chairs ran half the length of the room and beyond that sat a young man at a large desk.

Standing up the young man beckoned me towards him "Come in Captain Raine."

I recognised him immediately from sketches in newspaper reports appearing in The Seaham Weekly News. This handsome young man about thirty years old, tall and slim and dressed in the most elegant of gentlemen's attire without doubt tailored in London was Charles Vane Tempest Stewart, 6th Marquess of Londonderry. Although he portrayed a warm smile as he shook my hand, I had a strange feeling that beneath this facade was a worried man.

"Captain Raine" he continued "You may be wondering why I have asked you here. First, come over here to the window" and he led me around his desk to a large picture window which allowed the afternoon sun to light up the room. The window afforded great views over the North Dock which his grandfather had built in 1828.

"From here I can see every ship entering and leaving my docks and I know what cargo every ship brings into Seaham. One hour ago I saw your ship, The William Thrift, towed in through the dock gates by my paddle tug "Harry Vane" and heading for a berth in the South dock. I have to admit, until that point, I was a worried man who was in the depths of despair. The sight of you entering port has given me a glimmer of hope that all is not lost. Please sit down and let me acquaint you with some facts which may help to explain."

Sitting down on a sofa facing this troubled young man I could not help but wonder why the sight of my ship should raise his spirits and without thinking I spoke out confidently "If there is anything I can do to help your Lordship I will gladly do it."

"Thank you, Captain Raine," he replied "but it would be better that you consider what I have to say first."

"First, you may be aware that my mother Lady Frances Anne brought the telegraph service to Seaham Harbour twenty years ago. She had become frustrated that anyone wishing to communicate quickly with traders and businesses in the town would have to send a telegraph to the telegraph office in Sunderland who would then despatch a rider on horseback for the six miles to our town. She thought this was an absurd situation for a town straining to move forward. Consequently, she financed the building of a telegraph service to Seaham Harbour. Well – thanks to our telegraphy service I received a telegram a few weeks ago from Lord Salisbury via the Admiralty before he set sail for Berlin on board HMS Galatea. In it he explained what had happened to Lieutenant Smith and the assistance you gave to him at great peril to your own life and how you succeeded in safely delivering Jack and the intelligence he possessed to Lord Salisbury. He further told me in that telegram that he had taken you into his confidence and that you are aware of my clandestine role in the security of our nation."

"I only did what any true Englishman would have done your Lordship" I responded "but I can assure you that I will never reveal those events or the part you play in security matters."

"Thank you, Captain. I am confident you will keep my activities and role secret but that is not the reason I asked you here" replied his Lordship. "It is necessary for me to reveal some more confidences that I would not normally speak about but which must be laid out so that you understand my dilemma."

Slowly pacing backwards and forwards in front of the sofa with his hands clasped behind his back his Lordship hesitated and continued.

"You may be aware that I have a number of residences which are favourites of the Prince and Princess of Wales. I entertain them at Mount Stewart in County Down in Ireland; at Londonderry House on Park Lane in London and at

Wynyard Park in Durham. It is no secret that the Prince of Wales enjoys the company of ladies and he has a number of lady admirers who are keen to please him. One such lady is Jennie, the American wife of my cousin Lord Randolph Churchill who is a stunningly captivating woman whose looks and demeanour make her almost irresistible to most men. She has powerful social and romantic contacts and has had affairs with a number of other men. Last month the Royal Party attended a seventh birthday celebration for Winston, the eldest son of Lady Randolph, at their London home. Included in the Royal party was Herbert von Bismarck, Under-Secretary at the German Embassy in London and son of the German Chancellor. Well – the inevitable happened and Lady Randolph spent the night in Herbert von Bismarck's chambers. Now, you may consider this sort of thing distasteful but there are certain aristocrats, certainly not I, who believe there is nothing wrong in behaving in this fashion as long as they are discreet. However, that is not the issue that concerns me. It was what Lady Randolph overheard that gives me great concern."

At this point I felt it was necessary to reassure Lord Londonderry so I interrupted "I do appreciate the sensitive nature of disclosing such information your Lordship and I can give you my word nothing will be spoken of it outside this room".

"Thank you, Richard, – do you mind if I call you Richard – I don't like unnecessary formality. Now, Lady Randolph heard something in Herbert von Bismarck's bed chamber which worried her greatly. She wrestled with the options of keeping quiet and protecting her reputation or speaking up to Lord Randolph admitting her indiscretion but that would probably put an end to her marriage. In a state of absolute desperation, she disclosed the information to my wife the Marchioness of Londonderry, Lady Theresa, who of course confided in me."

“I see your Lordship. What did Lady Randolph hear that was so significant that she even contemplated jeopardising her marriage” I asked?

Lord Londonderry continued “von Bismarck had thought Lady Randolph had just left his bed chamber by an ante-room door when he had a visitor. He received this visitor in the drawing room - it was none other than General von Caprivi, Head of the Imperial German Navy. Lady Randolph however had re-entered the bedroom from the ante-room door looking for her necklace and bracelet which she had left on a dresser. The door to the drawing room was slightly ajar. Lady Randolph has travelled widely around Europe and is fluent in German and she overheard General von Caprivi discussing certain plans with von Bismarck. There were no specific details discussed but the name “ Worth” was heard and that something would happen on May 29th in Dundee, Scotland that would rock the British government to its core and destabilise the government leading to a state of anarchy. May 29th, Richard, that is in four days’ time”.

“Is there anything that can be done your Lordship” I said whilst at the same time wondering why Lord Londonderry had confided in me.

“As soon as I was told this information I despatched a newly gazetted naval third lieutenant to Dundee to reconnoitre and try and flush out any subversive activity so that we could call out the militia and prevent it happening. That was two weeks ago and I have had no reports from my agent and I suspect foul play. Lieutenant Jack Smith is in Berlin with Lord Salisbury; the agent I sent to Dundee has disappeared. When I saw The William Thrift entering harbour this afternoon my spirits were lifted that you might give assistance in this matter. Could I ask you to be of service to your country one more time? There may be great danger involved. I would respect your decision if you feel unable to help but whatever lies in store in Dundee in four days' time may be catastrophic for our country."

Lord Londonderry looked at me. He said nothing more but I could see the tension in his face as he waited for my reply.

I knew what I should do as soon as the question was asked. How many people are given the opportunity to be of service to their country even once in their lifetime? This would be my second chance. Without hesitation I replied "When do you want me to leave for Dundee your Lordship and how will I explain matters to Mrs Anderson? "

"I knew I could rely on you" he replied smiling. His relief in hearing my reply was clearly visible. "The sooner you get to Dundee the better. Can you leave within the hour? Any later and you will miss the tide and will not be able to leave harbour until early tomorrow morning. I will ask Mr Eminson to contact Mrs Anderson and tell her we have chartered her ship for an urgent cargo of linen from Dundee. She will be well recompensed and will have no objection."

"Right then" I exclaimed "I had better get back to my ship and make ready to sail. It is about 114 nautical miles sailing to Dundee on the Firth of Tay so if I can leave harbour now I should, with fair weather, be there in a day and a half. Jeremiah Hall will be closing the dock gates in fifty minutes so William Sheridan will have to put me next in turn to leave harbour and arrange for the tug."

"I shall send a runner down to the Harbourmaster's office and the necessary arrangements will be in place as soon as your ship is ready to sail" declared his Lordship.

Lord Londonderry shook my hand firmly "Good luck Richard. God protect you. Let me know by telegraph the moment you discover anything".

Quickly walking out of the Londonderry Offices, I half wondered if I had time to rush home and tell Isabella and the children that I had to sail immediately and that they should not worry. However, time was of the essence. I had to leave now.

Rushing on board The William Thrift I shouted all hands-on deck. "How are we placed for water and provisions Mr Marwick" I asked "Can we sail now?"

With a puzzled look on his face my mate replied "If you mean this precise moment Captain then yes, we have sufficient stores to last us about five days".

"Well, the tug will be with us in the next few minutes. Make ready to sail. We are bound for Dundee to pick up an urgent cargo of linen for Lord Londonderry. I am sorry lads that we have not had an opportunity to go ashore. I will make it up to you when we return."

Within ten minutes the paddle tug Harry Vane had puffed its way from the North dock to join us and we were soon passing a puzzled looking Jeremiah Hall who waved over to us as he prepared to close the dock gates. Looking over our stern as George slipped off the tow rope and the stiff breeze filled our foresail I thought I could make out a figure waving at the first-floor window of the Londonderry Offices overlooking the North dock. Did I really meet and talk with the 6th Marquess of Londonderry just half an hour ago or was I dreaming? Was there ever a more friendly, simple and unaffected member of the aristocracy. I had been filled with admiration at this great patriot; a great and devoted public servant. I could not contemplate failing him in this adventure.

Chapter 8

The international conspirator

Over the course of the next hour the crew went about their duties in silence. They were disappointed at not being able to take shore leave in their home port. I debated whether I should confide the events that had unfolded in the Londonderry Offices to George Marwick. If he understood the urgency and importance of our mission, he would not feel so disappointed and he could be a great asset in my search for the events that would "rock the British government to its core leading to a state of anarchy" whatever that might be. However, I decided not to say anything but to wait until we arrived at Dundee and I would reassess the situation. I had been made privilege to a lot of sensitive and personal information from Lord Londonderry and I would have to take care how much George and the crew were told.

Tom, who had busied himself tightening a head sail rope through a cleat on the bulwarks, took the opportunity of looking over my shoulder as I was consulting my charts.

"What heading are we taking Captain" he asked.

Used to Tom's natural inquisitiveness I was happy to pass on any knowledge I had which would make him a better sailor. "Well Tom. The charts tell me that Dundee is 56 degrees 30 minutes north, 2 degrees 58 minutes west but if we took that direct heading, we would sail straight into the cliffs off Bamborough Castle" and I showed him where we were on the chart and where that course would take us. "That is the final compass bearing and we need to chart a course that avoids any natural hazards on route. As you know we change course many times during a voyage until finally we reach our destination. Visibility is not too good at the moment so I am charting a course that will keep the coast in sight. In that way I can be certain of my position from prominent landmarks on the coast. I will point out to you the hazards we need to avoid on route."

"Thank you, Captain. I find navigation fascinating. I will have to learn more" replied Tom and he continued around the ship tightening the head sail ropes.

"George" I said turning to my mate behind me "I have decided on our course and have written it down so the lads can follow it when they are on watch. Can you come over here and I will talk it through with you." George joined me at the wheel.

"Right now, bearing in mind there is a stiff westerly breeze at the moment we need to follow this course."

	25th May	Leave Seaham Harbour	
4.00 p.m.	25th May	North by West until Tynemouth Haven	10 miles
7.20 p.m.	25th May	North by East until Coquet Island	20 miles
2.00 a.m.	26th May	North North West until Alnmouth	4 miles
5.20 a.m.	26th May	North by East until Bamborough Castle	15 miles
8.20 a. m.	26th May	North North West until Holy Island	5 miles
10.00 a.m.	26th May	North West by North until Berwick	9 miles
12.40 p.m.	26th May	North North West until Eyemouth	8 miles
3.20 p.m.	26th May	North West by North until Firth of Forth	29 miles
1.00 a.m.	27th May	North East by East until Firth of Tay	14 miles
6.00 a.m.	27th May	Arrive Dundee Roads	

"There are a few observations I would make about this course George just so the crew know what to expect. When proceeding towards Coquet Island I would advise that we go to the northward of the island as the passage is safer than the other between the island and the shore. There are a number of shoals and reefs to be aware of between Holy Island and The Farn Islands. The Parkdyke reef is the southernmost and is about two miles to the North of Emmanuel Head. The least depth is two fathoms and you can mark the point when you make a triangle between the east point of Bamborough Church; the low water mark of Emmanuel Head and Lindisfarne Castle to the East. We should be crossing the Firth of Forth mid-afternoon so when passing the Bass Rock on our port side we should take a heading for the lighthouse on May Island on the other side of the Firth and we should avoid the majority of steamers sailing out of Leith. Do you think the lads will have any problems with our course?"

Shaking his head and pursing his mouth George thought for a minute "None at all Captain. I will take the middle watch just after midnight when we are sailing off Bamborough Castle. There will be very little moonlight shining through the cloud cover but it will be dawn about 5.00 a.m. so the lads should be all right from there".

Next afternoon we passed through Farn Sound between the Megstone Rock and The Farn Islands. The Sound is a breeding colony for grey seals. Billy Booth stood on the prow staring over to the rocks in awe of the size of the bull seals and laughing at the antics of the young pups majestically swimming at speed around the William Thrift as we passed through with full sails tight to the wind. That evening I arranged with George that I would take the middle watch for the crossing over the Firth of Forth and I was really tired when I returned to my cabin at 4.30 a.m. I fell into my bunk exhausted.

"Captain Raine" Bob Mustard shouted through the cabin door. "It's 5.30 a.m.; its daylight and I have your breakfast".

"Come in Bob" I wearily replied "Is everything shipshape on deck? I am starving – what are we having for breakfast today?"

As I ask the same question every morning Bob laughs out aloud and replies "Everything is fine on deck. Mr Marwick has asked me to tell you we are about three miles south of the bar on the River Tay. You are having porridge and a mug of tea for breakfast."

I wash and dress and climb up the companionway and step out onto a bright sunny deck. The sky is clear and the wind is warm and fresh pushing the William Thrift along at a steady pace. Joining George at the wheel I look over to the estuary of the Tay. More water flows into the German Ocean from this river than from any other river in the British Isles.

"Shall I take the wheel into Dundee, George" I asked "It gets a little tricky from here".

"Aye aye Captain. I could do with a mug of tea before we berth in harbour" he replies.

The entrance to the river deepens to five fathoms but then decreases to three fathoms as we approach the Horseshoe Shoal. It deepens again to eight fathoms between Broughton Ferry and the black Fairway Buoy. The steam ferry is constantly plying the two-mile journey across the Firth and ships sailing upstream have to be wary as unusually the ferry commands right of way.

Picking up our pilot who must be more than seventy years of age but still as alert and fit as any of the younger pilots we sail directly towards the harbour which is on the northern bank of the River Tay. There are four docks. The Earl Grey Dock; the King William IV Dock; the Victoria Dock and the recently completed Camperdown Dock. There is a separate landing for the Tay Ferry to Newport and a Graving Dock and shipyards. Our pilot directs us towards the Craig Pier where the ferry lands and into the Tide Harbour, through the lock gates and into The Earl Grey Dock. Our route passes by a line of lofty warehouses for bonding corn, wine and other imports. Within the hour we are moored alongside a whaler which has forty or fifty sailors scurrying about on deck preparing to leave harbour. Of course, a whaler doesn't need that number of crew to sail her but they do need that number when they are out in their long ships in pursuit of a whale.

Now that I have safely arrived at Dundee, I can give my secret mission the full attention it deserves. Looking out over this busy dock with so many ships of all sorts, sailors and dock workers all going about their business I begin to realise the enormity of the task I was undertaking. Finding a needle in a haystack continually came into my mind. Where should I start? What information did I have? It was now mid-morning on the 27th May and all I had was the name "Worth" and something that may happen the day after tomorrow. But first I must carry out the usual formalities necessary when a ship arrives in port so I visit the Harbourmasters office to register my berth and organise the cargo loading arrangements. I frequent this harbour five or six times a year and know the harbourmaster, dock workers and layout of the town quite well and no one should think it unusual to see me or my ship. Waiting for me in the Dock Office is a Mr Wallace, a clerk from the Linen Mills, who advises me that upon instructions from Lord Londonderry his employers are presently arranging to transport rolls of finished cotton cloth from the factory which should arrive at the dock tomorrow. This rough linen is the sort of cloth previously used for slave clothing but since the abolition of slavery in Britain it is now used for soldier's shirting, bagging and sail cloth. I hurriedly return to the William Thrift and let my mate know the cargo arrangements and give him the good news that I have arranged for a watchman to come aboard so that the crew can have the rest of the day and evening ashore. A loud cheer rings out and the crew dash into their quarters to change into what decent shore clothes they have and within minutes they are making their way along the quayside singing and laughing and heading for the town centre.

Thinking hard about the options available to me I decided that the most likely place to find someone, or to find out about someone, would be to ask in the public houses, beer houses and inns. The characters that frequent these places tend to know everything and everybody in the town. A logical route to take would be Craig Street, Union Street, Whitehall Street, The Green Market, High Street, Castle Street, Exchange Street and Castle Lane. It would be a long, hard task so as soon as the dock watchman was on board at 11.30 am I set off along Union Street calling into to every hostelry on route. My enquiries began in a low-key fashion as I did not wish to draw attention to myself or alert the unknown Mr Worth who could be listening to me making these enquiries. By late afternoon I was almost at the end of my search route making my way down Exchange Street and beginning to feel quite despondent. Walking through the door of The Anchor Inn I sat beside a group of sailors that looked familiar and who I had probably met sometime before in a remote bar in some forgettable remote port.

"Hello lads" I quietly asked "Do you know of a Mr Worth? I need to see him urgently. Any idea where I can find him?"

Blank looks and shakes of the head were beginning to haunt my search. To my surprise I suddenly felt a hand on my shoulder. A waitress had been clearing the table behind me and heard my question.

"Do you mean the American?" she said in a broad Glaswegian accent. "If it is Mr Adam Worth you are looking for he is staying here at the Inn. He is in Room six on the first floor. Would you like me to call him down? He is in his room now"

My heart skipped a beat. Could this be the person I was seeking? I would have to be careful I did not alert this Adam Worth until I found out a little more about him.

The waitress was a good looking well built, buxom woman with rosy cheeks and a white apron tied around her waist. For some unknown reason I decided to adopt Mrs Anderson's technique and so I looked deep into her eyes without averting my stare. "Yes, that is probably the man I am looking for. He has compromised my sister and made off with a necklace passed down from our grandmother and I am trying to recover the piece so my sister can put the whole sordid business behind her. Listen – could you point him out when he comes down? There will be a half sovereign in it for you."

"No problem, sir. I always thought he looked the shifty type" she whispered "He tends to come down for his evening meal about six o'clock so if you sit over there at that table, I will point him out to you. Would you like a tankard of ale while you are waiting?"

Exactly on the hour a man came down the stairs and into the bar. My waitress friend nodded towards him. So, this was Adam Worth. He was about five feet eight inches tall of medium build with brown hair and a large moustache and dressed in a well-worn brown suit, white shirt and tie. Walking past me into the dining room of the Inn he sat himself down at a table in the window and overlooking the ferry landing. The waitress smiled at me as if to say "well go on then" and spurred on by her prompt I climbed the stairs onto the first floor. Room six was at the end of the passage and was unlocked. Slowly opening the door, I poked my head inside and to my relief the room was empty. My mind was churning over what I was doing there but suddenly it became clear. I had to find out who this man is and why he is here.

There was nothing but clothes in the wardrobe and in the chest of drawers. His lunch tray with dirty plates, cutlery and an empty tankard stood on the dresser. Looking under the bed was a small suitcase and a valise. I opened the suitcase and carefully searched through more clothing. Touching something cold and hard I lifted back a shirt and to my total surprise I found a revolver - fully loaded. After a few moments I searched further and came across a file full of newspaper cuttings. Scanning quickly through these cuttings a picture of Adam Worth began to take shape. This man was clearly so arrogant and egotistical that he had kept a scrapbook of newspaper articles about his exploits. He was an American who was originally born in Germany. When he was seventeen years old he lied about his age and enlisted in the Union army. Within two years he had become a bounty hunter enlisting in one regiment, collecting the bounty and then deserting to enlist in another under a false name. After the civil war he became a pick pocket in New York and he then began to organise robberies and heists. He was discovered attempting to break into the Boylston National Bank in Boston and he was caught, put on trial and jailed but made a daring escape with the aid of some unknown accomplice. Further newspaper reports associated him with a daring theft of raw cut diamonds from a bank in Philadelphia in which the vault doors were completely blown out by explosives. The American newspaper reports then speculated that he had left the country for Europe. More newspaper cuttings from the London Evening Standard dated one year later referred to a number of major robberies in Mayfair which no doubt had his hand on them. It was clear that Adam Worth certainly considered himself an international criminal mastermind.

Carefully replacing everything in the suitcase the way I found it I turned to the valise which was full of papers, letters and files. I quickly began scanning through the papers looking for anything of significance when I came across a typed document with a very fancy letterhead which read "The Reich Club, Upper Belgravia, London." It was addressed to Adam Worth and signed by the Chairman of the club Sir Archibald Heywood-Gloyne and it set out the principles, mission and rules of the club. It dawned on me that this was an anarchist group. Their constitution made it clear that the group was dissatisfied with the present government (*British parliamentary democracy is failing the ruling classes of this country)* and that they were obsessed with anti-Semitism (*A world Jewish conspiracy*). Their inspiration was the crisp, clear, lines of authority and government practised by the German aristocracy with whom the *Reich Club would seek to forge an alliance*. Sir Archibald then mentioned in his letter that the agreed sum of £1,000 would be paid in cash to Adam Worth on the successful completion of his mission.

Suddenly I heard footsteps at the bottom of the stairs and I quickly returned the papers to the valise and replaced it together with the suitcase under the bed. By now the footsteps were at the top of the stairs and I could not step back out into the corridor without being seen by Adam Worth. A broad Glaswegian voice called out from below "Mr Worth, will you not take a tankard of ale to your room as usual" and to my relief I heard his footsteps going back down the stairs. I left the room and slipped into the broom cupboard opposite which was ajar when I first came along the corridor. Adam Worth passed the cupboard and went into his room and I returned downstairs. Returning to my seat I called my new found friend over and slipped a half sovereign in her hand which she gratefully accepted giving me a knowing wink.

"I just need to find out who Adam Worth is now seeing so I will sit here with a tankard of ale until he leaves the Inn" I whispered "Can you fetch me an ale" and I once again looked deep into her eyes which made her cheeks flush a definite pink.

An hour later Adam Worth left the Inn and I followed at a discreet distance. By now it was after eight o'clock and I had difficulty in keeping him in sight as he wandered in and out of the shadows casting shapes along the dark back streets towards the docks. Suddenly he stopped outside a derelict warehouse, furtively looked around, hesitated and then lifted aside a board covering the entrance and went inside. I waited for a minute or two and then I followed. Inside I could barely make out anything in the darkness but I heard voices in a distant room. Peering through the door hinge I noticed two hurricane lamps were lit in the room and I could make out Adam Worth and three burly, scruffy looking men who spoke with strong Irish accents. They were inspecting brown glossy sticks of something about eight inches long which were stored in a box.

"I told you it would be easy to break into that explosive store and get this dynamite" laughed one of the Irishmen. "The Harbourmaster forbids explosives to be stored on board ships overnight in the dock so the shipment from the Midlothian Gunpowder and Dynamite Works is kept in that store just outside of the town until the point of embarkation, just before the ship sails. By the time they have carried out an inventory tomorrow afternoon it will be too late"

"It certainly has made our task easier and will help to further our Irish Republican Brotherhood cause" quipped Adam Worth.

Wait a minute I thought. He is trying to make out he is a Fenian – an American with Irish roots who is working to support armed rebellion in Ireland. He is nothing of the sort. He is using these Irish Nationalists to carry out an insurrection under the guise of the Brotherhood when in fact he is being paid to mastermind some atrocity by the Reich Club.

"Are you sure you know how to use this explosive Mr Worth?" asked his nervous looking companion "Is it safe to handle?"

"Don't worry Patrick. I have used this type many times before when I took part in a Fenian raid across the border at the Niagara River into Ridgeway, Canada. We blew up a number of government buildings" replied Adam Worth. "Broadly speaking there are two kinds of explosive – extremely rapid burning as in the case of gunpowder and detonating as in the case of dynamite. An ordinary dynamite stick can be set on fire by a match without great danger but will explode with shattering force in response to a fulminate detonator cap. Now we've also stolen plenty of blasting caps. Here they are" and he held up a thin device that looked like a nail about four inches long "They are a small primary explosive which when pushed into the dynamite stick can explode on shock or impact and so detonate the main explosive charge. This 50 lb. box of dynamite is enough to obliterate a whole block of buildings."

Turning to the third Irishman Adam Worth asked "Seamus. Have you sorted out where to strap the dynamite container so that the contact detonators will be struck with maximum impact?"

"I sure have Mr Worth" Seamus replied "We can pack the dynamite into the metal container tomorrow morning, carry it to the site, insert the detonators and then find a safe point to retreat and watch the explosion that will underpin a new beginning for Ireland. The other two Irishmen uttered a confident "to be sure, to be sure" in support of Seamus's declaration.

"Right then" exclaimed Adam Worth nodding in agreement as he began to put the sticks of dynamite back into the box. "Let's get this lot hidden out of sight under this old sailcloth and we will come back tomorrow morning to pick it up."

Quietly slipping through an adjoining door I waited for a few minutes as the group left the warehouse and I could no longer see the light from the hurricane lamps or hear their voices as they made their way along the dark, narrow streets. I retraced my steps back to the Earl Grey Docks and climbed on-board the William Thrift. By now it was just after 10.00 p.m. but it was a clear sky and the deck was lit by moonlight. The dock watchman asked hopefully if he was needed any longer and was relieved when I told him he was finished for the day. I desperately needed a drink and time to think about the extraordinary course of events that had unfolded since I left the ship at mid-day. In my cabin I poured a noggin of rum and took a long drink. Reflecting on my discoveries I was quite proud that I had found "Worth" and uncovered a plot by the Reich Club to get Worth to persuade a group of Irish nationalists to steal explosives and blow something up tomorrow – but what was to be blown up? Should I contact the officer in charge of the Dundee Rifles Volunteer Battalion now or wait and see if I could find out their target tomorrow and then inform the Dundee Rifles? Yes - that would be better. Wait until I know what the target is. I would keep Adam Worth under surveillance tomorrow morning and he would be sure to lead me to the three Irishmen and the intended target.

Hearing noises and footsteps on the deck above I climbed up the companionway.

"Good evening, Captain" chirped George happily as he held up Billy under one arm and Tom under the other. Behind him Bob Mustard had stopped to steady himself on the binnacle. "I will just get the lads bunked down for the night. Can I have a word with you when I come back?"

"Of course, George" I replied "Seems like you have all had a good time. I am pleased you have been able to enjoy your shore leave"

A few minutes later and George returned. "You will never guess who I bumped into tonight captain. We were doing the rounds of the ale houses in Dock Street and as I walked through the front door of the Red Lion there at the bar was that big ugly brute – the German sailor that we fought with on the top of Whitby cliffs. He was singing and drinking with a number of other German sailors."

"Did he see you George" I worriedly asked.

"No captain. He had his back to the main door so as soon as I saw him, I turned the lads around and we went on to the next ale house. I thought we had seen the last of that lot when HMS Galatea shattered the main mast of their ship the Ernst Friedrick."

George could see the worried look on my face. Could this have anything to do with the explosives plot I thought? It may just be a coincidence but I could not take the risk and had to check it out.

"This could be very significant George. First thing tomorrow morning give instructions to Bob, Tom and Billy for the loading of our cargo of linen. Then I would like you to walk around the four docks; the shipyard; the ferry landing, and the tide dock and report back to me as soon as possible if you see the German barquentine, the Ernst Friedrick. I suspect that this means trouble so make sure you are not spotted. Now let's get to our bunks. I have been awake since 4.30 this morning and tomorrow is going to be another long day."

Returning to my cabin I quickly undressed; collapsed on my bunk and putting my head on the pillow I tried to rationalise plans in my head for tomorrow morning. Alas, sleep overcame me within minutes.

Chapter 9

Time is running out

The sound of voices and footsteps on deck woke me from a deep sleep. Surprisingly, despite all of the questions going around my head I had slept very well indeed. The time was just after six o'clock and I quickly washed and dressed and made my way up on deck. Bob Mustard had heard me moving around my cabin and had made his way to the galley and poured me a hot mug of tea.

"Good morning, Captain Raine" Bob announced as I stood looking out over the River Tay "Drink this fresh cup of tea. It has just been brewed" and I gladly sipped away at the refreshing cup.

"Where is Mr Marwick. Is he in his quarters?" I asked Bob

"No sir. He was up early and after setting out the orders of the day he left the ship; it must have been about an hour ago now"

Well done, George, I thought, as I looked at my sketch of the river and the harbour area. Whenever I have a few moments spare in port I always try to document the layout of the docks for future reference in case I make a return visit and have to moor up in a different dock. Now where, I wondered, is the intended target of these maniacs?

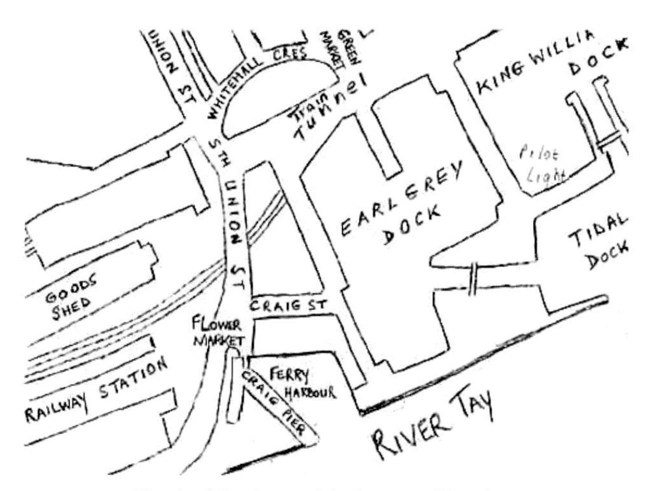

Sketch of the river and docks area of Dundee

Unsurprisingly I heard no answer to my question so I resolved that the most sensible course of action would be to make my way to the derelict warehouse and await our Irish friends collecting the explosives and then follow them to their destination. As soon as the target was revealed I could go straight to the Militia and reveal the plot. Fifteen minutes later I was outside the warehouse. It was not yet 7.00 a.m. so I assumed it would be a while before they arrived and so I moved the board covering the doorway to one side and entered. Sunlight was streaming in through the broken, high windows and from the holes in the roof where the tiles were missing and I crept silently towards the room where I had observed Adam Worth and his henchmen the night before. Peering through the crack in the hinged door I could see the room was empty but – to my horror – the sailcloth had been pushed aside and the box of dynamite and detonators was gone. I was too late. They had already picked up the explosives and were on their way to the target wherever that may be.

Dashing back to the William Thrift I was beginning to feel a sense of hopelessness. Their plot was to be executed sometime today and now I had no idea where they were and, even worse, what was their target. Just as I reached the gates into the dock George Marwick came running up behind me shouting "Captain, I have found the Ernst Friedrick although they do not call it that – they have replaced the nameplate on the stern and bow quarters with a new one; The Altmark from Hamburg – but it is the Ernst Friedrick alright. She is berthed in the Camperdown Dock undergoing repairs to the main mast."

"Well done, George" I sighed with relief "You stay on board until I return. I am going to see what that Kapitan Sturm is up to in this harbour. I should be back by mid-morning so take charge of the loading of the cargo. The shipment of linen should be arriving at the dock at any moment now" and I made my way along Dock Road to the Camperdown Dock.

Just inside the dock I stopped in my tracks and instinctively threw myself behind sacks of raw jute which had just been unloaded from a steamer newly arrived from Bengal, India. Just fifty yards ahead of me was Adam Worth striding along the quayside carrying his brown suitcase and valise. Following discretely behind I made sure that I was obscured from his view if he turned around. A further five hundred yards further on and Adam Worth stopped at the gangplank of a barquentine - The Altmark. George was right - it was unmistakably the Ernst Friedrick as there were carpenters and dockworkers climbing all over her main mast which was being fitted with new spars and rigging. Climbing up the gangplank Adam Worth reached the main deck and there to greet him was Kapitan Ernst Sturm.

A steely determination took over my mind. I had to find out what was the intended target of Worth's planned atrocity. This might be the only opportunity I would have of gaining a clue. It was not the time to hesitate and exercise caution. It was too late for that. I stuffed my jacket and cap behind stacks of timber, rolled up my shirtsleeves, picked up a five-foot spar and joined a number of other Dockers carrying new rigging on board. I approached the

German sailor on watch at the bottom of the gangplank and followed behind the other Dockers. With my face hidden by the spar I passed by the sailor on watch and climbed up on deck. To my horror the tall, brute with the broken nose we had crossed paths with in Whitby was sitting on deck smoothing a length of wood with a spokeshave plane just twenty yards beyond the main mast. If I hesitated, he would surely see me so I purposefully laid down the spar on the deck beside the main mast and walked straight into the open doors leading down the companionway and into the corridor serving the crew accommodation area. I stopped for a second to see if any of the crew had seen me and had followed me down to see what I was doing. I glanced around quickly. I could hear voices at the end of the passage so I crept silently towards the bottom door which I presumed must have been the master cabin. Hearing footsteps approaching the companionway I pulled open a sliding hatch a few feet away from where I was standing. Without looking into the hatch, I jumped in, dropped onto bilge boards in the hull and pulled shut the hatch above me. Listening intently, I held my breath as the footsteps walked around above my head and then climbed back up onto the main deck. Suddenly, I felt a sharp kick on my shins which buckled my legs and knocked me on my back. Quickly recovering from my sudden fall, I sat up and, turning on to my knees, I peered into the blackness but I could see nothing.

"Who's there" I whispered.

A muffled, indistinct noise came from a few feet away. I shuffled forward on my knees and groped in front of me with arms outstretched in the dark not knowing what to expect. My right hand touched something and I pulled back before moving forward again. It was a head – a head with a scarf or something covering the mouth. Untying the knot at the back of the scarf a voice whispered "I presume you should not be on this ship otherwise you would not be creeping around down here".

“Never mind about me” I replied “Why have you been tied up and left down here”

“Those Germans have held me prisoner for the last two weeks. I was beginning to think I was done for. Do you think we can escape off this ship?”

Untying his hands and feet I helped the stranger to stand. For a few moments he struggled to balance himself because his legs had been tied and strapped with both knees bent. Listening for any sound above I pushed back the sliding hatch, looked out and pulled myself up and out of the dark hull compartment. Bending over the hatch I offered my hand down to the stranger and pulled him up beside me and then closed the hatch cover behind him.

“If we go up on deck the crew will spot us straight away” said the stranger looking cold and weak after his two-week ordeal in that dark hole. “Let’s look through that door behind the companionway stairs” and we tiptoed along the corridor and slowly opened the door. This room was at the ship’s prow and stored spare anchors and chains. To our delight, high up on each side of the prow were small watertight doors about eighteen inches square used for manipulating mooring ropes when berthing in an awkward part of a dock.

“Do you think you could squeeze through one of those doors” I said turning to the stranger. Looking down at his slim frame he grinned back at me and said “What do you think?”

Releasing the lock bar, I pushed open the watertight door on the opposite quarter to the dockside. Rigging a rope and slipping it through the small door I whispered “Try to make as little noise as possible when you enter the water. Swim as close to the hull as you can and around the back of the ship tied up in the next berth” and without another word I squeezed through the small door; slid down the rope and slipped silently into the water followed by the stranger.

After three or four minutes of slow, quiet swimming; treading water and frequently gazing upwards at the bulwarks of the German ship we reached the ship behind and we swam around it until we reached the dockside. I climbed up a ladder tied against the dock wall and stepped up onto the quay followed by my slim friend. Grabbing my coat and hat from under the stacks of timber I motioned him to follow me and we hurriedly ran back to the Earl Grey Dock.

Climbing on board The William Thrift my mate strode towards me "What has happened to you Captain. You are dripping wet and so is your friend".

"I will explain later George. I am going to my cabin. Can you ask Bob if he has anything hot for my friend to eat and I would love a mug of tea?" I turned to the stranger. "I have some clothes that should fit you. Come on down to my cabin"

I threw the stranger a dry towel and asked "Are you the agent that Lord Londonderry despatched to Dundee?"

A look of shock came over his face. "How would you know that?"

So, I was right. I smiled as I slipped off my wet clothes. "Because Lord Londonderry has received no word from you and, assuming the worst, he asked me to find out what was happening here. By the way my name is Richard Raine. I am the master of this ship The William Thrift. What is your name and how did you end up doing this sort of work? You seem to be a little young to be endangering your life like this"

"I am a newly gazetted third Lieutenant in the Royal Navy Captain Raine. I am keen to earn a reputation and make my mark in the world so I volunteered for special assignments. This is my first and I ended up being discovered and imprisoned by those Germans. My name is Alexander John Smith and I hail from London."

I stared at Alexander John Smith. Yes – there was definitely a likeness. The same colour hair; the same nose; slim but muscly and with that same confident air about him.

Breaking off my stare I continued to rub my hair with the towel and asked "Do you have a brother called Jack?"

Alexander gasped and looking totally surprised replied "How on earth would you know that Captain. Yes, I do have a brother called Jack. He is about six years older than myself and he is a Lieutenant Commander in the Royal Navy."

"Well, it is just that I met Lieutenant Jack Smith a short while ago. Is he in the same line of business as yourself?"

"Special assignments" replied Alexander chuckling "Goodness me no. Jack is a career naval officer on board HMS Galatea. He will follow the traditional naval officer's promotion route and I am sure he will make flag officer before he is forty years old."

Smiling to myself I reasoned that if Jack had decided not to tell his brother that he undertook clandestine and special assignments then I would not reveal his secret.

"Now then Alexander. Let me tell you what I have discovered since berthing here two days ago and I explained how I had found Adam Worth and discovered his background and his assignment from Sir Archibald Heywood-Gloyne; how I had spied on the Irish Nationalists in the disused warehouse and overheard the plot to use dynamite and finally how I found Adam Worth boarding the Ernst Friedrick and being greeted by Kapitan Ernst Sturm.

Listening intently Alexander spoke up "I would dare bet that Worth has planned to make his escape on the German barquentine leaving the Irish Republican Brotherhood to take the blame and be hunted down for the conspiracy."

By now Alexander was dressed in dry clothes. “Captain Raine” he said “I think I should send a telegraphic message immediately to Lord Londonderry and pass on everything you have discovered. We have very little time left and we have no clue to help us discover the location of the planned explosion so I propose we inform the Militia as soon as I leave the telegraph office.”

“I agree Alexander. That is the best course of action to take. I will wait here for you to return” and my new friend left the ship to make his way to the telegraph office.

Thirty minutes later I was on deck looking out over the dock when Alexander came running down Union Street towards the ship. Dashing up the gangplank he blurted out “Captain Raine, Lord Londonderry knows Sir Archibald and he also knows that his brother-in-law works in Buckingham Palace in the Lord Chamberlain’s Office. The Lord Chamberlain organises all of the Queens’ engagements so Lord Londonderry thinks it reasonable to assume that Sir Archibald knows, through his brother-in-law, where Her Majesty will be on any particular day. He has checked with Buckingham Palace and today the Queen is on her way to her Scottish home at Balmoral for her summer vacation. Could that be of any significance?”

Thinking aloud I gasped “Alexander – the east coast train line from London to Balmoral Castle used to cross the Tay Railway Bridge across the river to Dundee and then on to Royal Deeside. That was until last year when during a fierce storm the bridge collapsed due to structural design faults. Until the new rail bridge is completed next year passengers have to get off the train at Newport on the south side of the River Tay and board the steam paddle ferry “The Fifeshire” known locally as “the Fifey”. It crosses the Firth of Tay to the ferry landing here at Dundee where passengers disembark and join the train to Aberdeen. If the royal party left London on the seven o’clock train this morning, then they would arrive at Tayport about 2.00 p.m. which was 30 minutes ago. If that is the case the royal party, including Queen Victoria, will be on the Fifeshire now."

Looking over my shoulder to the River Tay Alexander screamed "Here it is now. It is only about a quarter of a mile off and will be here in less than fifteen minutes."

"George, bring my telescope over here" I shouted and raising it up I began to scan the area around the ferry landing.

After a few moments my eyes focused and I detected some movement beneath the ferry landing stage. "Something is going on underneath the landing stage Alexander. I am going over there to investigate. The militia should be here any moment. Tell them to proceed to the landing stage with all haste and to watch out for and arrest three Irishmen and an American" and I took off at full speed towards Craig Pier.

Two hundred yards before I reached Craig Pier two of the Irishmen clambered up from the wooden beamed structure followed by the third and they slowly walked towards the flower market. I had no time to deal with them I thought but at that exact moment a squad of Dundee Rifles came marching around the corner from South Union Street. Alexander shouted "There they are" to the Militia and he shot off in pursuit of the Irishmen followed by the soldiers.

Seconds later I had reached the ferry landing stage. The Fifeshire blew its whistle twice as it entered the ferry harbour. It would be landing at Craig Pier in about two minutes. The deck of the paddle ferry was packed with commuters and passengers keen to resume their train journey to Aberdeenshire. I climbed down onto the wooden beams where the Irishmen had alighted from and crawled under the wooden framed landing stage. With only the light between the planking above to guide me I strained my eyes to look for an explosive device. After a few moments, which seemed like minutes, something glinted in the sunlight about six feet ahead of me. Pulling myself along the beam I reached the object. It was a milk churn which I assumed was filled with dynamite. It was strapped firmly to a pylon with stout rope. Reaching into my jacket for my pocket knife I froze. I had lent my pocket knife to Tom Colling yesterday and there was no way I could untie the tight knots. I could see the paddle ferry edging closer and closer to the pier side; then it touched with a bump. My mind began to rationalise. Why had the dynamite not exploded? Looking up to the top of the container I saw two contact detonators had been pushed into dynamite sticks and were protruding about one inch above the ferry landing platform. At that moment I could hear the ferry doors opening with a rusty creak. I thrust my hand between the planking and pushed the two detonators a further two inches into the dynamite just as the ferry ramp dropped with a loud thud onto the ferry landing. I closed my eyes and waited. My heart was thumping and my legs were like jelly. After a few minutes I regained my composure and crawled back along the wooden beam and climbed up onto Craig Pier just in time to see our great Queen Victoria and her party making their way to the railway station just thirty yards away.

Rushing over to me Alexander was all smiles. "We apprehended all three Irishmen Captain Raine. They put up a fierce fight but what happened to the dynamite. Did you find it under the ferry landing?"

"Alexander, you have no idea how close they were to blowing the Pier and the steam ferry to pieces together with our Queen, the royal party and all of those passengers. They had placed the contact detonators so that when the ferry ramp dropped onto the landing stage it would strike the detonators with maximum impact and trigger the main charge underneath. With only seconds to spare I pushed the detonators further into the dynamite so they were just below the planking and would not be in contact with the ramp when it dropped. We had better speak to the Militia. They will need an ordnance officer to arrange to dismantle the explosives."

"What about Adam Worth" Alexander exclaimed "Where do you think he is?"

"I think that having watched his accomplices make their way under the ferry landing to assemble the bomb he will have left the scene so that he would not be implicated if they were discovered. Probably he made his way back to the Ernst Friedrick."

I shouted over to the colour sergeant to accompany us with some of his men to the Camperdown Dock to arrest the main conspirator and we ran as quickly as we could along Dock Road. Alexander led the pack and this young, agile man was more than twenty yards ahead of us as we ran into the dock gates and along the quayside. Then I saw Alexander stop in his tracks. As we reached him, I could see why. The Ernst Friedrick was setting full sails as she slipped out of the tidal dock and into the river heading out on to the Firth of Tay.

"That's it then Captain Raine" Alexander said dejectedly "They have got clean away"

"Don't be too despondent Alexander" I replied "Just look at what we have achieved. We came here not knowing who it was we were looking for and what they intended doing. We have discovered their plot, caught them in the act and prevented an act of terrorism that would have rocked the British Empire to its foundation. Although Adam Worth has not been apprehended, he will be a wanted man wherever he sets foot on British soil. He will be caught and brought to justice very soon - I am sure of that. Let's get back to my ship. We deserve a good meal and a long glass of rum or two" and with a smile and nod of agreement Alexander Smith and I made our way along the quayside to the William Thrift.

Two days later and we were being towed towards the lock gates at Seaham harbour. I had enjoyed Alexander's company and we had made good friends on the voyage home. We had talked about all manner of things but I did not reveal to him that I was also a good friend of his brother Jack. One day perhaps he will hear from Jack about our adventure off Whitby. Jeremiah Hall waved us through the dock gates and we berthed in the North dock. Leaving George in charge of unloading our cargo of coarse linen Alexander and I climbed the steps to the top of the dock and made our way to the Londonderry offices.

Standing at the front entrance to the porch holding the door open was the clerk in the brown suit that I met on my last visit here.

"His Lordship has asked me to take you straight up to see him. Follow me gentlemen" and he led us upstairs to the boardroom.

As we entered the room Lord Londonderry strode towards us and shook our hands vigorously. His face was beaming and his eyes were darting and flashing uncontrollably.

"Well done Richard and Alexander. There are people in the cabinet office; in the Houses of Parliament; at Buckingham Palace and around the British Empire that will breathe a sigh of relief that you were able to uncover and prevent a plot to destabilise the monarchy and the democratic process of British politics. Sir Archibald Heywood- Gloyne has been arrested together with his brother-in-law and they will stand trial for high treason. We have searched his office and apartments in Upper Belgravia and found anti-Semitic and pro-German literature, posters and leaflets but we found no details of other members of the Reich Club. He must have the membership book hidden or in a bank vault."

"What about this your Lordship?" I interrupted "When I was searching through Adam Worth's valise, I came across a list of the members of the Reich Club which Sir Archibald had sent to Worth to give to his German contacts.

Presumably the list would identify pro-German sympathisers who could be used for further subversive activities. I stuffed it into my jacket pocket just as I heard Worth returning to his room in the Anchor Inn. I had forgotten all about it until now."

Eagerly scanning the list of names Lord Londonderry's eyes lit up and he sat on the nearest chair.

"I am absolutely astounded at this list of members of the Reich Club. There must be sixty or seventy names on it but just look at who they are" and he read off a dozen or so extremely well-known names in British society, politics and the military?

"Lord Galloway, Lord Sempill, Lord Redesdale, Lord Carnegie, Admiral Hugh Jefferson, Marquess of Grantham, Sir Thomas Walcott and the list goes on. All disaffected aristocrats and senior politicians who presumably would act after the death of our monarch by inviting the German government to help prevent anarchy in our country but who would in fact remove the British Parliament. They would substitute their own brand of democracy following Reich Club principles and values. It would in fact be a bloodless take-over of Great Britain by Germany. Although it may be unlikely that we can convince a court of law that these Reich Club members knowingly participated in the Dundee conspiracy I will make sure these people are removed from any position of authority in Parliament or the military and that they are treated as social pariahs in society. They will rue the day they ever signed up to be members of the Reich Club."

Despite my involvement in thwarting this assassination plot the international significance of a successful outcome by The Reich Club had not dawned on me until now. This could have affected the future of every level of society in Great Britain including my own family and children. This sudden realisation brought a cold shiver to my body and a deep desire to hold close my dear wife and children.

“Lord Londonderry” I asked “If I could beg your leave. I have not seen my family for more than five weeks and my wife will have heard by now that the William Thrift is in the harbour. She will be expecting me calling at any time.”

“Of course, Richard” he replied with a smile “You must get home as soon as possible. Perhaps you can call tomorrow and we can talk some more about your adventure. You have been of immense service to your Queen and country and I would like to explore how your country can reward you.” Turning to Alexander he continued “I have no doubt that their Lordships in the Admiralty will be following your career with interest. In the meantime, I am going to open a bottle of the finest champagne and we will sit here and reflect on the amazing events of the last week”

Alexander walked me to the door and shaking my new friend’s hand I said goodbye and briskly walked along North Terrace, passing the Londonderry Arms Inn and up Church Street to my house. Isabella and the children would be overjoyed when I walk through the hall into the sitting room and I was excited, relieved and happy to be home as I turned my key and opened the front door.

CHAPTER 10

A holiday with a sting in the tail

Three weeks later the family were looking forward to a long-overdue holiday. The children William, Elizabeth Ann and young Richard Henry skipped out into the street followed excitedly by Isabella. "Have you checked the train timetable Richard? We don't want to miss the early train. The carriages will be full after 10.15am particularly today when Sangster's Circus is visiting Sunderland."

As I pulled the front door shut and turned the key I thought momentarily and answered "Yes dear. We will have plenty of time to catch the Hartlepool train".

Isabella was right of course. Six months earlier "Lord George Sanger" had brought his circus and world-famous menagerie to Seaham Harbour. He wasn't a real Lord but a self-proclaimed "Lord" of the showman's guild. At the time the streets of Seaham Harbour were buzzing with thousands of visitors from outlying towns and villages keen to see the carriages, trappings, clowns and artists in clothes of a most elaborate character. A procession of numerous caravans drawn by forty-five powerful and valuable horses formed an imposing cavalcade along North Terrace. One immense caravan was drawn by nine horses. The splendid band carriage behind it was drawn by three camels and the whole procession was headed by two very large elephants. The menagerie included birds, beasts and reptiles from every continent and a favourite with the crowds were the trained dogs and monkey acts.

Isabella and I walked hand-in-hand up Church Street passing St Johns Church and into Marlborough Street with the children skipping ahead. As we approached Mrs Anderson's house, I asked them to continue on to the railway station just fifty yards away and I would join them in five minutes. I knocked on the polished bronze rapper and Mrs Anderson opened the door with a welcoming smile. “Come in Richard. You are on time as usual “. I followed her into the parlour and placed the account books on the table.

“Would you like a cup of tea”, she asked as she beckoned me to sit down on the sofa.

“No thank you” I replied. “Isabella and the children are waiting for me at the station. They are very excited that they are going to spend a few days at Isabella’s sister house in Hartlepool. It has been a while since they had a holiday and they have been talking about it all week.”

“And what about you Richard” she said with that searching look that always makes me feel uncomfortable. “Will you be taking a well-earned rest while the William Thrift is in the dry harbour.”

“I am pleased to say everything went well yesterday” I replied. “After the dock workers discharged the silver sand for the Bottle works, George Marwick and the lads made their way home to spend some time with their families for the next three days. I have told them to report back early Wednesday morning so we can catch the tide for our next voyage. I stayed behind and waited until the tug towed the William Thrift into the dry harbour. Mr Potts the shipbuilder was there himself. He has assured me she will look splendid by the time I return but I only intend to stay one night in Hartlepool as I want to make sure the work on the William Thrift is done to my satisfaction. I will be back on Sunday to review the work as it progresses.”

“Very well, Richard, but you must try and enjoy the next few days. You don’t often have the opportunity to relax. This is the perfect chance to spend time with Isabella and the children and to forget the day-to-day problems of the life on board the ship”.

Leading me to the front door she smiled as she bade me goodbye and I made my way up Marlborough Street passing the Station Hotel and onto the platform where the family were patiently waiting.

Right on time as the station clock chimed nine o'clock the train slowly pulled up at the platform with wheels screeching on the rails and steam hissing from the locomotive. "All aboard for Seaham Colliery, Ryhope East and Hendon Burn" the stationmaster cried and without a moment's hesitation the children were climbing into a carriage followed by Isabella and myself. Fortunately, the carriage was unoccupied so we had the luxury of space and comfort for the short journey to Ryhope East station. I explained to the children that this railway was one of the very last "private" railways left in the country. Most had been bought out by the big joint stock railway companies such as the North Eastern Railway Company, Great Western Railway etc.

"But who owns this one daddy?" asked William inquisitively. "This railway is the Londonderry Seaham to Sunderland Railway" I replied. "It was built by the 3rd Marquess of Londonderry. He opened it over forty years ago to transport coals and goods from Seaham to Hendon Burn Station which is near to the docks and coal staithes at Sunderland. But it isn't connected to any of the other main lines so we have to change trains at Ryhope East station, cross the tracks using the footbridge to Ryhope West station where we board the Sunderland to Hartlepool train going the opposite way and operated by the North Eastern Railway."

Elizabeth Ann looked puzzled but didn't say anything. Soon we were approaching Ryhope East so we picked up our luggage and prepared to disembark. Within fifteen minutes the train from Sunderland approached the station. Boarding our second train we patiently waited a good ten minutes for the Postmaster to arrive with his sacks for the mail van. Then at last the engine slowly left the station and we gathered speed travelling south, in the right direction, for Hartlepool passing Seaton, Murton and Shincliffe on the way. I smiled at Isabella as she passed the time playing "I spy with my little eye" with the children. Looking out of the carriage window my thoughts drifted back to the cliffs at Whitby and the docks of Dundee. Events like that rarely happen to ordinary people. Did that really happen I thought?

As we approached West Hartlepool I looked down over the expanse of the bay and the docks. It seemed strange looking at this panoramic view from the headland. My usual approach to the piers and harbour, and the only approach I have experienced, is sailing the William Thrift into port from the sea. Hartlepool has had a harbour for two to three hundred years but it was originally, chiefly, a fishing port. The piers were constructed with great difficulty considering the ever-changing nature of the sand dunes and the variable nature of the winds and sea currents along this part of the east coast and the Tees Bay in particular. A series of inner piers form a series of wave traps in the outer harbour so that the lock gates can be operated at ease and in safety at all times. I was always impressed when I sailed past Heugh Lighthouse. At its base are two guns with a fan blast for heating shot and further north are batteries for the coast brigade, the naval reserve and the artillery volunteers. There are also recently erected barracks nearby for the accommodation of the Durham Artillery Militia. With great similarity to Seaham Harbour the population of the town exploded from about 400 to 15,000 when the Clarence, Stockton and Hartlepool railway began transporting coal to the docks. There are numerous staithes, coal drops and ballast cranes which are now as familiar to me as any in the docks along this coast.

A screech of brakes and a hiss of steam signalled our arrival at the station. Leaning out of the carriage window I could see a number of people on the platform either waiting to greet arrivals or waiting to board the train. Isabella had the carriage door opened as soon as the train came to a halt and was swiftly onto the platform with the children in tow. As I stepped out with the luggage a high-pitched shout. "Isabella, Richard". pierced the air and there striding quickly towards us was a smiling Peggy, Isabella's younger sister, with her two young children. Warmly embracing Isabella for what seemed an eternity Peggy turned to welcome me, William, Elizabeth Ann and Richard Henry. Clearly the two sisters had missed each other and chatted incessantly as Peggy led us from the station to her cottage in Lumley Street. Peggy was a widow but had successfully raised her family and through good management and judgement was financially comfortable. John, her late husband, was a shipowner and captain of the Ocean Queen that left South Shields for Shoreham-on-Sea five years ago but floundered in heavy weather with all hands lost. I had recently read an editorial in this month's Northern Pilot commenting on the dangerous work of a mariner. Apparent a Parliamentary Commission had reported that in the last year the annual mortality rate in maritime occupations was 2%. i.e., two out of every one hundred seamen are drowned or fatally injured each year. A sobering statistic I thought.

Today it is market day and the streets are thronging with shoppers looking for fresh vegetables, meat, bakery products and clothes and idly walking in and out of the stalls in the market square looking for a bargain. We passed the popular Temperance Hall at the bottom of Lumley Street and surprisingly the lecture hall and club room was well supported. A number of Durham Artillery Militia Volunteers from the artillery depot and drill ground in Baltic Street were seated proudly wearing their smart uniforms and sporting the new-fashioned Imperial military style moustaches. Following along behind the children who were chattering and skipping ahead of us we soon arrived at the gate to Peggy's house which was liberally covered with an arch of roses and carnations. Opening the front door, we were ushered into the cottage by Peggy and shown to our pleasantly furnished clean and tidy bedroom. In no time at all our luggage was unpacked and both of the sisters were sitting in the garden with cups of tea and freshly baked cake and the children were playing with their toys leaving me to relax and enjoy the sunshine, fresh air and my own company. The afternoon passed quickly and as the sun set on the Cleveland Hills we retired indoors and had a very tasty dinner of roast beef and vegetables followed by plum pudding made from the abundant fruit harvested from the plum tree at the bottom of the garden. After dinner we all sat comfortably in the drawing room. Isabella touched my shoulder and apologized that she had spent so much time talking to Peggy. I gave her hand a reassuring squeeze and whispered "I am enjoying listening to your reminiscences. You haven't seen each other for nearly two years so it is understandable you have lots to talk about. I am fine sitting by the fire reading my book."

Early next morning we were awoken with the smell of freshly baked bread and the sound of sausages and bacon sizzling in the frying pan coming from the kitchen. We eagerly dressed and went downstairs looking forward to the promising meal that awaited us. Peggy knew I enjoyed a hearty breakfast and my plate was overfilled with her delicious cooking.

Pouring me a second cup of tea Peggy said "Richard, Isabella tells me you have to return to Seaham Harbour this morning. It is a shame you can't stay longer but I must thank you for bringing her here with the children. I hope you have enjoyed your short stay. It has been good to see you again."

"It is lovely to see you and the children again Peggy. I have really found it relaxing and I will remember your delicious cooking with great affection but yes, I have to return, my ship is on the grid-iron in the dry harbour."

Looking puzzled Peggy asked "What exactly is a grid-iron, Richard?"

“It is a cradle like contraption” I replied. “The ship is floated over the grid-iron and at low water the ship rests on it about three feet above the harbour bottom. This will allow Robert Potts and his ship repairers to carry out below the water-line repairs. Mrs. Anderson has also commissioned him to replace all of the rigging with new mainsheets, block and tackle and some of the sails so I have told him I will be around for the next two days in case he has any questions about my preferences in the execution of the work. I know how much Isabella has cherished this visit so you must promise that you and the children will visit us at Seaham Harbour.” Peggy and Isabella looked at each affectionately and nodded approvingly.

The morning sun was warm on my face and the smell of the jasmine and honeysuckle climbing up the garden wall was exquisite as I kissed Isabella and the children goodbye. Isabella confidently reassured me “Don’t worry about me and the children. We will be alright to make the return journey by ourselves on Tuesday. Our plans have already been made for today. We are all going to attend the Sunday service at the United Methodist Free Church in Frederick Street. Peggy tells me that some of the Ministers are from the same Methodist Connection that visit our chapel in Seaham Harbour. Now, you must promise me that you will try and relax. You are supposed to be on holiday”.

Waving her goodbye I took one last look at the charming old-fashioned garden with its smooth lawn, variegated flower-beds and colourful shrubs and set off for the train station with a happy, contented and exhilarated disposition.

Just ten minutes later my contentment was shattered!

CHAPTER 11

The international conspirator returns

There he was as bold as brass striding towards the railway station as though he was just going to the office. The bell on the newsagent's door pinged quietly as it closed behind me. I stood transfixed as he approached me. What should I do? Should I make a quick retreat and consider my options or should I confront him? This man, Adam Worth, had attempted to assassinate our gracious Queen Victoria on the Fifeshire ferry on the river Tay just six weeks ago and every Harbormaster, Customs and Excise Officer, Police Officer and Naval Agency had been alerted to find and apprehend him.

After a few moments hesitation it occurred to me that Adam Worth had never seen me. I had shadowed him as he carried out his evil deeds in Dundee but there was no way he could have seen me or recognize me now. I was just another man in the street so I turned my back and looked inquisitively in the tobacconist's window as he drew closer. He had made very little attempt to disguise or conceal his appearance. He still wore the same well used brown suit, shirt, tie and shoes but his large moustache was gone and he was now clean shaven. Clearly, he was so conceited and self-confident he considered it unnecessary to conceal his identity.

His two companions walked by his side. Gazing intently at the reflections in the window I could see that one of the men was dressed in quite fashionable clothes, was tall and upright and about thirty years of age. He appeared to be leading or guiding an older, middle-aged smartly dressed man by the elbow who looked uncomfortable walking in between them. They continued their conversation as they reached the tobacconists shop and although I could not hear what they were saying it was quite apparent from the accent of the taller man that he was Irish. Immediately the question ran through my mind. Was this international conspirator involved in another Fenian plot against the British government? I shivered at the thought of the havoc and chaos that followed in the wake of this man and the potential catastrophe that could lie ahead if his activities could not be stopped.

I followed at a discrete distance as they walked towards the railway station and climbed the steps to the booking office. My first thought was to immediately communicate the presence of Adam Worth to the authorities but if I left him now, he would vanish into the background as he has done so many times before. The booking office was bristling with passengers as they made their way to the ticket office window. Thankfully, through a lull in the chatter I heard Adam Worth clearly request "three second-class tickets to Sunderland" and I took the decision to follow them to their destination and inform Lord Londonderry or the authorities at the earliest opportunity. The train was preparing to depart when the three men boarded the third carriage down from the engine and as the stationmaster's whistle blew, I hurriedly stepped on board shuffling ahead of a number of other travelers. To my relief this was a corridor train and I could see Adam Worth entering an empty compartment. These corridor carriages have only recently been introduced by the North Eastern Railway Company. Each carriage is divided into six separate compartments each designed to seat six people with a sliding door opening onto a narrow corridor running along the full length of the carriage. I positioned myself at the end of the corridor so that I could monitor their movements and follow them if they abruptly left the train. The train was busy with day excursion travelers heading for the circus at Sunderland and the compartments had quickly filled up leaving many passengers with no option but to stand in the corridor for the fifty-five-minute journey to Sunderland.

Upon arriving at each station on the route I anxiously gazed past the bodies of people disembarking and alighting and temporarily blocking my view of the carriage door just ten feet away. I remembered the disappointment on Lieutenant Alexander Smiths face when he saw the Ernst Frederick sailing out of the tidal dock at Dundee on the River Tay and I was determined that this time I would do my utmost not to lose them. This time Adam Worth and his accomplices would be brought to justice. My thoughts were temporarily distracted as we pulled into Seaton station. For two and a half miles down the track to Ryhope West the gradient reaches 1 in 44. Recently the express bound for Newcastle from Liverpool had descended Seaton Bank and was derailed at the sharp curve at its foot injuring 101 passengers. As a result, the North Eastern Railway realigned the curve and they say it is now much safer. Thankfully, I could feel the locomotive gently applying its brakes on the descent down Seaton Bank to Ryhope West and we slowly pulled up at the platform. From this point on to the terminus at Hendon Burn, Sunderland the two tracks run parallel with each other. Apparently, the North Eastern Railway had refused to share their station at Ryhope or their existing tracks with Lord Londonderry's railway. This not only necessitated a second station at Ryhope but also a second bridge over the dene and a second set of tracks from there to Sunderland.

Our arrival at the terminus was heralded by a general noisy commotion, clamoring movement and frantic crowding in the corridor as all the passengers left their compartments to disembark the train. Taking care that I did not compromise my surveillance of the three suspects I allowed the day trippers behind me to pass. The Irishman exited the compartment first with the older man followed by Worth and they stepped out on to the platform. I followed a few yards behind. I became conscious that the Irishman was both leading the older man by the arm and aggressively pushing him along. Most of the crowd were making their way to the Brick Field where the sounds of pipe organ music and steam driven rides could be heard from Sangers Circus. The familiar sight of Hendon Docks could be seen a few hundred yards to the East but Adam Worth was making his way past the old windmill, along Hendon Valley Road and heading for the old quarter of Sunderland. Arriving at Henry Street they climbed the steps of a ramshackle tenement building and knocked on the door. An unkempt, poorly groomed woman with a scruffy hat and apron beckoned them to enter. From my viewpoint behind the gable end of Addison Street just thirty yards away I had a full view of the house and noted that a few moments later a gas light was turned up in a room on the second floor. Clearly this house was to be the base for their plan of action but how could I communicate with Lord Londonderry without breaking off my surveillance and allowing them the potential to disappear.

Looking at the sad scene along Henry Street of decrepit housing with unpaved streets and communal standpipes for drinking water I wondered how people could live in these conditions. I recall reading in the Seaham Weekly News that Henry Street was the scene of a horrific smallpox outbreak ten years ago. Conditions had deteriorated as a result of unregulated development. Many of the streets had been built in the 1850's and medical investigators acting on behalf of the Local Health Board became aware of an all-pervasive smell of sewerage within these houses. An interview with a builder who had constructed some of the properties revealed that a pipe drain which ran under the floor of each property to draw off moisture from the foundations had not been fitted with a syphon where it joined the sewer allowing both sewer gases and contagion to enter the dwellings. Twenty yards along the back street a group of children were playing at marbles and I could hear the familiar names of the marbles shouted as they played along the back lane such as the pottery-clay "stoney", the common marble "Jack-ally" and the most valuable marble the "blood-red ally". My presence behind the gable end of their street must have stood out as unusual as two of the group broke off from their game and they slowly wandered over to where I was leaning against the wall. “What’s up Mister. Do you want something?” asked the young girl. For a moment I was confused and searched my brain for the right response. I had a dilemma. I needed help to get a message to Lord Londonderry but at the same time I did not want to disclose the importance of my mission. Without any further hesitation I blurted out “yes, I do need some help. Do you live around here? I need to know who lives in that house and I pointed to the house around the corner.”

“My brother Joseph and I live just over the road from that house” she replied. “Mrs. Calhoun lives there but she is not a very nice lady and is always in trouble with the local Bobby because she gets into arguments and fights when she is drunk which is nearly every night.”

“What is your name” I asked while not releasing my gaze from Mrs. Calhoun’s house. “I am Francesca Cooper” she replied. “Can we help or can our dad help. He is laid off work at the docks so he is available to do any sort of work you need. I gazed momentarily at the well-groomed and neatly dressed brother and sister and thought how similar in age they were to my older two children and I resolved to accept their offer.

“Go and fetch your dad” I blurted out. “Tell him I need his help urgently” and they both dashed over the road and into the house opposite.

Moments later a tall stocky man with a broad belt around his waist, sleeves rolled up his forearms and no collar on his shirt returned with the children. “Good afternoon, sir. Francesca and Joseph tell me I might be able to assist you. My name is John Cooper and I can turn my hand to any work. What can I do to help?”

I had no option now. I had committed to engaging John Cooper's help and the only way forward was to be honest with the circumstances that brought me to Hendon in Sunderland. I introduced myself and briefly explained that the man in the house opposite was wanted by the authorities and that he and his associates posed a potential danger to the nation. I felt a sense of relief now that I had shared these fears with someone else.

"What puzzles me John" I added, "who is the older man? He doesn't seem to be a willing companion of Adam Worth or the Irishman. I need to find out what he has to do with this matter."

John confidently replied. "Let me find out for you Captain Raine. I know that building and I can find a way inside. Mrs. Calhoun rents her rooms out but only to the Irish. If we wait an hour or so Mrs. Calhoun will be making her early evening visit to The Boar's Head and then we will only have to contend with the other two boarders. In the meantime, come inside my house. The front door of Mrs. Calhoun's can be seen from my kitchen window and you can warm yourself sitting next to the fire range."

The cup of tea in front of the blazing heat of the kitchen fire was most welcome and I took the opportunity to find out a little more about John and his family. He was looking after his two children on his own and from my perception of their neat and tidy home and the good manners, nature and character of Francesca and Joseph he was making a successful job of it. As we talked, Joseph began quietly playing an old piano in the next room. For such a young boy he was rendering an almost perfect piece by Debussy punctuated by at least half a dozen piano keys that did not work. Working at the docks as a trimmer, John told me that his job was hard and tiresome work but it was the best work he could get in the area although he was not guaranteed regular hours every week. He had plenty of work when ships sailed in to Hudson Dock to take on a cargo.

However, if the weather was stormy or there was an unusually bad swell that prevented the dock gates from opening the ships could not enter or leave port. In those circumstances which mainly occurred during the late autumn and winter months he was laid off because there was no work available. He confided in me that his main regret when his wages were short was that he could not afford the school fees of three pence each day for Francesca and Joseph. That amounted to a hefty two shillings and sixpence per week. They both enjoyed school and were keen to learn and were disappointed when they were sent home by the headmaster because they didn't have the school fees.

At that moment John blurted out excitedly "there she goes Captain Raine" and I dashed to the window to see Mrs. Calhoun descending her front doorsteps. She was heading for the public house but also accompanying her was the tall Irishman who was evidently keen to also spend an evening in The Boar's Head. That was a bit of luck I thought.

"This is our chance to find out about Adam Worth's reluctant companion" I said to John. "Now, I need to get inside that house and subtlety and delicately have a private word with him. How can I do that John?"

"Well - each house in Henry Street has a coal drop in the back lane. The coal merchant dumps coal down the drop into the cellar and every cellar can be accessed from the kitchen. So, let's take a look in the back lane and see if the trap-door to the coal drop is locked. I dare bet it's not because there won't be any coal in that cellar. Mrs. Calhoun would rather go cold without coal than miss her gin."

"Francesca and Joseph, we have a couple of jobs for you to do" John said crouching down and looking at his children intently. "Now - Francesca. We know that the gas light is turned up in the second-floor room." Turning to me he said "we can safely assume that they have the middle-aged gentleman in there".

Returning his gaze to Francesca he continued, "we now need to know if Adam Worth is in the ground floor front room where another gas light is on. Although you wouldn't recognize him, I think it's safe to assume if someone is in there it would be him." I nodded in agreement. That seemed a fair conjecture. He continued, "take your skipping ropes with you and try, without being too obvious, to see if there is anyone in that sitting room."

Without a moment's hesitation Francesca dashed out of the door with her skipping ropes. Two minutes later she was back panting heavily. "Yes dad, there is a man sitting in there reading a newspaper and smoking a cigarette."

"Right Joseph. You stand on the corner of the back lane watching me and Captain Raine. When you see us going down the coal drop into the cellar, run around to the front corner and signal to Francesca who will be skipping around at the bottom of Mrs. Calhoun's steps. Francesca, when you see Joseph's signal go and knock on the door to attract Adam Worth to open the front door. At that point he will be in the hall with the inner hall door and the stairs behind him. Engage him in a conversation. I am sure you can think of something. Right - does everyone understand what we are doing." We all nodded in agreement.

Following behind my new friend we walked around to the back lane. John looked around furtively and then lifted the coal drop door. He was right. It was not locked and we both slid down into the cellar. At that moment Joseph sprinted at top speed to the front of the street and signaled to Francesca who climbed the steps and knocked on the front door. John and I stealthily made our way out of the cellar and through the kitchen. We waited for the knock on the front door and the sound of footsteps walking through the hall and the front door opening. We could hear Francesca asking if she could speak to Mrs. Calhoun. "My dad has some herring for sale. They were caught this morning and Mrs. Calhoun enjoys fresh herring" Francesca asked. Silently but quickly, we crept through the hall while Adam Worth listened to Francesca and swiftly climbed the stairs onto the second floor. Although the door to the first room was locked a key was sitting on the table by the door. Opening the door, we could see a well-dressed middle-aged man with a winged collar and bow tie dozing on an old threadbare armchair. Not wishing to alarm him, or allow him to give the alarm, I gently placed my hand over his mouth and shook his shoulder to wake him up. His eyes opened behind heavily pebbled lens and he panicked momentarily. Quietly I asked him not to be afraid. "We are here to help if we can. Are you in trouble?

He nodded slowly and I took my hand away from his mouth. I quickly introduced myself and John and explained that I had previously experienced the underhand and treacherous activities of Adam Worth. "Now what is he up to and why has he got you involved?" I asked "and be assured we will help in any way we can".

He replied with real emotion in his voice "My name is John Holland and he has my daughter Helen held hostage. I don't know where she is but he has threatened that she will be punished if I do not comply with his wishes. My daughter means the world to me and I am terrified in case she is harmed so I am obliged to do everything he tells me without question."

"But why" I asked. "What does he want from you"

"I am a mathematician and an engineer" he replied. "For almost two years I was working for a company run by a consortium of entrepreneurs in New York City in the USA. I was employed on a secret engineering project to build a submersible boat and which the U.S. Department of Defense were beginning to take a serious interest. We were progressing very well and, in my opinion, no other company was as advanced in the field of submarine engineering. The prototype I was working on was almost ready to be trialed when I discovered the source of the funding for the project. The so-called entrepreneurs were the Fenian Brotherhood. They had no intention to form a partnership with the U.S. government. They intended to use my submarine boat against the Royal Navy in their insane, murderous campaign to free Ireland from British rule. Jeremiah O'Donovan, one of the leaders of the Fenian Brotherhood, who is here with Adam Worth is intent on striking a blow at Britain's maritime supremacy and he and his consortium raised a "skirmishing fund" to finance the submarine project. I built my prototype, which O'Donovan calls the Fenian Ram, at Delamater's Iron Works at a cost of $20,000. It is thirty feet long, displaces 19 tons with a crew of three, and is powered by a 15hp Brayton 4-cylinder petrol engine. The boat is armed with a 9-inch pneumatic cannon known as a 'dynamite gun' that fires a six-foot projectile through an eleven-foot-long tube with a watertight cap that can be opened and closed by a remote-controlled mechanism in the bow."

Taking off his glasses and rubbing his eyes he continued. "At first, I was skeptical when I was informed that the Fenian Society were financing the project. However, a British naval attaché, Captain William Arthur, secretly contacted me at my apartment in New York and showed me copies of documents that confirmed this was indeed the case. I immediately made arrangements with Captain Arthur to return to Britain with my daughter and with all of my plans and drawings. All of my other possessions I left in my New York apartment. Jeremiah O'Donovan employed Adam Worth to track me down after I arrived back in this country. He not only found me but he kidnapped my daughter Helen. He has told me he intends to hold Helen hostage until I return to New York with him and complete the Fenian Ram project. He told me that after I left the USA one of the members of the Fenian consortium, John Breslin, became impatient and according to O'Donovan tried to launch the submarine but not one person knew the controls or how to operate her without my guidance. She was towed up the East River into Long Island Sound where they completely messed up her trial and she sank. She was raised and now sits in a lumber shed on the Mill River at New Haven until O'Donovan and Worth return with me to finish her development and hand over the completed project including operating and technical specifications."

"You are in a predicament my friend" I quipped. "But could they not use another engineer to complete your prototype and make the Fenian Ram operational?"

"No not really" he answered. "This is a very specialized area and I only know of two other engineers - one in Sweden and the other in France - who would have the technical knowledge to even remotely understand the issues of submersible boats.

He gripped my forearm and pleaded "How can I get my daughter back safely Captain Raine?"

"Well John" I replied "we can't make a move until we know where they have interned her. When John and I leave here we will alert the authorities but we will tell them to take no action until Helen is safe. Have you overheard any careless comments that might help us to locate her?"

"Not that I can think of but Adam Worth's room is just next door. You might find something in there".

"Right" I said to John "Let's have a look in his room. Now don't you worry. We will lock you in here so they will not know their plans have been compromised. We will be close at hand at all times until we are ready to make our move" and we crept out of the room locking the door behind us and replacing the key on the table.

The room next door was in darkness. John pulled the curtain to one side which let in a swathe of light from the street lamp just outside the window. There was nothing lying about in the room except an old admiralty chart. Worth must have the submarine plans and designs with him downstairs I thought. John took hold of my arm and drew my attention to the old map. "Look Captain Raine. This chart of the Northumberland coast has a ring drawn around Coquet Island and inside the ring is written Area 55. Do you think that could be relevant?"

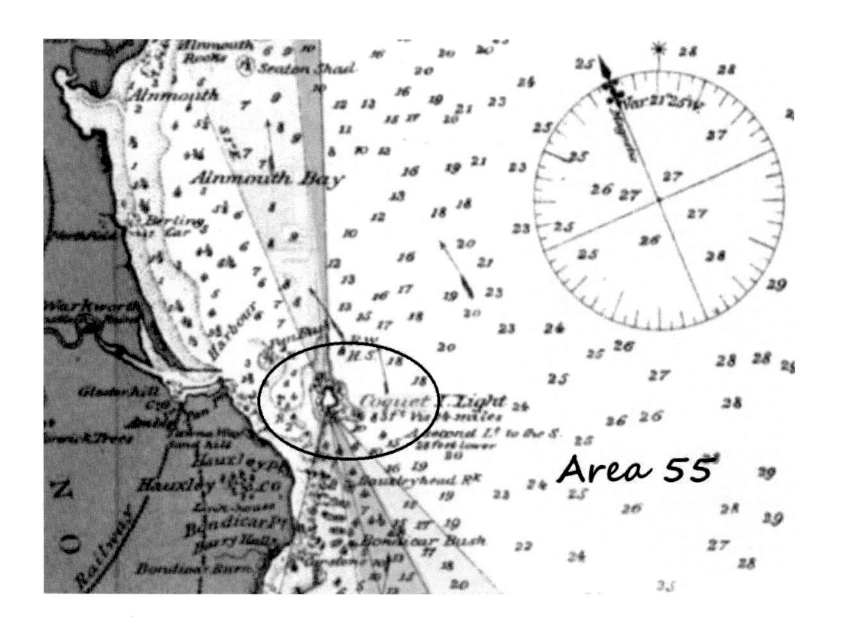

The Admiralty chart in Adam Worth's room

"Quite possibly, John. Let's get out of here before we are discovered." Stealthily we crept down the stairs, along the hall and through the kitchen to the coal cellar. Quietly closing the coal drop hatch behind us we made our way back to John's house.

We sat with Francesca and Joseph and ate a tasty supper of baked herring and bread and butter in front of the fire. After a while John turned to Francesca and Joseph and quietly asked them to put on their night clothes for bed. "Do some reading for half-an-hour and then put the light out and get some sleep". "Yes dad" they politely replied giving him a hug and they made their way up the stairs. Turning to me he asked "What do we do now Captain Raine".

"I need to get a telegraphic message to a friend of mine who is involved in the security service and tell him what we have found here" I replied "but the Post Office telegraph in West Sunniside Place will not be open until 8.00 am tomorrow morning. If you can continue to keep a watch tomorrow morning, I will make my way there and I will return as soon as possible."

We moved an easy chair to face the kitchen window overlooking Mrs. Calhoun's house. Around 11.00 pm Jeremiah O'Donnell and Mrs. Calhoun returned quite the worst for wear with drink and soon after all of the lights in the house were turned down. John wrapped a blanket around himself and took the first watch in the easy chair. I stretched out on the settee in front of the fire and sleep soon took over my overworked thoughts and my tired body. Two hours later I took the watch and John got some well-earned rest. Throughout the night and into the early morning we monitored every movement in that house until dawn broke.

Francesca and Joseph were washed and dressed and helping set the table for breakfast when I awoke at 6.00 am. Francesca's golden-tinged long hair was brushed neatly just off her shoulders and shone as she walked back and forth past the sunbeams breaking in through the window. I walked over to John who was gazing intently out of the kitchen window to the house opposite. "All quiet Captain Raine. Nothing to report yet" he said as Joseph brought him a mug of tea and Francesca beckoned me to the breakfast table. She is just like my daughter Elizabeth Ann I thought. She knows I always feel so much better in the morning after a hot, strong drink of tea.

As the time approached 8.00 am I set off along the road for the General Post Office less than five minutes away. As soon as the large double doors of the Post Office opened, I strode across the mosaic tiled floor and handed my message to the clerk at the telegraph counter. It read: -

To: Lord Londonderry, Seaham Hall.

"Adam Worth located at 27 Henry Street, Sunderland.

He has detained an engineer, John Holland.

Holland's daughter is held hostage.

Keeping watch from 18 Addison Street

Await your advice."

Richard Raine

Ten minutes later the chatter of the telegraph key brought a reply.

To: Richard Raine, Sunderland Post Office.

"Captain William Arthur has been looking for Holland.

Holland went missing two weeks ago.

Captain Arthur here at Seaham Hall

He is leaving in my carriage now.

He will rendezvous with you in one hour"

Londonderry

I returned to Addison Street and sat waiting with John who had continued his watch on the house across the road. Just over one hour later a knock on the back door proclaimed the arrival of Captain Arthur. He had requested Lord Londonderry's coachman to stop two streets away so that the coach did not attract any unnecessary attention. He was a middle-aged naval officer with a stout portly waist. He informed me that he had been recruited for this assignment because of his knowledge of naval architecture and naval warfare studies. Although we had no information on the whereabouts of Helen, John Holland's daughter, Captain Arthur recommended that we immediately enter Mrs. Calhoun's house and apprehend Worth and O'Donovan. At least John Holland would then be free from Fenian control and would be safely in the hands of British Naval authorities. At that moment there was another loud knock on the door. A sergeant from the local police station accompanied by six young, burly constables presented themselves to Captain Arthur. Their inspector had instructed the local force, on the authority of an important dignitary, to lend any assistance necessary to Captain Arthur in a matter of National security. Captain Arthur explained the situation in the house over the road and within a few minutes the plan for a trap was laid. Three constables and the sergeant crossed the road, climbed the steps and entered the front door of the house whilst the other three constables entered though the back door. John Cooper and I followed closely behind Captain Arthur up the front door steps. Within a matter of minutes, the whole house was searched and the occupants were apprehended after a fierce struggle and brought before Captain Arthur in the front room. To my horror only Mrs. Calhoun and Jeremiah O'Donnell were found in the house.

"Where is Adam Worth?" Captain Arthur barked at O'Donnell.

Shaking his head defiantly O'Donnell replied "That snake crept out of the back door half an hour ago. He gave no indication of where he was going but I have suspected for some time that he had no real enthusiasm for the Irish cause. I hope you catch the rat."

I looked at Captain Arthur. His face was white and he was clearly in shock. He knew Worth had escaped his clutches. Worse still he had John Holland with him. Holland's daughter was incarcerated somewhere and Adam Worth was at liberty to bring pressure on Holland to do whatever he commanded. This was possibly the worst imaginable outcome for Captain Arthur.

My new friend John Cooper turned to me. "Captain Raine. What about that admiralty chart we saw in Worth's room?"

"Yes, that could be the answer" I replied. "Captain Arthur, we saw an old map in Worth's room and Coquet Island on the Northumberland coast was circled in pencil. Could Worth be heading there with John Holland? If he is then it's a fair bet, he will be leaving from the Central Station in Fawcett Street. That is the only station with trains heading north of Sunderland."

"It's worth a try. Let's get to the Central Station straight away" he said hopefully. I shook John Cooper by the hand and promised I would be back to see him when all of this was over and ran out the door behind Captain Arthur who was already in full flight.

Catching up to my portly companion I uttered through panting breaths that Adam Worth could have had no knowledge of our planned entrapment in Henry Street. He obviously intended to leave without O'Donnell anyway and so he would be thinking everything was going as he had planned. He still had not seen me and, Captain Arthur confirmed, Worth had never seen him. If Worth was at the station there was every chance we could once again put him under surveillance and reclaim the advantage.

But a doubt ran through my mind. Was Adam Worth at the station?

CHAPTER 12

The escape to Northumberland

The route to the Central Station took us past the Town Moor where people were congregating to enjoy their pastimes in the early morning sun. Looking down to the mouth of the river I could see the ballast keels leaving the harbour to discharge their ballast. Light colliers were running down the River Wear under sail to anchor in the roadstead. Both young and old are let loose on this Moor to enjoy themselves each day. Quoits were being played by the men and, as we passed, I could hear some complaining that a quoit had been thrown but the players foot was not kept against the hob until the flat ring was released. A number of old men were playing bowls on a course running from north to south. A tracker was pointing out to the bowler the best spot to throw his next bowl. A group of young ladies were drawing sketches and painting on canvas in the far corner of the Moor overlooking the Ropery. Captain Arthur was panting heavily after his initial sprint past the old Barracks and he was obviously exhausted. Nevertheless, we passed the bull bait ring at a brisk pace. The last bull bait in Sunderland was over fifty years ago and I could see the anchor, still sunk into the ground, with the ring attached to which the bull was fastened with ropes. Only the owners of the bulldogs that were to be set on to the bulls were allowed in the circle drawn around the ring and heavy betting was made on each dog. Apparently, after some time the bull became fagged and the bulldogs were called off. The bull was then led away to the slaughter house. A barbaric sport that is now best left to history I thought. Continuing along Church Walk we approached Fawcett Street and the impressive railway station built only two years ago came into view. Entering the concourse, I could see a two-island platform with one track running south and one running north beneath an arched roof springing from the brick retaining walls. At the end of the concourse was the booking office with a gently sloping ramp to the platforms. Scanning the platform from our elevated position Captain Arthur shouted in horror "He's not there Richard. We've lost him" and he threw up his arms in dismay. I didn't respond but strode onto the north-bound platform and approached the small waiting room behind the booking office. I beckoned my companion over motioning for him to be quiet. There in the corner was Adam Worth appearing as though he hadn't a care in the world with John Holland sitting in silence next to him.

Captain Arthur was panting loudly as we entered the booking office. His face was red and he sat down on a seat to steady his shaking tired legs. "I think we can make the assumption that Worth is heading for Coquet Island"

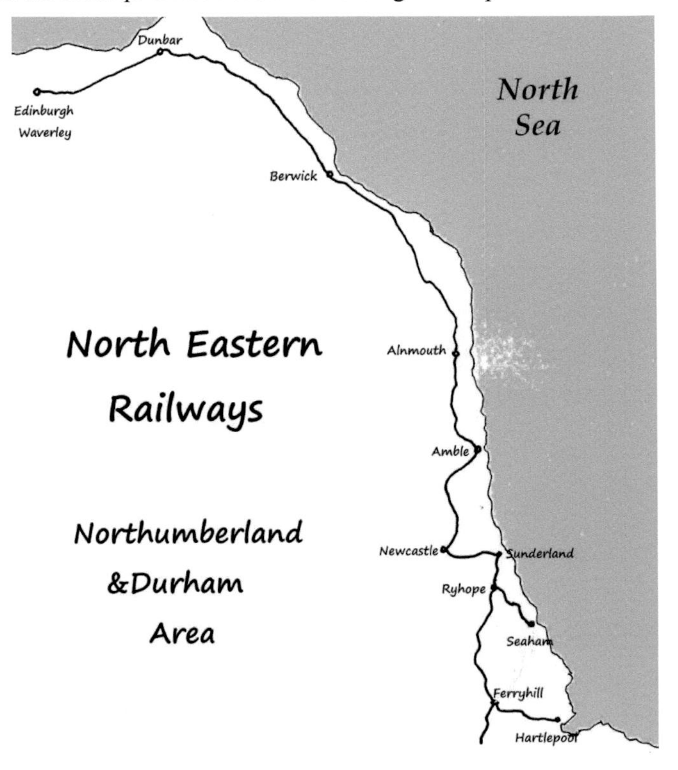

Railway map on the wall of the booking hall

I looked at the railway map and timetable pinned on the wall of the booking office and consulted my watch.

I whispered. "The next train travelling north according to the notice board is the 11.35 am to Edinburgh Waverley station. Consulting the railways map on the wall It was clear that the 11.35 am train stopped at Amble about 30 miles north of Newcastle. "Right. I will buy two tickets to Amble which is the nearest railway station for Coquet Island and we will stay as close to them as possible until we have an opportunity to apprehend Worth and release John Holland." Captain Arthur nodded in agreement and I made my way to the front of the booking hall to buy the tickets. On my return I sat down beside Captain Arthur. From his seat he could clearly see into the waiting room. We tried to stay out of the line of sight of John Holland in case he inadvertently gave our presence away to Worth. Ten minutes later the two of them stood up and walked out of the busy waiting room and on to the platform. We slowly followed as the North Eastern Railway train from York to Edinburgh hissed and spluttered as it pulled into the station and stopped at platform two. Worth and Holland climbed into one of the carriages and Captain Worth and I moved forward and approached the train. This was not a corridor train. We had no option but to take a seat in the next compartment which by good fortune was still unoccupied. Although we couldn't see Adam Worth from our compartment, we knew that as long as we watched carefully from our window at each stop, we would see him if he left the train. The locomotive began to pull us out of the station and built-up speed as it took us through the suburbs leading to Gateshead and Newcastle and then onwards from Newcastle Central Station and over the border to Northumberland. We soon arrived at the coastal fishing town of Amble. On the outskirts of the town were row after row of well-kept allotment gardens with their eager owners weeding and tending their plots. Through the opposite carriage window, on the other side of the track, I could see dozens of coal trucks in the sidings waiting to be shunted down to the harbour. The rest of the town was now visible from our carriage. Walworth Castle stood sentry over the town. We passed an impressive church and Rectory, the Blue Bell Inn, the Mason's Arms, the Radcliffe Arms, the school and many shops in the Main Street. A number of goods sheds, cranes and the brick works came into view. The train slowed down with buffers clanking loudly as it pulled into Amble station which was only a few hundred yards from Radcliffe Quay and Broomhill Quay at the mouth of the River Coquet. This was an area I was most familiar with from my visits to deliver timber to the shipbuilding yard near Warkworth Harbour and to take on cargoes of coal from the staithes.

We carefully watched for any movement in the carriage next door. I asked myself, "Are they going to leave the train here. Have we made the right assumptions about Coquet Island?" After a few moments I had the answer. The carriage door opened and John Holland got off the train followed by Worth. We walked behind at a discrete distance as they made their way past the Customs House and the Coastguard Station towards the far end of the harbour.

The quayside was littered with cobles and small boats that had been hauled out of the water for repair and fishing nets were stretched out over the ground to dry in the afternoon sun. The familiar smell of fish, seaweed, tar and bitumen hit my nostrils as we bent low behind stacks of old fish crates. Captain Arthur blurted out "Richard. There is a small boat tied up on the South Jetty and they are making their way down the steps to board it."

"Yes, and look at those six sailors manning the oars" I replied. "If they are not German, I'm a Dutchman. Has Adam Worth hoodwinked the Fenian Brotherhood once again and is he again in league with General von Caprivi and Kapitan Sturm of the Imperial German Navy"?

Captain Arthur nodded and added despondently "well what do we do now. We have lost them" as the boat pulled away from the South Jetty and out of the mouth of the river heading for Coquet Island in the distance.

"All is not lost. We're not going to give up quite that easily" I answered. "I know the harbour master Lieutenant Thompson. His office is just around the corner. He is also the officer commanding the local Royal Naval Reserve Volunteers. We can consult with him and enlist his help. I am sure that he can quickly assemble a detachment of able men."

Striding into the harbour master's office we discovered that Lieutenant Thompson was not on duty. Captain Arthur explained our predicament to Ben Jefferson the assistant harbour master who immediately sent a message to the Lieutenant that he was needed urgently. As would be expected Ben Jefferson was also second in command of the local RNRV and he immediately sent runners around the town to muster as many of the volunteer reserves on a matter of national emergency. This was just the sort of situation that the RNRV was first created for over twenty years ago. In the late 1850's, Napoleon III, the nephew of Bonaparte, began his war-mongering and sabre-rattling against a number of European nations including threats of invasion against Britain. The Commander-in-Chief of the British armed forces, the Duke of Wellington, was very concerned that most of the British Army and Royal Navy were garrisoned around the world and involved in overseas campaigns. To bolster home defenses, the Volunteer Act was passed through parliament in 1859 which allowed counties and shires to raise their own naval, rifle and artillery volunteer brigades. I was a member of the RNRV at Seaham Harbour and I knew how well trained and disciplined were all the Volunteer Forces.

Captain Arthur and I stood with Ben Jefferson outside the coastguard station as one by one the lads from the local RNRV arrived with a variety of old-fashioned muskets, re-conditioned carbines, muzzle-loading rifles but some with the latest snider breach-loading rifles. Each volunteer was hastily briefed as soon as they arrived. I could sense an air of excitement building up as these men realized that they had been training for just this sort of action for many years. In every county around Britain volunteer reserves had reported to drill halls and drill sheds for two evenings every week to train in sabre practice, musketry and rifle shooting and learning every conceivable nautical skill sometimes from experienced and disciplined Royal Navy instructors. At least twenty men had answered the muster call with more appearing every minute by the time Lieutenant Thompson arrived and took over command of his detachment. Quickly briefed on the situation by Captain Arthur he immediately instructed his second-in-command to take a message to the chief magistrate, Mr. Robson, who was also acting Major in command of the 2nd Northumberland (Percy) Artillery Volunteers based here in the town to mobilize his gunners.

I looked out beyond the navigation light at the end of the north pier towards Coquet Island and wondered "what is going on over there?"

CHAPTER 13

The mysterious events on Coquet Island

Coquet Island off the coast of Northumberland

The early afternoon sun was bathing Coquet Island in light. In any other circumstances the view before us would calm any troubled mind but Captain Arthur and myself knew that Adam Worth was on that island and capable of committing the very worst of atrocities against our country.

Beyond the island I could see three cobles with fishermen throwing their lines into the water and hauling in their crab and lobster pots just two hundred yards from the landing stage of the lighthouse. Watching them for a few minutes I thought, "hang on, they don't look like local fishermen. Does anyone have a telescope?" Ben Jefferson passed me his pocket telescope.

"Look at those boats Captain Arthur. I may be mistaken but those men are dressed like German sailors and it looks like they are taking depth soundings with a lead line around the approach to the landing steps. Why would they be doing that?" I asked.

Captain Arthur replied, "You are right. They must be determining the depths and the composition of the seabed for anchorage and pilotage around the lighthouse. They could be establishing the rise and fall of the tide at different times of the day. We have to find out what the devil they are up to?"

Gathering his naval volunteers together Lieutenant Thompson introduced Captain Arthur and myself and asked them to listen carefully. I appraised them of the importance of their task and that there was one person on the island called John Holland who was very important to the British government. He had been coerced into accompanying Worth to Coquet Island because his daughter had been kidnapped. Only Adam Worth knew of her whereabouts. The essential goal to be achieved by this squad was to get on to Coquet Island, release John Holland from the clutches of the German navy, capture and detain Adam Worth and, hopefully, find out what has happened to Helen Holland. I could hear the men muttering together excitedly and their exuberance and eagerness to get into action shone like a beacon.

"Right, we need intelligence to plan our next steps. Does anyone know the layout of the island" I asked.

A young fresh-faced volunteer with a cutlass under his belt and a muzzle-loading carbine slung over his shoulder stepped forward. "I used to visit the island with my father many years ago when he delivered the provisions and stores for the lighthouse. I know how the land lies because I used to wander off and play in the sand dunes with my older brother while we waited for dad".

"Perfect, that is just what we need to know" replied Captain Arthur. "Tell us everything you remember"

The young lad continued, "The island is uninhabited and it has been for many years. At one time the only regular inhabitants were a religious order who, in Norman times, built a monastery on the east side facing the North Sea. About fifty years ago a cottage, dwelling house with a tower and a lighthouse were built from the stone remains of the Norman monastery. Next to the lighthouse is a large, well-made landing wharf that dad used to moor up to when loading and unloading stores. The light keepers are old Ned and George Wood who have been working there for over twenty years. There used to be a third brother but he died. The two brothers have no affection for life on the mainland and according to dad they were happy with their own company living a solitary life enjoying every season surrounded by the sea. They are supplied with oil and provisions from the mainland once a month and they rarely leave the island. Trinity House makes a yearly inspection of the light facilities and arrange for any necessary repairs to be made. I remember being taken up to the watch-room at the top of the lighthouse by old Ned and my dad. The floor of the watch-room is made of iron and is reached through a trap-door at the top of a very steep metal ladder leading from the stone steps running up the side of the lighthouse. I understand that the two brothers take equal watches of four hours each and the lamp is lighted at sunset and extinguished at sunrise leaving the rest of the day for the brothers to carry out any maintenance or just to relax."

Just then another lad joined in. "We did a study of Coquet Island in our geography class when I was at school many years ago. I remember our teacher telling us the island belongs to the Duke of Northumberland and is covered with a thick grass with many deep depressions where the monks dug for peat that they used for fuel on their fires and for cooking."

Another volunteer added. "I used to fish around the island. It is about two-thirds of a mile from the mainland so it can take a good fifteen minutes to row out to it, perhaps longer when the current turns. It is about sixteen acres in extent and stands about thirty-five feet above high water but at low-water the ledges dry out which almost doubles the size of the island. I remember we had to take great care when approaching Coquet roads because there is foul ground to the eastward channel and Hauxley rocks to the west has only eight feet spare above bottom rock when allowing for the lift of the sea."

"All of this is very useful" Captain Arthur said addressing the volunteers now approaching about thirty in number. "Have we sufficient boats to get us all over to the island?"

Lieutenant Thompson looked around at his volunteers and loudly replied that there were plenty of boats on hand for the men to use. Nearly every man was a seaman or a fisherman and they all had their own boats. Captain Arthur continued "I suggest we do not use the landing stage. We don't know what to expect when we get there or how many German sailors are on the island. It's low water now so I recommend we land on the ledges facing the mainland."

Looking out at the North Sea I felt the wind becoming fresher and blowing from the east. It was bringing with it a blanket of thick sea mist. That might be just what we need I thought to myself.

Organizing his men into the boats Lieutenant Thompson gave the order to cast off and row for the island. Captain Arthur and myself sat in the prow of the second boat with Ben Jefferson. "Lend me your telescope Ben" I asked and I scanned the approaching shore, lighthouse, house and cottage. From this viewpoint Coquet Island looked like a vast black-backed fish basking in the sun with the mist rolling in behind it. The white-walled lighthouse, cottage and house looked like a whitish fin just behind a fish's head.

"So careless" I said to Captain Arthur. "Not one person is keeping watch on the approaches from the mainland".

The boats pulled up onto the exposed rocky outcrop on the land-facing shoreline. The rocks were covered with thick kelp and seaweed. The men promptly dashed for the cover of the small cliffs protecting the fields above the narrow beach. Reaching a depression in the cliff Lieutenant Thompson led his men up and into the fields above. The young lad was right. There were many areas of land that had been dug out for the valuable peat and which provided the perfect cover to advance towards the house and cottage. Reaching the grey stone wall surrounding the lighthouse I beckoned everyone to keep their heads down while I carried out a surveillance of the area.

Six German sailors were hauling three cobles onto the small beach below the landing steps. Another five or six sailors were sharpening cutlasses and cleaning carbines by the door of the house and another two sailors were busy attending to food cooking on an open fire.

“There he is” I muttered to myself as Adam Worth opened the cottage door. Behind him I could see John Holland standing with his back to the fireplace as Worth closed the door behind him.

“Stand easy lads” I whispered to the squad. “John Holland is in that cottage. Don’t advance until I give a signal that he is safe”.

“I’m coming with you” insisted Ben Jefferson. “You will need someone to watch your back” and he handed me a Snider breech-loading rifle and an ammunition belt of cartridges which I slung over my shoulder. I didn’t argue. His support was very welcome.

We crept behind the wall until we reached the cottage and, making sure there was no one looking in our direction we slid over the wall and behind a hand cart in the yard. The cottage door was only ten yards away but was that door locked I asked myself? It was not the time to procrastinate so with a nod from Ben, we dashed for the door and turned the handle. The door opened and we rushed inside. Ben peered outside and with relief indicated that we had not been seen.

Startled but clearly overjoyed to see me John Holland sprang up from the table where he had been sitting eating a bowl of soup and some bread.

"Captain Raine. I had given up hope that you would still be around to help. When Adam Worth took me to the railway station at Sunderland, I thought I had no chance of getting away from this evil man and finding my daughter. Have you brought help?" he hopefully asked.

Ben Jefferson smiled and confidently answered. "We have a squad of naval volunteers assembled close by waiting for our signal to launch an assault." I quickly asked, "How many German sailors are here on the island and, apart from the men outside, where are they?"

"I have seen about two dozen foreign sailors and most of them are billeted in the house next door" he replied. "While sitting here at the window eating my soup, I saw a sailor carrying more bowls of soup to the lighthouse so there are more people in there."

Turning to Ben I said "I think we need to see who is in the lighthouse. It must be someone who can't sit and take their food with the other sailors. It's a bit of a risk but let's find out. We can't leave you here Mr. Holland. Stick close behind us" and I peered out of the door at the sailors cooking on the open fire in the courtyard.

We waited for what seemed an eternity until those sailors hanging around watching the food being cooked filled their plates and disappeared into the house next door to eat. The two men who were cooking sat down by the open fire with their backs to the cottage. Here was our chance.

"Right. Let's go. Be as quick and quiet as you can" I pleaded and we dashed out of the door towards the lighthouse just ten yards away.

Rushing through the door at the base of the lighthouse we surprised an unsuspecting sailor sitting on a sack of flour and before he had the opportunity to gather his wits Ben Jefferson struck him on the forehead with the butt of his rifle knocking him senseless onto the floor. There was no one else in that room. A further door stood before us with a key in the lock. Cautiously unlocking the door, I detected three people in the dim light of two candles. Levelling my rifle into the room I shouted "Come out here where we can see you."

Into the light shuffled the two lighthouse keepers, Ned and George Wood, and a young teenage girl.

"Helen" cried John Holland. "Are you all right. I have been worried sick since they absconded with you. I feared I may never see you again." The two embraced and both were engulfed in tears.

At that moment the lighthouse door opened and another sailor appeared. Although he was taken completely by surprise at our presence, he dashed back out of the door screeching at the top of his voice and giving the alarm to his comrades in the house next door.

"Quickly Ben" I shouted. "Barricade the door". Without another word all five of us stacked the table and chairs, furniture and sacks of provisions against the door. We could hear the commotion outside and Adam Worth's voice loudly prompting the sailors to break down the door. The heavy glass window to the side of us was smashed throwing shards of glass across the floor. We both raised our rifles and let off a volley through the broken window to hopefully give us some breathing space to collect our thoughts. It made no difference. The barricaded door was beginning to weaken.

"Everyone - get up the lighthouse steps" I shouted.

I followed Helen and the two lighthouse keepers running up the stairs going up the side of the lighthouse with Ben Jefferson right behind me.

The door below crashed to the ground and a rush of men barged into the room swinging cudgels and cutlasses. Backing up the stairs slowly Ben and I had the advantage that only one man at a time could challenge us because of the narrow stairs. We had not been able to reload our rifles since that first volley but we made good use of the long reach of the rifle butts against the oncoming heads and we accounted for five or six German sailors who collapsed on the stairs holding their bleeding heads.

Ned Wood shouted down, "Quickly. We are in the lamp room. Climb up the metal steps and we can close the lamp room trapdoor. That will hold them off"

The iron steps leading to the lamp room trapdoor

"Go on Ben. I will be right behind you" I panted and with that Ben shot up the steep steps like a monkey while I continued to batter the next assailant trying to reach me with his cudgel

I made a dash up the steps and as I threw myself inside the lamp room at the very top of the lighthouse, Ned slammed the trapdoor shut. Although the trapdoor could not be locked Ned shuffled a twenty-gallon oil drum over the hatch. "That should hold them" he exclaimed.

But unfortunately, it didn't. The stoutest of the sailors stood at the top of the steps with his shoulders pushing up on the trapdoor. He dislodged the oil drum and was able to throw his muscly tattooed arm through the opening. In his hand was a revolver and he was manipulating his hand to point the gun towards us when Helen bravely stamped on his fingers. A shot rang out from the revolver prompted by his involuntary pull on the trigger. The bullet ricocheted with a ping twice off the metal casing of the lamp room and then, with a thud, embedded itself in a timber beam. Following up her first kick Helen stamped once again on his hand and his arm disappeared as he lost his hold on the steep steps below and he fell on his companions.

I was aware of gunfire outside. Alerted by the volley downstairs Captain Arthur and Lieutenant Thompson had decided to launch their assault and gave orders to open fire on the German sailors gathered around the base of the lighthouse. The German foe in the courtyard quickly dived for cover collecting their carbines and returned heavy fire that pinned down the volunteers behind the perimeter wall. I could hear Adam Worth barking out orders in German at the base of the lighthouse. In response the sailors trying to break into the lamp room ran down the stairs to reinforce their comrades defense of the courtyard area.

I stepped out onto the viewing platform to see what was going on followed by Ben Jefferson. From our high viewpoint I could clearly see everything on the island. The German sailors were returning rapid fire against Lieutenant Thompson's forces. Each one of them had the very latest of carbines and their rate of fire was twice that of our men some of whom had been issued with out-of-date muzzle loading muskets. Even though we had superior numbers in terms of men we were at a disadvantage. "I don't like it Ben" I exclaimed. "We can only hold our line if we increase our rate of fire".

"That's the least of our worries," shouted Ben. "Look at that" and he pointed out at sea. Approaching the island through the sea fret and mist was a German barquentine in full sail. It was unmistakably the Ernst Friedrick probably with Kapitan Sturm in command.

"Is he mad?" I exclaimed. "He will flounder on the rocks if he continues on that course". The Ernst Fredrick dressed down her sails and slowly maneuvered through the North Channel into Coquet roads keeping the island ledges to the eastward and the Pan Point to the westward. The ship slowed down further until it was about three cables to the northward of Pan Point where she drew up safely at the anchorage in Coquet Road.

"Kapitan Sturm must have had intelligence from those depth soundings to make that maneuver" I mumbled. "He has dropped anchor and three jolly boats are being lowered."

About twenty men armed with breech-loading rifles climbed down into the jolly boats and the boats pulled towards the landing stage. This is not going well I thought. If those sailors join the fight we are finished. Suddenly, a boom rang out from shore. Turning towards the town I could see a cloud of smoke on the shoreline and a shell whistled over the lighthouse and over the square-rigged foremast of the Ernst Friedrick.

The 68-pdr muzzle loading gun of the Artillery Volunteers fires a first volley at the German Barquentine

Ben leapt into the air with a whoop. "Good old Major Robson. He has mustered his brigade of artillery volunteers at the practice battery. They must have been watching the action on the island through their telescopes and he has seen the danger unfolding when the Ernst Friedrick launched her boats. He has readied the guns on the shore battery for action and his first shot from the 68-pounder gun has overshot the German barquentine. The battery sergeant major will be sure to drop the angle of elevation and hit the target on his next shot."

"I hope not Ben." I exclaimed. "We are right in the line of fire. The last shot whistled only yards above us. If the gun elevation is lowered the next shell will take the top off this lighthouse". Ben looked at me in horror. He knew I was right.

Returning our gaze to the Ernst Friedrick we could see that the intervention of the artillery volunteers had caused a dramatic change to their plans. Officers on board were screaming for the boats to return to the ship. There was no way Kapitan Sturm was going to risk his ship being pummeled by 68-pounder shells.

The sound of the retreat shrieked out over the waves from the bosun's whistle. Hearing the call to retreat the sailors below broke off the firefight against our men at the perimeter wall and they all ran to their boats. Some returned covering fire to protect the last of the sailors as they scrambled on board the boats, including Adam Worth, and they pulled away furiously towards their ship. The German barquentine was now hauling its anchor and there was a scurry of activity as men were shuffling along the yards and letting loose the mainsails which quickly filled in the fresh breeze. The sailors from the boats scurried aboard the Ernst Friedrick as its sails filled and it began to gather speed. The last few men in the boats managed to pull themselves on board including Adam Worth who threw himself over the bulwarks clasping his valise and John Holland's chart and design case under his arm. Through Ben Jefferson's telescope I could see Worth turn and look towards Coquet Island with a look of anger and indignation on his face.

At the sight of the German ship in full flight a cheer rang out from Lieutenant Thompson and his men. A cheer that echoed from island to shore and then was accompanied by celebrations from the shore battery. A cheer that none of them would ever forget.

"For God's sake let us get down from this lamp room" I shouted "before that battery sergeant major fires another shot" and we all quickly descended the iron steps and stairs and joined the rejoicing volunteers in the courtyard.

CHAPTER 14

Rendezvous with the 6th Marquess of Londonderry

Returning to the mainland the volunteers were in boisterous spirits as they entered the mouth of the River Coquet and tied their boats up at the Radcliffe Quay. Lieutenant Thompson had arranged for a dozen armed men to stay on the island for a few days with Ned and George Wood just in case Kapitan Sturm returned. A secret signal was agreed between the lighthouse keepers and the naval and artillery volunteers. Clearly suspicions would be aroused and the alarm would be raised if the lamp was not lit at sunset each day. But, in addition, Ned and George would place a black flag in the lamp room, visible from the shore battery, if there was any danger or if they needed assistance from the volunteers.

It was past seven o'clock when Captain Arthur, John Holland and his daughter and I left the joyous volunteers in very high spirits and walked into the town. The last train had left Amble station half an hour ago so, on Ben Jefferson's recommendation, we booked rooms in the Blue Bell Inn and spent a very enjoyable few hours recounting today's events, eating supper and drinking a very nice local ale. For the first time since I had met John Holland, he looked relaxed and contented and did not show any signs of anxiety or mental strain. It was pleasing to see him and his pretty daughter Helen holding hands, smiling, laughing and talking to each other. No one would have believed they had both been through such a torturous experience.

I apologized for interrupting their conversation but I had to get something off my chest. There was one issue that was suppressing the euphoria and elation that I should have felt.

"After a day when we have achieved so much my only regret is that Adam Worth has not only escaped, but he has taken the plans and drawings of your submersible - the Fenian Ram - and they are now in the hands of the Imperial German Navy. All of your hard work for the last two years has been compromised. It must be very upsetting to you that they will now have the advantage of your skills and knowledge in the race to perfect submarine technology".

John Holland looked at Captain Arthur and they both smiled at each other. "Forgive Captain Arthur and myself Richard. Allow us to share with you why we can display a little bit of self-satisfaction in today's events. We have previously discussed my work on the Fenian Ram in great detail. As you know Captain Arthur is also an authority on submersibles." He looked up at me with a wry smile.

"From a design concept I knew that the vessel had a number of technical shortcomings but I had new ideas and thoughts on how they could be remedied. I had never expressed or even hinted at those new ideas let alone incorporate them in my plans and original drawings. Although my prototype performed satisfactorily under water, she was terribly slow and her weapons system was never perfected. I always intended to build a bigger and more sophisticated boat at a later date. Once the hatch at the top of the submarine was closed the Fenian Ram was "blind" when she submerged. My intentions were to build a sort of conning tower that would incorporate a telescopic periscope to view shipping on the surface thereby enabling the submariner to see above the waves without having to break cover. The dynamite gun concept would have been replaced with new developments in torpedo warfare that could fire torpedoes even when submerged. That alone could create one of the world's deadliest weapons. In addition to the internal combustion engine for propulsion on the surface I planned to add an electric motor powered by an electric battery as an alternative method of propulsion when submerged. My next prototype would also have positive buoyancy so that if the engine failed it would automatically rise to the surface and it would have a fixed center of gravity to make it much more maneuverable. Luckily no-one in the consortium knew of these planned improvements. The fact that Worth has my drawings in his possession gives the German navy no advantage. They could in fact have obtained copies of those drawings from the USA Patents Office. But one fact Adam Worth did not take into account. He forgot that I am a mathematician. I have developed an algorithm of matrix multiplication that has been applied to all of the measurements shown in the plans that he has taken. I know how to apply that algorithm to reveal the correct size, volume, angle or weight to be used and it isn't the figures shown in the plans."

Captain Arthur added, "John agreed to work with the British Government on his submarine project some months ago and we were working towards that aim when Adam Worth kidnapped Helen. We have established a top-secret government team in a shipyard in Barrow-in -Furness, Cumberland which will build a new submarine incorporating all of John's new plans. Tomorrow morning, we will be taking the Borders train to Carlisle from Newcastle Central Station and then the branch line train for Barrow-in-Furness. So, as you see, Adam Worth has gone to a lot of trouble for no advantage. I wonder what the boffins in the Imperial German Navy think of the plans and drawings he hands over to them and they find that the one-inch hexagonal nut on a ballast pipe does not fit on the three-quarter inch ballast pump. They will spend months trying to make sense of the specifications in the drawings."

I laughed out aloud. That news was so pleasing.

"Well, I don't know about you three but I am going to have an early night" I said. "It's been a long, long day".

Next morning, I awoke completely refreshed after a good night's sleep. I dressed and left the Inn and took a brisk walk through the Main Street which was quite busy with people going about their daily business. I arrived at the Post Office just as the assistant manager was opening the large double doors. I handed a telegram request to the counter assistant and waited for the reply. Ten minutes later the reply from Lord Londonderry read: -

"Glad to hear of your successful encounter with Worth.

Tell Captain Arthur I will arrange to see him next week.

I would welcome a debriefing of yesterday's events.

Please disembark at Seaham Hall station.

My carriage will collect you."

Londonderry

I rejoined my friends in the dining room of the Inn and passed on Lord Londonderry's message to Captain Arthur. After breakfast we all made our way to the railway station to catch the 10.15 am service to Newcastle. On our arrival at Newcastle the train for Carlisle was just preparing to leave. I quickly bade farewell to my companions and waved them off as the Borders train pulled out of the station. Very shortly afterwards I left on the next train stopping at Sunderland Central. It was only a short walk to Hendon Burn Terminus where I found an empty carriage on the Londonderry Seaham to Sunderland railway. It seemed such a long time since I had followed Adam Worth to Coquet Island but that was only yesterday.

I felt quite privileged and important as the train slowed down and stopped at Seaham Hall station. Most of the passengers were straining from their carriage windows to see who was disembarking. This stop at the small, pretty platform and waiting room is exclusively reserved for Lord Londonderry and his family at Seaham Hall. Waiting on the platform was a footman in full livery from the manor house who greeted me and led me to a waiting carriage drawn by two splendid, grey horses.

The three-quarters of a mile drive along "Lord Byron's" walk brought us to the entrance gate for Seaham Hall and its park where once you could find the quaint old village of Seaham. This small hamlet was long since swept away a century ago to lay out the lawns and gardens leading down from the much-extended hall to the brook and dene. A group of gardeners turned and doffed their caps as the carriage drove past at "Lady Byron's Well" the reputed scene of Byron's twice repeated proposal of marriage to Lady Milbanke.

The grand facade of Seaham Hall

As the landau carriage approached the big house, I could see that Seaham Hall presented a curious patchwork of styles. The coachman stopped outside the stately Grecian portico flanked by tall windows.

I could see on the right side were buildings of a much older and plainer house. The butler in his fine tails, wing collar and tie and silver-buckled shiny shoes opened the carriage door and welcomed me.

"His Lordship is expecting you, Captain Raine. Please follow me" and he led the way through a spacious hall lined with glass cases containing stuffed animals. Passing through this I was led through a smaller inner hall lit by the glazed roof above with pictures of scenery, principally of Ireland, adorning the walls. A grand staircase presented itself before us and to the right the great folding mahogany doors to the dining room were swept open. This was a long and lofty room hung with paintings illustrating the history of Seaham and with a large portrait of Lady Frances Anne Vane, the grandmother of the current Marquesses, hanging over the fireplace. Another portrait of his grandfather, the third Marquess, seated on a horse in the market square at Durham City hung at the far end of the dining room. To the left of the staircase the beautiful ballroom showcased a great window looking out to a stunning view of the sea and the coast to Hartlepool and the Yorkshire moors beyond. As we passed the billiard room and the music room the butler turned and quietly said, "His Lordship is in the library" and he knocked, opened the door and announced "Captain Raine your Lordship" and he bade me to enter. This was such a pleasant room I thought with another large bay window looking out over the terrace garden and Dene. In the distance, lit up by the furnaces and lights from Seaham Colliery I caught a glimpse of Christchurch built by Lady Frances Anne as a lasting memorial to her husband. There were bookcases on every wall filled with books of all ages and sizes, Empire chairs of classical shape with the sphinxes head forming the arms and the caduceus forming the back were arranged around the room.

As I entered the room the young Marquess sprung to his feet and strode over to warmly greet me. "Richard" he said vigorously shaking my hand and forearm as though I was a long lost relative. "It's so good to see you again. Since your telegram telling me that you had encountered Adam Worth in Hartlepool two days ago, I have been on the edge of my seat waiting for any news."

Just then the under-butler entered the room with a tea tray. "That will be all Thomas" he said to his servant. "We can manage ourselves thank you" and he began to pour two cups of tea.

Waiting until the servants had closed the library door, he turned to me. "Now sit down with your cup of tea and tell me absolutely everything that has happened. I cannot wait another moment longer."

I began to relay my tale starting with my first encounter with Worth when I saw him walking towards Hartlepool railway station on Sunday morning until he was last sighted sailing away from Coquet Island with his tail between his legs late yesterday afternoon. At every possible juncture his Lordship asked questions, or for clarification, so that he had the fullest briefing and understanding of the events that took place. I also explained how I was initially disappointed that Adam Worth had escaped with John Holland's plans and designs but Captain Arthur had reassured me that the German High Command would get no advantage from them. Lord Londonderry seemed to be fully aware of this. He also knew of John Holland's future intentions and that he had agreed to work with the British Government in the top-secret establishment in Barrow-in-Furness. Clearly, he and Captain Arthur, had been negotiating that part of the plan for some time.

“What I don’t understand your Lordship” I asked. “Kapitan Sturm and Adam Worth have gone to a lot of trouble and effort to steal these submersible designs. Are they really that important?”

I could see Lord Londonderry pondering for a few seconds.

“I think I know you well enough now Richard” he exclaimed. “I will take you into my confidence and it may answer your question. The British Naval Intelligence Service has been aware of major German naval activity in the German Bight area of the North Sea for some time. You will recall your friend Lieutenant Jack Smith.” I nodded. “Well. About six months ago Jack sailed across the North Sea with a friend in a twenty-foot ketch. For the benefit of any German customs officers or harbour officials that may have asked, they were on a sporting vacation sailing around the German Frisian Islands. They spent three weeks visiting every sandbank, cove and inlet on the islands. You may know that the German Frisian Islands provide the only access to the North Sea from mainland Germany. Every other German naval port is on the Baltic Sea so strategically the Frisian Islands are very important. You will also know that they are in an area of rapid and constant change with mudbanks and sandbanks around every island so while Jack Smith was “enjoying his vacation” he was also making up-to-date charts of the islands for the Admiralty. To sail into the Frisian Islands requires great care and skill to use the narrow approach channels that twist and turn for miles. The tidal streams in those channels meet or divide at a watershed often drying out to about half a fathom in depth. It provides a fascinating world that changes with each tide and challenges any navigator at every turn. Luckily, Jack Smith is one of the best navigational officers in the fleet. This is the typical topography of all of the Frisian islands.

Jack Smith detected unusual activity on Sylt, an island located about six miles off the mainland. The island itself extends for about twenty-four miles in a north-south direction and its shape constantly shifts with the tides over time. The German High Command call this Area 55.

I interrupted Lord Londonderry at this point. "Adam Worth had an old chart in his room in Henry Street and it had "Area 55" marked on it. Could that be significant?"

"That is the very same thing" replied his Lordship. "One night Jack and his comrade navigated their way through the tidal channels of Sylt and discovered a labyrinth of concrete pens, wharfs, workshops and an excavated deep-water harbour. This is where the Imperial German Navy intend to base their new submarine service. Perhaps you can now see that stealing John Holland's designs was only one part of the jigsaw. The German High Command know that they cannot match the number and might of the Royal Navy dreadnoughts and battleships. They are deficient in numbers of capital ships and firepower. However, if they had a flotilla of submarines armed with torpedoes, they could cause havoc and inflict serious casualties and damage to the Royal Navy. They call this the Area 55 Project. The island of Sylt embraces Latitude 55 degrees North on sea charts and if you look at the same latitude on the north-east coast of England it covers the area from Coquet Island down to Hartlepool. A flotilla of German submarines operating in that area could intercept all Royal Navy ships sailing south from their safe anchorage at Scapa Flow or vessels moving north from the Channel Fleet to embargo German ports in the Baltic Sea. In addition, no British naval ship could sail within four miles of the island. There would be no way they could enter the shallow channels of the islands whereas submarines with their shallow draft could enter and exit Sylt through dredged channels and be free to slip into the North Sea and roam undetected in Area 55. The damage that a submarine fleet could cause to British trade could also prove to be disastrous to our economy. The majority of the fuel used to power British manufacturing and industry is coal, and most of that, is shipped from the ports in Area 55 such as Amble, Blyth, Newcastle, South Shields, Sunderland, Seaham and Hartlepool. If those coal supplies were interrupted, or prevented, it would cripple British industry. Richard, your intervention on Coquet Island has thwarted Germany's master plan to have a new submarine facility operating in Area 55. Without John Holland they could spend years in developing their new war machine."

"I can see why it is so important to the German naval plans to become leaders in the development of submarine warfare" I replied. "In some ways we were fortunate, or rather extraordinary lucky, that I was walking to the railway station at Hartlepool at exactly the same time as Adam Worth. Perhaps fate intervened to prevent an aggressive, war-monger state from riding roughshod over other countries. Let us hope that with the help of John Holland and the technical expertise of Captain Arthur and the Royal Navy's new submarine facility in the shipyard at Barrow-in-Furness we can, at least, neutralize any threat from the Imperial German Navy in the North Sea."

At this point I thought about the contribution made by John Cooper and his family in Sunderland. "Could we make some gesture to reward them for their help?" I asked. "He is a stout, upright and honest man who has brought up his daughter and son single-handed and deserves a step-up in the hard life he lives."

The young Marquess nodded and after a few moments said, "yes, it would be right to make some gesture. I will speak with my Chief Clerk. He is on very friendly terms with Lord Lambton's chief agent at Hendon Docks. I am sure that they will be able to find a permanent position for John Cooper so that he does not have to endure the uncertainty of unemployment every day. I will also ask him to arrange payment of the daily school fees for Francesca and Joseph until they reach school leaving age. You also mentioned that Joseph was becoming proficient on the piano. There is a recently tuned upright piano in the music room that is no longer used since we acquired a new grand piano. I will arrange to have that delivered to their house In Addison Street."

"Perfect" I replied. Thank you so much your Lordship. If you will now excuse me, I would like to return home. Isabella and the children will be returning soon and I would like to have the house ready for them."

"Of course, Richard. The last few days must have been exhausting for you," he said. "Why don't you call into the Londonderry Offices on North Terrace with Isabella on Friday afternoon and we can raise a glass or two. She may not be aware of the reason for the celebration but I am sure she will enjoy it. "

Lord Londonderry pulled the tassel by the fireplace to summon his butler. I followed him through the impressive halls and corridors back to the main entrance of the manor house. The waiting footman opened the carriage door for me and within minutes the coachman had crossed the Pack horse bridge over Seaham Dene. Passing the "ice house" used by the cook at the manor the horses strained to pull the carriage up to the New Drive built by Lady Frances Anne as a more direct route to her Londonderry Offices on the sea cliffs. A train was just entering Seaham Colliery railway station as the landau carriage trotted past and carried on along Harbour Walk to the docks. I shouted to the coachman to stop. It occurred to me that the crew would be rejoining the ship tomorrow morning. Yesterday, I had intended to visit the shipyard and make sure that Robert Potts and his men had satisfactorily carried out the work to the William Thrift. This was the perfect opportunity. As I climbed down the steps leading to the dry dock, I could see the William Thrift sitting on the gridiron above the waterline.

Robert Potts was inspecting the work on the hull as I approached the ship. "Ah - Captain Raine" he chirped. "We are almost finished the repairs you specified. I had expected you to check on our progress yesterday but no matter. We were able to complete the list satisfactorily."

Robert Potts was originally a shipbuilder. Seaham Harbour once built ships. Not large ships, but fine wooden sailing ships. The first ship built at this shipyard was "The Wansbeck" almost fifty years ago. Since then, William Henzell built and launched seventeen schooners, brigs and snows until Edward Potts took over the yards completing another seven ships. Robert took over from his brother in 1861 and built ten ships. Mrs. Anderson told me that orders for new wooden slips from British yards collapsed in the 1870's when the British government levied a tax on imported timber. This made it cheaper for Mrs. Anderson to order a vessel to be built in continental Europe. As a consequence, Robert Potts had no option but to change his business to focus on ship repair rather than shipbuilding.

I followed Robert Potts around the William Thrift as he pointed out the work his men had carried out. The copper skin on the hull had been cleaned of seaweed, barnacles and mollusks. That should reduce the drag in the water and speed up our voyages I thought. I looked over the new cleats and jammers and checked that new blocks and ratchets had been fitted. There is nothing more irritating to George Marwick and the lads than halyards or control lines that slip particularly if they are working at speed to complete a maneuver. Absolutely nothing had been overlooked on the masts, booms and bowsprits. Old sheets, spreaders, stays and trapeze wires had been repaired or replaced. The caulkers had made a good job of sealing joints and the riggers had taken down and renewed the endless number of ropes that had been chafed or worn down.

"You have done a fine job Mr. Potts. Will you need a hand to haul the William Thrift out of the dry harbour when the lock gates are opened?" I asked.

"Don't worry about that Captain Raine. My boys will get the Harry Vane paddle tug to haul her into the South Dock. She will be as good as new and ready for work first thing tomorrow morning. But - before you go, I need to show you something and I followed him into the forward bulkhead". There standing majestically in the corner was a new maritime water closet. Our very own toilet.

"Mrs. Anderson ordered the closet and asked me to fit it. She thought you would be pleased".

"That is brilliant Mr. Potts. The lads will be delighted to throw the old bucket and rope overboard" I said with a chuckle.

I left the busy docks behind me and with a spring in my step I walked along South Terrace. I turned the corner at the Vane Arms at the bottom of Church Street, crossed the road and called into Thompson's Stores to buy some fresh milk and bread. Finally arriving at my house, I sighed with pleasure as I turned the key and went inside. At last, I could relax in my own home. After such a catalog of events over the last four days I desperately needed some relaxation time. Fortunately, I had cleaned and prepared the fire before we left home last weekend and very quickly, I had the fire lit and roaring up the chimney. The kettle was filled with water and placed on the trivet of the fire range to heat. I took off my coat, put on my slippers and sank into my easy chair in front of the fire. In a matter of seconds my eyes closed and I drifted off dreaming of my adventure on Coquet Island.

I awoke with a jolt. Richard Henry had leapt into my lap followed closely by Elizabeth Anne and they were both laughing and playfully cuddling me. Thankfully William had restrained from joining in but nevertheless was pleased to see me. Isabella shouted from the hall as she took off her hat and coat. "We're home Richard. The train was packed and we couldn't get a seat until we reached Murton."

She gracefully entered the sitting room wearing the dark green dress that she knows is my favorite and with a broad smile on her face she affectionately tousled my hair.

"You look very relaxed Richard" she said, "have you enjoyed your little holiday whilst we have been away."

I looked up at her and with a smile I simply replied, "Yes, dear"

I had no idea then that just one year later the lives of my crew would be in peril and that my ship, the "William Thrift" would be stranded and wrecked.

CHAPTER 15

The Initial Inquiry

It was a particularly unhappy occasion for me, not just because of the incident itself but because this ship had made many voyages with a happy and contented crew which is something that every good sailing master seeks to achieve. The incident happened during one of those "great storms" that every mariner remembers for life. All along the east coast of England sailing ships were driven ashore and those that sought refuge got foul of each other on entering harbour. Those that made it into harbour had lost bowsprits; stauncheons, masts; bulwarks and quarter boards were broken with the strength of the south easterly that had blown all day. In a formal investigation held at Lowestoft on 7th December 1882 a Court of Inquiry, as demanded by the Mercantile Marine Act, was commanded to look into the circumstances attending the stranding and loss of the sailing ship "William Thrift" off Pakefield, on 28th October 1882. I attended the hearing with the owner Elizabeth Anderson. We travelled to Lowestoft on the Great Eastern Railway to Norwich and then took a tiresome horse drawn omnibus to Oulton Broad. We had booked accommodation in the Wherry Hotel overlooking the Broad for the evening and we enjoyed a very pleasant evening meal of braised mutton and vegetables. Mrs Anderson could sense my anxiety at the forthcoming inquest and I knew she was trying to reassure me that the outcome would be satisfactory.

All master mariners fear such hearings as the outcome can often destroy a master's career for ever. I knew that there were only three possible outcomes to an inquiry called under the Mercantile Marine Act to investigate the stranding and wreck of a ship. The best possible outcome is that the master and crew were in no way to blame for the incident. Secondly, that the master was to blame but with mitigating circumstances in which case the master is suspended from taking charge of a vessel for six months or so. Finally, the worst possible outcome, that the master was completely at blame and that his certificate of competence is to be completely revoked. Despite Mrs Andersons' reassurances I did not sleep at all that night and on that bleak, cold December morning we made our way to the inquiry which was to be held before Mr H.C. Rothery, Wreck Commissioner assisted by Captain Knox R.N., and Captains Kennedy and Hyde as Assessors. Mr Mansel-Jones and Mr Howard Smith appeared for the Board of Trade and handed in to the Chairman a statement of the questions that the Board of Trade desired the opinion of the Court.

In an upstairs chamber of the Lowestoft Shipping Offices Mr Rothery, Wreck Commissioner, opened the proceedings and introduced the Court of Inquiry members. The walls of the chambers were decorated in ornate mahogany wood which complemented to great effect the shiny brass door furniture. Solicitors and legal representatives sat in anticipation with their clients and witnesses. Behind sat the general public and at the back of the chamber in a separate section sat members of the local press.

"Is the Master of the "William Thrift" to be represented by counsel or solicitor" asked Mr Rothery in a gruff voice. "No, I do not have any representative" I replied wondering whether the Chairman's obvious animosity would cloud his judgement.

"Well, let us begin. I am informed that the "William Thrift" is a wooden brigantine originally registered at the Port of Dundee. She is 151 tons gross and was built at Perth in the year 1852. Is that correct?"

"That is correct sir" I replied but worryingly the Chairman glared at me and remarked "Speak up otherwise we will be here all day"

"Now, who is the owner" he barked. At this point Mrs Anderson stood up, looked directly at Mr Rothery, and confidently replied "I am sir; my name is Elizabeth Anderson of 28 Marlborough Street, Seaham Harbour." This brought a curt nod and a smile from Mr Rothery and my hopes were raised that Mrs Anderson's flashing eyes had hit the mark and that his mood was taking a turn for the better.

"I am directed by representatives of the Board of Trade to enquire into the circumstances surrounding this case. Will you be providing these facts Captain Raine?" I simply answered "yes sir" but then he continued "before you give your statement, I should remind you that the Board of Trade have produced three witnesses who have given statements and if your evidence conflicts with theirs, I may have to call them for cross examination. Do you understand?" Again, I answered "yes sir"

"Very well." He said "You may begin by telling the court the facts and do not waste our time by giving your opinion. That will be for my colleagues to decide"

I took a deep breathe. Thought for a while where I should begin and having decided I then gave my statement.

"We left Seaham Harbour for London on the 24th October with a crew of five hands, including myself, and a cargo of 260 tons of coal."

"I take it both yourself and your first mate have valid certificates of competence" he interrupted "You will need to provide the clerk of this court with your registration numbers"

Nodding to confirm I continued "Three days later on the 27th we were brought up in Corton Roads, a few miles north of Lowestoft. The weather had been very heavy. The "William Thrift" had been driven by a great storm for the previous two days. The gale had lasted so long that the crew were suffering from the effects of the hard work. All hands were constantly on deck with the roaring seas and the raging wind. There was no opportunity to go below and dry out clothes. It had been two days since the crew had eaten a hot meal as the seas were continually breaching the decks and the galley was constantly swamped with water. I decided at 9:00 am that we should drop anchor and let the gale blow over so we dropped the port anchor with sixty-five fathoms of chain. The wind at that time was blowing a strong breeze from South to South, South East.

However, by 4:00 pm on the 27th the strength of the wind increased and so twenty more fathoms of chain were paid out on the anchor and because of the movement of the ship in the water a spring was put on the cable with a nine-inch coir hawser.

At noon the next day, on the 28th there had been no easing in the gale and the wind had now veered to North East by East becoming even stronger. It was at this time that I saw a schooner drifting down upon us and to avoid a certain collision I ordered the crew to slip the chains on the anchors and to set the main and fore topmast staysails. My intention was to run before the wind until we arrived in Lowestoft roads opposite the entrance to the harbour. We dropped the starboard anchor and seventy-five fathoms of chain and I hoped that when the tide allowed, we could be towed into harbour if a tug could get out to reach us.

I ordered the crew to get two warps and a tow line and fasten them onto the spare anchor which we dropped and paid out eighty fathoms of chain. By 5:00 pm the tide turned to the south and with the wind increasing and the waves becoming mountainous both cables broke. Seeing that there was nothing more we could do, both anchors having gone, I decided that there was only one option available to us. I determined that I would beach the "William Thrift" at the most convenient spot and accordingly I decided to put her ashore about a mile and a half southward of the south pier between Kirkley and Pakefield where I knew there were sand and shingle beaches. By now everything on deck had been washed overboard including the jolly boat.

While drifting towards the shore we kept lighting flares but the furious waves continually breached the decks and extinguished them. When at last the ship's hull touched bottom the sea was roaring and the swell was mountain high and there was no way we could make it to the shoreline. We were obliged to take to the rigging and for the next hour we shouted for assistance. The rut of the sea was great and the waves were breaking upon our ships quarter and the scuds of wind whistled through our yards making our shrouds rattle with a dreadful ferocity.

Illustration of the "William Thrift" from The Shipwrecked Mariner (Quarterly Maritime Magazine)

Eventually we could see the people on the shore carrying a small lifeboat to windward but such was the violence of the gale that they could not launch it through the violent surf. Our souls were beginning to despair and we remained clinging to the rigging with our hands numb with the cold and wet sea. The thunder grumbled so horribly and at the same time lightning was illuminating the sky and shoreline and black seas were swamping the decks below us. About half an hour later the coastguard brought the rocket apparatus up on the beach and within a very short time the first line was fired over the rigging which my first mate secured to the yards of the foresail. A breaches buoy was attached to the line and paid out to the ship and one-by-one each of my crew was hauled to the shore. I was the last to leave the ship and was landed on shore at about 9:00pm.

Within minutes of our rescue a huge wave turned the "William Thrift" over on its port side and soon the raging swell turned her into a total wreck as her planking was torn from her and she broke up in the waves."

The Court of Inquiry had sat motionless and silent all the way through my account of that dreadful storm and the terrors which my crew had endured. After a few moments the Wreck Commissioner, Mr Rothery, quietly said "Thank you Captain Raine. You have provided this Inquiry with an excellent account of the events that led to the stranding and loss of your ship. You may sit down now. The Court of Inquiry will now adjourn and consider Captain Raine's evidence" and simultaneously the panel rose and left the room.

During the course of the next hour my mind was swirling with questions. Had I done everything I could to prevent the tragedy? Had I made errors of judgement during that voyage? What would other master mariners have done if faced with that situation? Mrs Anderson could see I was in torment and she tried to engage me in polite conversation but my worst fears were slowly overcoming my very consciousness.

The members of the Court of Inquiry entered the room and solemnly took their seats. The Wreck Commissioner began "We have heard the account given by the master of the "William Thrift" and we have consulted the evidence provided by the three witness statements brought to this court by the Board of Trade. We can confirm that Captain Raine's account has been completely verified by witnesses on shore and in other vessels in the vicinity during that terrible storm. We are now in a position to give our decision."

Raising his voice and projecting it so that the gentlemen of the press at the back of the room could hear without error he began "In the matter of The Merchant Shipping Acts, 1854 to 1876 a Court of Inquiry has considered the events of the sinking of a sailing vessel and to decide who is at fault in causing the stranding and loss of the vessel. The verdict of the court, having carefully inquired into the circumstances, have found that the stranding and loss of the William Thrift was due to the parting of the cables by which she was riding in Lowestoft Roads and that **"no blame attaches to the master or any of the officers for the casualty, the vessel having been brought up in a safe and proper anchorage, and having been navigated with proper seamanlike care and skill."**

My relief upon hearing this verdict was indescribable. I had been punishing myself for days to the point where I had almost convinced myself that the loss of the "William Thrift" was through my negligence. Elizabeth Anderson smiled and simply said "I told you everything would be fine. Now let us get out of this dreary place and take a pot of tea at the nice corner tea room" and with that my ordeal was over.

It was a sad day for the crew, Elizabeth Anderson and I when our ship went down but alas, it is all too common in this life we choose to live, coasting coals and timber along the wild and unpredictable east coast of England. Still, I had my reputation and Masters Certificate of Competence untarnished, and intact, and it should not be long before both the crew and myself gain a new berth although it would be unlikely that we would all sign on to the same ship. Nevertheless, I carried an emptiness away from that Court of Inquiry. Was the feeling of emptiness caused by the memory of that dreadful storm and the trauma of the events outside Lowestoft Harbour or was it the loss of a good ship and the near loss of my crew? Something was bearing down on my mind and body and I couldn't shake off that feeling of total loss.

However, there was one more twist in this tale: events that were still to unfold in the case of the stranding and loss of the William Thrift. I had never been a cynical or angry person but the facts that came to light within the next week could well have driven a weaker man to seek retribution, reprisals or revenge. Those events were to be made public over the course of the next week.

CHAPTER 16

The full story is made public

Richard took great pride in his position as ship's captain and he was deeply hurt when the William Thrift was stranded and lost off Pakefield beach, Suffolk on that stormy night of 28th October 1882. The stigma of losing a ship, even though the Board of Inquiry had made it clear that he was in no way to blame, was a heavy burden to carry amongst his fellow Master Mariners. When he heard that a "further" investigation was to be carried out by The Board of Trade he resolved to travel to Lowestoft and attend the Inquiry so that he could give whatever assistance necessary to the proceedings. Mrs Anderson declined the opportunity to attend this second hearing – she had indicated that she was happy with the initial verdict of the court and knew that Richard Raine no longer needed support to protect his professional credentials. That had already been secured from the first Inquiry.

The Board of Trade Inquiry was held in Lowestoft one week later on 13th December 1882. Richard Raine was particularly keen to be there as he had heard that the inquiry was instituted to "ascertain why it was that assistance had not been promptly afforded to the William Thrift and other vessels which were wrecked in the immediate neighbourhood of Lowestoft on that night". Richard once again took a room in the Wherry Hotel at Oulton Broad on the evening before the Inquiry. On this visit he was able to appreciate the peace and tranquillity of the wildlife, the beautiful scenery and the antics of amateur sailors attempting to sail pleasure boats on the Broad. He remembered none of this from his previous visit but then his mind had been otherwise preoccupied with more serious thoughts.

The breakfast at the Wherry Hotel next morning was substantial and tasty and he felt fortified and ready for the long, tedious day ahead of him. The journey to the town centre of Lowestoft was a short one and he soon arrived at his destination. On entering the upstairs chambers of the Shipping Offices at Lowestoft he was aware that a large crowd of spectators and members of the press had taken seats to watch the proceedings. The large number of people in the room surprised him as there was less than half that number at the original Inquiry. As he sat down the Wreck Commissioner, Mr H.C. Rothery saw him and immediately came down from the bench and strode towards him.

"Good morning, Captain Raine" he said "I am so pleased you have been able to come here today. You may hear something of interest to you. The Board of Trade has presented the Court with a number of questions that they would like answers to and I shall take great pleasure in eliciting the answers from the witnesses we will be calling before the Inquiry today."

Returning to take his seat on the bench he called the Inquiry to order and introduced his colleagues. They were the same members as previously except for the addition of Captain W Eames RN and once again Mr Mansel-Jones and Mr Howard Smith appeared on behalf of the Board of Trade. Speaking clearly and with volume he announced "We will be calling Mr Preston, junior who is counsel for the coxswain of the Lowestoft lifeboat; Mr Woods who is counsel for the coxswain of the Pakefield lifeboat and Mr Warman, Acting Secretary of the Pakefield Branch of the Royal National Lifeboat Institution. In addition, I must ask these persons to take care when presenting their evidence as the Board of Trade has produced and examined eighteen witnesses and so any evidence given today will be either be confirmed or refuted by their statements.

Mr Rothery then read to the Court a report prepared by Mr Balfour, the Receiver of Wrecks at Lowestoft summarising the shipping losses along the

Suffolk coast during that terrible storm. It read "The Receiver of Wrecks informed this court that on that Saturday evening of 28th October, 16 vessels were wrecked and most, if not all of them, were showing signals of distress. From those vessels 18 persons were saved by lines from the ship to the shore, 28 by the rocket apparatus and 17 by the lifeboat. The loss of life was very great with 22 known to have perished besides the whole of the crew of a foreign vessel called the "Anna" and possibly also that of a schooner whose name is unknown."

Pausing to look through his papers Mr Rothery then said "The Board of Trade has selected three cases for inquiry, the "Isis", the "William Thrift" and the "Secret" and by looking at these three cases we may identify the cause of the great loss of life. I am told the "Isis" went ashore at 7:30 pm on the south beach, the "William Thrift" went ashore at about 8:00 pm on Pakefield beach and the third vessel the "Secret" struck at about 8:30 pm on the Newcome sands from where she drifted to Kessingland beach."

Taking off his spectacles and looking up to the three witnesses called before the court he sternly announced "The first question I have to ask and which the Board of Trade also require a full account is this. What was the reason, when signals of distress were exhibited from the Isis, the William Thrift, the Secret and all of those other vessels that the Lowestoft lifeboat did not proceed to render assistance before 11:30pm on that day?

Standing up to answer the court Mr Preston junior representing the coxswain of the Lowestoft lifeboat informed the court that at Lowestoft there are two lifeboats both belonging to the RNLI. Both are under the control of the local committee resident on the spot. The larger lifeboat; the "number one" which alone has to do with this inquiry was entrusted to a coxswain, a local innkeeper called Robert Hook whose duty was to keep her in a state of cleanliness and efficiency and to respond to any vessels in distress, assemble the crew and launch the boat. For this he was paid eight pounds per annum for his services. As regards the crew it was the practice of certain persons called beachmen to man the lifeboat and for each launch to a wreck they were paid a bounty of one pound per man by the local committee.

Mr Preston junior then directed the Court of Inquiry to an incident earlier in the year. On the 7th March a small fishing smack called the "Alert" had grounded on Newcome Sands and a yawl manned by lifeboat men from Lowestoft put off from the North Beach to go to her assistance. However, they found it impossible to board her and returned to shore and got out the number one lifeboat and proceeded towards her. In the meantime, the lifeboat from Pakefield had gone out, arrived before them, and succeeded in getting the Alert off the sands and had received a salvage award of £105 for their services. Subsequently the Lowestoft lifeboat secretary sent in the application to the local committee for the usual allowance of £1 per man for going out to a wreck. The local committee came to the conclusion that it would not be justified in recommending the full allowance for the service as they had already paid the Pakefield lifeboat men but they decided that they should receive the level of remuneration when the lifeboat is taken out on exercise i.e., 5 shillings per man. The men from Lowestoft lifeboat refused this sum and returned it to the parent society. The result was that so strong a feeling of dissatisfaction was created amongst the beachmen that the men refused to haul the lifeboat out of the lifeboat house on 1st October, as was the custom, ready for the winter storms. The lifeboat remained in the boathouse when these unfortunate casualties occurred. Finishing his statement Mr Preston stood silently whilst Mr Rothery conferred with his colleagues. "You may sit down Mr Preston junior" and then he referred to his notes and read "From the witness statements provided by the Board of Trade it was about 5:00pm when the first vessel went ashore and between that hour and half-past seven no less than six vessels went aground on the South Beach, all of them showing signals of distress. Can I now ask if Mr Sparham, a carpenter living in Lowestoft is present? I understand you have presented some facts to the Board of trade representatives."

Mr Sparham stood and replied "Yes sir, I am here".

"Let us have your view of events Mr Sparham" said the Wreck Commissioner.

"Well, there was great excitement in the town and many of the townsfolk could see those ships in distress amidst the mountainous seas" began Mr Sparham. "There were loud calls for the lifeboat to be got out and launched but the lifeboat men and beachmen refused thinking they had been unfairly treated in the affair of the "Alert". A gentleman named Mr Hazard, a visitor to the town, was on the South Pier at the time, and seeing that assistance should be rendered without delay was determined to make an effort to get the lifeboat out. On arriving at the lifeboat station, he found the doors to be locked and was directed to Mr Hook the Coxswain's house, a little inn nearby, where he found Mr Hook smoking a pipe and serving his customers. Mr Hazard endeavoured in every possible way to induce Hook to take the boat out but he refused. Very strong language was used by both men. Mr Hazard then offered as an inducement £1 a head to any men who would crew the lifeboat and a Mr Stacey who was standing nearby offered to give another £1 per head. Eventually the boathouse was opened and the volunteers hauled her down the beach. It was now between 7 and 8 o'clock at night. The surf had become so strong by this time that it was found impossible to launch her and she was thrown broadside on the beach and it was not until about 11:30 pm that she was fairly afloat."

The Pakefield Lifeboat "James Leath"

Thanking Mr Sparham for his very clear account Mr Rothery again turned to his notes and read "The second question this Court of Inquiry must establish is whether proper assistance was rendered by the rocket apparatus, under the control of the chief officer of the coastguard? Can I ask Mr Symes to stand and respond to that question from the Board of Trade?"

Mr Symes, the chief officer of the Lowestoft coastguard stood and began to read his statement "At about 4:45 pm on that day and within a very short time of the first vessel the "Messenger" going ashore, I brought the rocket apparatus on to the South Pier and having thrown the line over that vessel we succeeded in landing from her 15 persons, namely her crew of eight and the seven beach men who had boarded her. I was then told that another vessel was ashore on the North Beach and proceeded immediately in that direction but on getting to the bridge I was told that the crew had been saved from the shore. A telegram from Mr Warford, coxswain of the lifeboat at Pakefield was put into my hands which read, "Brigantine ashore- lifeboat been off but cannot break through surf- can render no assistance - Send life apparatus at once" We accordingly galloped our horses to Pakefield and arrived there about 9:00 pm, just in time to throw a rocket line over the vessel, which turned out to be the "William Thrift". Despite the raging waves and gusting winds, we were able to rig the breaches buoy and rescue her crew of five hands before the vessel's masts went, and in ten minutes afterwards she was a wreck on the shore. In all, the coastguard crew was engaged with the rocket apparatus from 4:45 pm till about 1:45 am the following day during which time we saved no less than 28 lives. I would also like to take this opportunity Chairman to speak of the efficient assistance I received from Mr Beaby who threw the rocket line so correctly that he never had occasion to throw it more than once at the object aimed at."

Thanking Mr Symes, the Wreck Commission asked him to be seated and then announced "My colleagues and I will adjourn and consider whether further evidence is required. This Inquiry will resume in one hour" and with that the panel rose and left the chambers. Richard Raine was uncertain what to do for the next hour. He could visit the little tea room at the corner of the Ipswich Road but then there was no guarantee that he would be back within the hour. Instead, he noticed a familiar face sitting two rows behind him – Captain Massingham – harbour master at Lowestoft and so he passed the time discussing the proceedings with him.

Exactly to the minute Mr Rothery and colleagues returned and resumed their places. Addressing the members of the press at the back of the room the Wreck Commissioner announced "This Court of Inquiry has concluded that the reasons why the Lowestoft lifeboat did not go out sooner to the assistance of the shipwrecked crews was because of the negligent actions of the Lowestoft lifeboat crew who did not get the lifeboat out of the station ready for the winter storms and who refused to launch her when those ships were in distress off Lowestoft and Pakefield beach. I am taking the unusual step of allowing Mr Mansel-Jones on behalf of the Board of Trade to address this Inquiry as I believe he has some very interesting views to tell the press which I, as Wreck Commissioner, am not at liberty to make but which I endorse whole heartedly. "

Mr Mansel-Jones stood up and with obvious anger and bitterness remarked "Thank you Mr Rothery. I would like to express the opinion of the Board of Trade that there seemed to be a somewhat objectionable trade-unionism among the lifeboat men and beach men of Lowestoft and to some extent they appear to have had "salvage" as their motive before the salvation of life. We consider that the conduct of the beach men was wicked in the extreme in refusing to lend a hand to launch the boat when they knew their fellow-creatures needed assistance. In our opinion the reputation of the Lowestoft life boatmen was more than tarnished by the events of that memorable night and it would be some time before the stigma which the conduct of those men had brought on the name of Lowestoft could be cleared. In particular we need to name one person whose actions, more than any other, contributed to the great loss of life in this incident; the coxswain of the Lowestoft lifeboat – Robert Hook whose behaviour was despicable and I do trust that the members of the press ensure that the people of Lowestoft are well informed of the part he has played."

The Wreck Commissioner thanked Mr Mansel-Jones for his comments directing personal criticism – something that he was not permitted to do. Speaking further he continued "It is our clear intention that the rules and procedures, training and leadership of the local committees at Lowestoft and Pakefield RNLI are rigorously reviewed. This tragic series of events must never be allowed to happen again. Finally, I would like to conclude by giving my thanks to Mr Hazard who is not here today but whose admirable spirit and perseverance saved at least seventeen lives. I shall personally write to Mr Hazard to express the gratitude of the people of Lowestoft for his heroic actions on that night. I would also commend Mr Symes and Mr Beaby of the Coastguard on the handling of the rocket apparatus and say that we are all agreed that theirs is a record of service of which the coastguard at Lowestoft, unlike the lifeboat crew, may be justly proud".

Richard Raine was stunned and in a state of shock when he left the chambers of the Lowestoft Shipping Office. In a daze he boarded the Great Eastern Railway train to return home to Seaham Harbour. Luckily the compartment on the train was empty as he could not have exchanged small talk with fellow passengers. He re-lived that terrifying experience all way home and the events laid out in that courtroom repeatedly taunted him as the same question came into his head. Why, Why, Why? He had hoped that he would have found answers that would lift the dark clouds hovering over his life since he lost his ship. Quite the contrary had happened. The inquest had not quelled the feeling of loss and broken pride in losing his ship – he was now angry. His ship, the "William Thrift" and fifteen other vessels along with twenty-two good sailors were lost because of the greed and animosity of the Lowestoft lifeboat men. How could those men have been so cruel and callous to ignore the signals of distress of sailors pleading for their fellow men to help them in their darkest hour – their last thoughts on this mortal world before they met their maker divided between their loved ones who would be left behind and cursing the sort of mankind on that shoreline who had not an ounce of humanity in their souls.

Richard Raine returned briefly to sea but these proceedings dwelled on his mind and he lost his appetite for fighting the sea and the elements. Six years later, in 1887, the year Richard's eldest son William was married, he left the sea and bought the Wellington Inn in South Railway Street, Seaham Harbour from William Henzell who had operated a small shipyard building wooden ships in the new harbour and had been the first landlord of the Wellington Inn since 1843.

The Wellington Inn, Seaham Harbour

It was later renamed the Duke of Wellington and then the Duke of Seaham and here Richard Raine and Isabella his wife worked out their "retirement" with their daughter Elizabeth Ann until she married in 1896 to James Robson, a marine engineer. His second son Richard Henry was married in 1898 and his family lived only a few doors away from the Wellington Inn at South Crescent.

Every evening Richard sat on a stool at the bar welcoming every mariner who walked through the door of the Inn. Most of them were his old shipmates and they would each re-tell the same old adventures together laughing at the golden days in the ports along the East coast but always skirting around the hard life and the battles with the wind and sea that every mariner knows only too well. Any new sailor visiting the Wellington Inn for the first time very soon received a very flowery account from Richard of the day Captain Knill of the "Annandale" broke the jib-stay mast of the "William Thrift" in harbour – after all, William Sheridan, harbourmaster, is no longer around to tell the tale. During the day the routine was always the same. Richard would walk hand-in-hand with his granddaughter Hannah down to the harbour. Their favourite spot was on the grassy bank above the North Dock where Hannah would make daisy chains and catch butterflies listening to grandfather re-telling his salty tales and shouting hellos and pleasantries to the men on the ships below in harbour.

By 1901 Richard's health was deteriorating. The hard life at sea was catching up on him and when Richards's daughter moved to Throston, Hartlepool where his son-in-law now worked Richard agreed with Isabella that they should move with their daughter. In addition, Richard's brother, Henry and his sister Elizabeth had moved from Sandsend many years before and were living in Hartlepool and Richard believed in trying to maintain close family ties. His two grandsons James and Richard were born in Hartlepool and he cherished seeing his grandchildren grow up and every day he would go for long walks with them.

When he was alone with his thoughts, he was still angry at the callous, mercenary selfishness of the Lowestoft lifeboat men. He could never forgive them no matter how many years had passed since the "William Thrift" was lost. There was plenty of harbour life at Hartlepool and he still saw familiar faces coming and going in port but it was not his favourite port. That accolade was reserved for Seaham Harbour.

Richard fought desperately to recover from a short but serious illness. He didn't want to give up. He desperately wanted to spend a few more happy years with his beloved grandchildren. It was there at 13 Bell Street, Throston, Hartlepool that Richard died of heart failure on 5th July 1906 aged 65 surrounded by his loving and adoring family.

CHAPTER 17

Captain Raine's story

It is November 2011 and my wife and I were on a short holiday to Southport in Lancashire on the North- West coast of England. My name is Fred Cooper and I am the author of this book. This is an account of the circumstances which prompted me to write about the life of Richard Raine and to reveal a story that has remained untold for many years.

I was born in Seaham in the 1950's and now live in New Herrington on the outskirts of Sunderland. Although Sunderland transferred from the County of Durham into Tyne and Wear when the new metropolitan counties were created in 1973, I still regard myself as a "Durham" lad who has his roots firmly planted in Seaham. I retired from my career as a Chartered Management Accountant eight years ago and spend most of my time researching the local history of Seaham. I am Chairman of the Seaham Family History Group and we meet in the new Library each Wednesday morning and we promote and assist members from Seaham in tracing their ancestry.

In Southport we were staying at the Prince of Wales hotel on Lord Street which is one of the most famous Victorian boulevards in the country stretching almost a mile from end to end with much of the pavement under cover. It's an ideal place to eat, drink and shop and at this time of the year Lord Street is decorated with Christmas lights in the trees and all the market stalls are selling traditional fare. Not that we needed to eat and drink anything when we were out of the hotel – we were booked on a "turkey and tinsel" all-inclusive package from Monday to Friday. I hadn't been on one of these packages before but for the uninitiated the Hotel cram the four festive days of Christmas all together in one package. So, Monday is Christmas Eve, Tuesday is Christmas Day, Wednesday is Boxing day and Thursday is New Year's Eve and the hotel put on appropriate dinners, entertainment, party hats, and decorations to suit the occasion. I can't explain how odd it was to be clasping hands in a circle with about one hundred other guests at 10:30 pm on a Thursday night in November singing "Auld lang Syne" but we really enjoyed our stay at the Prince of Wales.

It was while my wife Margaret was shopping in Lord Street that she suggested I looked around the many bookshops along the boulevard. Margaret enjoys "browsing" in the unique boutiques, designer shops and high street stores when she shops and is always keen to get rid of me so she can have a good rummage. Willingly I agreed and made my way along the street calling in to each book shop along the way. Eventually I came across the Royal Arcade bursting with antiques and collectables. If you are interested in history, as I am, it sells a wonderful mix of eclectic goods and any history anorak could spend hours in this Aladdin's cave. Weaving my way through the Arcade I came across four boxes full of old picture postcards of almost every town in the country. This was just down my street I thought as I browsed through each card desperately seeking old picture postcards of Seaham. Alas, I was not to find any. Then I started looking through the shelves of books and was delighted to see so many very old editions of books that were clearly no longer available from modern book stores. There were books on the floor; on shelves; on tables; even in the alleyway leading into the entrance of the Royal Arcade. Such was the range of old books on offer I quite happily took my time, in particular selecting old volumes that to me are so much more interesting than modern literature.

After an hour or so, or it may have been longer as I was in a world of my own, I came to the books in the entrance to the alleyway. These books were on shelving covering both walls leading along a fifty-yard passage. There must have been around 10,000 books, magazines and atlases of the world which clearly were left in the passage in all weathers but which were protected from the rain by the alleyway roof. I can only presume the bookstore owner left the books where they were; year in and year out, and simply locked the alleyway gate each night. This is where, quite by chance, I was browsing through each book, carefully turning each fragile cover over when I realised, I had turned two books over. Picking up the two books I noticed that one of the books had "fused" onto the back of the other probably because of the dampness and the pressure of so many books that had been squeezed onto that shelving. Carefully prising the second book away from the first I found that it was more of a journal than a book and it was handwritten in wonderful copperplate style handwriting. The front cover of the journal was entitled "A Master Mariners Tale". I opened up the first page and began to read "My name is Richard Raine and I am the Master of the collier brigantine "William Thrift" sailing out of Seaham Harbour in the County of Durham and this is my journal for the year of our Lord 1881".

I reeled back on my heels. What an amazing coincidence. Here I am, a Seaham lad, visiting a coastal town on the other side of the country and I had stumbled across a journal written in 1881 by a ship's captain sailing out of Seaham. I began to read the first page but the more I read the more excited I became as the words on the page hit me time and again with place names and descriptions of the town that I know so well. At that moment I decided I had better buy this journal. For some reason I had a fear; an illogical notion that the journal would disappear or disintegrate unless it belonged to me and I looked around for the owner of the bookstall eager to lay claim to the book. Sitting at a leather-clad, study desk inside the shop sat an elderly gentleman thumbing his way through an old volume with broken spine and loose pages. From the care he took in turning the pages he clearly loved old books and was without doubt the owner of the bookshop. His mannerisms and charismatic appearance reminded me of little Nell's grandfather in The Old Curiosity Shop.

"Excuse me" I said "I don't want to interrupt your reading but could you tell me how much this book is please" and I handed him the old journal with the hard back, brown cover.

Looking at the book he turned it over, then looked at the front again; opened it to look at the first few pages and then the back pages. "Umm" he said "I didn't buy this book because I always leave some mark to remind me what I paid for it. If I sell books for less than I buy them for I would be out of business" he said jokingly. "My father must have bought this one. Shall we say seven pounds". For some reason I said without thinking "Would you take five pounds". My wife Margaret is an expert at bartering and years of listening to her negotiating a bargain must be rubbing off on me. Then it suddenly occurred to me that I might offend this old gentleman by trying to "chip him" and he could then refuse to sell me the book. "Umm" he said again "Yes, five pounds will be fine. Would you like me to wrap it for you?" With a sense of relief, I declined and paid the five pounds. The journal was now mine and with a spring in my step at my new acquisition I left the arcade and wandered through the nearby designer shops until I found Margaret.

It was still mid-afternoon and the weather was sunny and mild for a November day. We decided that we should not miss the opportunity of walking along the famous Southport pier so we walked to the end of Lord Street and then through the stunning greenery of Hesketh Park towards the pier. The pier is Britain's second oldest and second largest and I was pleased to see a pier tram almost ready to set off along the one-mile structure. When we reached the end, I looked out towards the sea and saw nothing but sands. The tide retreats so far on this coast that even at the end of a one-mile pier you have to wait for the tide to turn before you can see the sea. I was tempted to take a seat inside the pavilion and open my new found treasure but I decided I would enjoy reading Richard Raine's journal when I returned home. On our return to the hotel, I placed it in my suitcase where it remained until we unpacked two days later.

The first thing I do when I return home from a holiday is to put the kettle on for a nice cup of tea. There is nothing better than a cup of tea made from your usual brand of tea in your favourite cup. Quickly emptying the suitcases, I returned to the sitting room with Richard Raines journal in hand and excitedly settled down to explore my new book with cup in hand. As I turned each page my mind was filled with Richard Raine's description of the town; the people he worked with and met in the harbour and the streets. I could not believe I was reading a day-by-day account of a sea captain's world written so long ago in 1881. At each mention of a building or place he visited in his daily routine my thoughts raced as I recalled those same places as they are now and mentally compared them with Richard's description. Then, I began to read his detailed account of a voyage in the "William Thrift" to Colchester in April of that year. As his account unravelled my heart began to beat faster and faster as his adventure on finding the "Neptun" abandoned and Lieutenant Jack Edward Smith left for dead in the hold began to leap off the pages and into my head. Then I began to read his entry in the journal for May1881 and was astounded at the events that unfolded in Dundee involving The Reich Club and the assassination plot. Finally, reading his exploits and adventure on Coquet Island in Northumberland were just incredible. It took my breath away. This journal was a first-hand account of a spy story – almost a James Bond tale of the Victorian era- and I could not put the journal down until I had read the whole book from first to last page. That night I should have slept well – back in my own comfortable bed after five nights in a hotel bed – but my thoughts were racing as I recalled Richards exploits bit by bit until I eventually fell asleep in the early hours of the morning. When I awoke the journal was still in my thoughts. Lying there in a half daze I thought to myself "I wonder what happened to the people he worked with and met. With my knowledge of genealogy, I should be able to easily trace them in census and civil records." With that thought in mind I drifted back off to sleep content that I now had such an interesting new project to occupy my time over the next few weeks.

At the earliest opportunity the next morning after completing my daily household chores, I picked up my laptop, sat on the settee in the sitting room and began my new quest. My objective was to find out as much as I could about Richard Raine; his crew; his ship and the characters mentioned in his journal. I have a full annual members' subscription to "Find My Past" which is a genealogy database with every ten-year UK census from1841 to 1911 and so my first search began with Richard himself. Ironically, he had recorded his arrival in port at Seaham Harbour on census day, Sunday 3rd April 1881 in his journal and had described how he had completed the census enumeration form and handed it to William Sheridan, Harbour Master on leaving port the next day. That census of 1881 would be the key document to cross reference with the named individuals in Richard's journal to see where they were on that day "according to the census". Every individual mentioned in the journal was found on the genealogy database in the places where Richard had seen them on that day. William Sheridan, Harbour Master; Jeremiah Hall, Dock Gateman; Elizabeth Anderson, Ship Owner; Reverend Angus Bethune, Vicar of St John's Church; the crew consisting of William Booth, Thomas Colling, Robert Mustard, George Marwick and Richard himself were all there on the census just as Richard had noted in his journal. In addition to the census records, I also had access to the civil records which began in 1837 of births, marriages and deaths and so I should be able to build up a framework of Richards life from cradle to grave with a census snapshot every ten years to show where he lived, his age and occupation.

Very soon I had built up an impersonal sketch of Richards's life from these records. He was born in 1841 in Lythe, a district of Sandsend, Yorkshire. Sandsend is only three miles from Whitby where his old shipmate Jacob Porritt, Master of the Ytham, lived and an area that Richard knew well as he described in his journal. His father was an Alum Rock labourer. Alum is a colourless crystal element that is used in the dye trade to stabilise colours and is a major industry in that part of Yorkshire. Richard lived with his parents and his four brothers William, Henry, John and Joseph. After Richards birth in 1841 came four more brothers Edward, Charles, Thomas and Henry and his one sister Elizabeth. Thomas had been Sexton of St Mary's Church just next door to the Reverend Angus Bethune's vicarage.

In 1863 at the age of twenty-two he married Isabella Thompson (nee Lister) in St Andrew's Church, Dalton-Le-Dale, Seaham and they had a son named William born 1864, daughter Elizabeth Ann who died at the age of two in 1871, another daughter again named Elizabeth Ann was born that same year and finally a son, Richard Henry born in 1874.

Finding out information about the "William Thrift" was an easier task. I searched for details of the ship on the Crew List Index Project website. This told me that it was a wooden brigantine of 160 tons built in Perth in 1852 and originally owned by the P M Duncan and GEM Line of Dundee. Undertaking a Google search on the ship's name brought up Wreck Report number 1612 held at Lowestoft on 7th December 1882 – the year after Richard's journal – and this gave me all of the sad details of the demise of his ship the "William Thrift". Bit by bit I had drawn together background information to Richard's life as a young man and then as a sea captain in command of a collier brigantine. But all of the facts I had collected were impersonal; none of it gave an insight into Richard as a person and I felt that I needed to fill that vacuum somehow and complete the picture.

If only I could find a living relative of Richard's they might be able to tell me of any personal reminiscences or have a photograph of him passed down through the family. Another long Google search produced a lead. Some five years earlier on 22nd October 2007 a request had been posted on Rootsweb, a genealogy support website, which read: -

"Hi, Can anybody find Richard Raine born 1841 in Lythe on the 1861 census?
Unfortunately, he may have been at sea as he was a Master Mariner.
Can anybody help?
Sue"

Luckily for me the website had Sue's email address and I wrestled with the idea of emailing her for at least a week. What would she think of receiving an email from a perfect stranger asking questions about her ancestor? Eventually I plucked up the courage; nothing ventured nothing gained I thought and so I composed an email. My finger was poised over the send button at least four times until I eventually plucked up the courage and hit "send". It was too late now I thought. For the next two days I looked at my emails every half hour to see if I had a reply. I sometimes forget that ordinary people have other things to do than consult their emails as often as I do. After two days I had begun to give up any hope of a reply until the "ping" went and there it was.

Apparently, Sue had been researching her ancestry for more than five years and had accumulated a wealth of information, not only about Richard but of all her ancestors and she was very interested in any information I had found. More importantly she had the very thing that would make my story complete. The family had photographs of Richard and his wife Isabella and she had no objection in letting me have copies for a book that I might write in the future based upon Richard's life and exploits. Fate seemed to be smiling on me at every step in this adventure. Richard's family had moved to Sunderland after Richard died in 1906 and Sue was living only four miles away from where I lived. The natural next step was to meet and exchange information. This was arranged at the first opportunity we were both free. Sue had agreed to ask her three cousins, David, Rene and Pat, who also had information about Richard and his siblings to join us. On the arranged day I was full of anticipation at meeting Captain Richard Raines ancestors and putting a face to this very brave man who had lived such an interesting and full life. The meeting was to be at Sue's house and I was overwhelmed at the warm welcome she and her relatives gave me and we seemed to talk for ages about our exploits into the world of genealogy. Sue and David were descended from Richard's children and Rene and Pat were descended from Richards's brother Henry. It was amazing to see that they were all present in this room four generations later. Eventually Sue brought out an old tea caddy that had been handed down each generation until it was finally her turn to be caretaker. Out of this box came a number of old sepia family photographs and quickly scanning through them Sue pulled out four and handed them to me.

"This is Richard as a young man. I believe he was only about twenty years old when this was taken."

I could see in the general demeanour of this young man a determination to do more with his life than to be an alum-rock labourer. He looked deep in thought; someone who was keen to learn and improve his prospects.

"This one was taken when he was captain of the "William Thrift" so that would be around 1880. He seems to be wearing tropical uniform so he must have been sailing in southerly latitudes."

Now here was a man, I thought to myself, who has reached a position of authority who enjoys the status of Master Mariner. He has worked hard to achieve his position and has an air of confidence which only comes when someone's ability has been tested by real maritime experiences

"This one is again Richard just before he died in Hartlepool in 1906."

This is the face of a man who loves his family I thought. Someone who has earned his retirement and now wants to rest his bones and put the troubles and hard life he experienced at sea behind him.

"This photograph is very faded but you can just make out Richard's wife, Isabella, taken about five years after Richard's death. She would be about seventy years old when the photograph was taken."

Yes – you can tell this is a devoted wife. A woman who worries and waits for her man to return safely from each voyage. A woman who waits for the man who has made a good home for herself and the children. A woman who trusts the man who tells her he is embarrassed when Mrs Anderson looks deep into his eyes.

"And finally, this is Richards's youngest brother, Henry who lived only a street away from him in Hartlepool

The likeness between Richard and Henry was striking. Yes – I am sure these two brothers were very close. Henry must have felt lost and alone when his elder brother Richard passed away.

At last, I was able to put a face to Richard Raine. For three months since that eventful day in Southport I had wondered what this man looked like and now I knew. His photograph's revealed him at the three stages in his life as a young man; as the sea captain who had experienced so many thrilling and frightening experiences at sea and then as a family man in his twilight years.

Sue then reached into the tea caddy and gently pulled out an old fading letter that was tearing at the creases. "This letter was written by Richard to his son William and it made me realise how very close Richard and Isabella were to their grown-up children and their grandchildren. The letter is dated 31st March 1901 and Richard asks if William's daughter Isabel, aged 11, can come and stay with them during the Easter holidays." Carefully she handed me the letter and I looked at the yellowing paper written in Richard's own hand – handwriting which I recognised instantly from his journal. It began with "Dear son and daughter" and ends "With all our kind love to you, your loving father and mother" and I could feel in those words the closeness of the family and Richard and Isabella's warm affection for their children and grandchildren.

"Well, I have something to show to you all" I declared with excitement "You may have wondered why I am so interested in your ancestor Richard Raine, a complete stranger to me until three months ago. Let me start by telling you about a short holiday in Southport last November" and I recounted the events leading to my discovery of Richard's journal in the Royal Arcade bookshop. Pulling the dark brown journal out of my briefcase I told them that Richard's account of his exploits against foreign agents had intrigued me so much I had to find out more about his life.

Richard's Journal

I looked up to see Sue, David, Rene and Pat looking at one another with a puzzled expression. David was the first to speak but I could see he was speaking for all of them.

"I am not sure what you are referring to Fred" and the others concurred "We have never heard of any story about Richard and foreign agents. Does this journal mention something about such an event?"

Strange I thought as it became clear to me that Richard had never spoken to his family about the day he had come across an abandoned schooner and of the adventure that followed.

"If you do not know about that then you are all going to be thrilled when you read Richard's journal" I replied "Unfortunately I did not make copies but I will take some copies and post one to each of you in the next few days. However, in the meantime could I suggest that one of you reads the journal out aloud to everyone?"

"I will read it out" Sue said eagerly and she opened the journal and intently began reading it out slowly and clearly. No one spoke a word as Sue recounted Richard's exploits in finding the Neptun abandoned; discovering Lieutenant

Commander Jack Edward Smith in the aft hold; dropping anchor at Whitby and sending the telegraph to the Admiralty. At this point Sue stopped reading and was visibly thinking about something.

“Hang on a minute” and she left the room and went upstairs returning after a short while with a box in her hand. “My grandmother left this to me. She said it was a family heirloom and I thought it belonged to her but it must have originally belonged to Richard’s wife, Isabella” and she opened the box and took out a beautiful black jet brooch.

The jet brooch inherited by Sue

“Look, the jewellers name is on the box” she said “W. Hamond, Hand Crafted Jewellers, 112 Church Street, Whitby. Established 1860”. It was without doubt the very brooch that Richard had bought in Whitby for Isabella.

Sue could hardly contain her excitement as she continued reading the journal while her cousins sat in stunned disbelief at the story unfolding before them. The near-death experience on Whitby cliffs; the chase by the German naval intelligence agent, Kapitan Sturm in the merchantman Ernst Friedrich; the arrival of HMS Galatea at the last minute and the meeting with Lord Salisbury had everyone rooted to their seats. To their astonishment a further adventure followed just three weeks later when the William Thrift returned from a voyage to the Baltic Sea and Richard Raine uncovered a plot to assassinate Queen Victoria in Dundee and the takeover of the British Parliament by a pro-German group of anarchists. Finally, they were all astounded to hear of the events on Coquet Island and how the Imperial German Navy attempted to steal the most advanced submarine prototype of its age.

As Sue turned over the last page of the journal, she looked at the front cover again and took a deep breathe "I just didn't know he had been involved in anything so dangerous and secretive. We all knew about his terrifying experience when the "William Thrift" was wrecked and lost at Lowestoft but this is something that has come as a complete shock". David, Rene and Pat all echoed the same sentiment and were astonished that this story had not been mentioned at all in the family because had it been known then they would have found out about it when researching the family history. At this point Pat looked at David and said "What about your letter David. Show it to Fred and see what he can make of it". With an acknowledging nod David looked into his bag and after a few moments pulled out a folded letter and passed it to me.

"This has passed down through each generation with a batch of other family papers but we have all looked at it and we haven't a clue where it came from or to what it refers" he exclaimed "What do you make of it?"

I looked at the folded letter. It was not like ordinary writing paper but much thicker – a sort of parchment with an oily texture. Not the sort of paper that would be used for everyday letters. I could see that it had been well looked after as it was in pristine condition for a document that was so old. Opening it up carefully I lifted it up to get the benefit of the light from the window. I slowly read the handwritten text and smiled to myself.

Robert Arthur Talbot Gascoyne-Cecil
Cranbourne House
Cecil Street
London
5th July 1881

My Dear Captain Raine,

I hope this letter finds you in the best of health. I have recently returned from my conference and I am pleased to tell you that the outcome could not have been better. I was able to persuade the delegates of the advantages in signing mutual interest agreements which of course has upset Otto.

I have been informed about the invaluable service you gave on your visit to Dundee and Coquet Island and my employer has instructed me to pass on his best wishes and grateful thanks. He apologises that he cannot personally acknowledge the contribution you made in these two ventures but I have told him I am sure you will understand.

By the way Jack sends his warmest regards.

Very best wishes from your grateful friend,

Robert Gascoyne-Cecil

Turning to Sue and her cousins I laughed "You have just read about the person who wrote this letter. He is mentioned in Richard's journal. Robert Gasgoyne-Cecil was the 3rd Marquess of Salisbury, Foreign Secretary of Great Britain and Ireland and the employer he refers to is the Prime Minister, William Ewart Gladstone. This is a thank you letter from Her Majesty's Government but because of the clandestine nature of the work that was involved it was couched in terms that only Richard would understand."

After a period of understandable silence, the room slowly began to chatter excitedly at the series of fantastic events that had just been revealed. “We had no idea we were going to find out such revelations when we came here today” admitted David “but why did Richard not tell the family about his amazing adventure?”

Shrugging my shoulders, I looked at all four cousins “If you remember that in his journal, he wrote that he accompanied Lieutenant Jack Smith and Captain Armstrong to the master cabin of HMS Galatea and there he was introduced to Lord Salisbury. After thanking Richard Lord Salisbury went on to say he deserved an explanation of the events of the previous two days but before he could reveal the full story, he needed to be assured that Richard would not betray his confidence. Lord Salisbury’s exact words in the journal were” and I turned to the particular paragraph and read “Do you understand the importance of my request that you keep this conversation to yourself and do not repeat what I am about to tell you to anyone my dear sir?” Richard’s reply was “You have made my part in this matter very clear your Lordship. I give you my word that I will not speak of this to anyone”.

“I can only presume” I continued “that Richard, being a gentleman; a man of honour; a family man who believed in the virtues of trust, honesty and integrity naturally believed that if gave his word he should keep his word. So, it is clear that he didn’t tell his crew of the meeting with Lord Salisbury, the plot by the Reich Club and the events on Coquet Island, nor did he tell his sons and daughters. Whether he told Isabella we will never know but I would dare guess he kept his word completely and said nothing. One thing I do know. The history books tell us that the skills that Lord Salisbury practiced in diplomacy were recognised by his contemporaries and he is regarded as one of the greatest statesmen this country has ever known. His work underpinning the Treaty of Berlin sought to conciliate and pacify whilst maintaining important national interests and kept many nations in Europe at peace for more than thirty years until tensions finally erupted causing the outbreak of the First World War. His contribution in safeguarding the security of our nation was recognised by Queen Victoria who awarded him the highest civil honour she could – The Order of the Garter.

The history books also tell us that the keel of the first submarine commissioned by the Royal Navy was laid at the Vickers-Maxim shipyard in Barrow-in-Furness at the end of the 19th century. That submarine was named HMS Holland 1 and she was the first of a six-boat submarine flotilla called the Holland class. In order to keep the boats construction secret HMS Holland 1 was assembled in a building labelled as the "Yacht Shed" and the parts that had to be fabricated in the general yard were marked "for pontoon number 1". A full century later the Institute of Mechanical Engineers awarded the Holland submarines a prestigious award. They recognised the engineering feat of John Holland and Captain William Arthur. The Institute said "This was the vessel that dragged the Royal Navy into the modern era".

I think we should now recognise the part that Richard played in making it possible for Lord Salisbury to successfully out-manoeuvre Otto von Bismarck and for foiling the plans of the Reich Club to assassinate the sovereign and overthrow the democratically elected British Parliament. Who knows what would have happened if Germany had succeeded in developing the science of submarine warfare and completed the Area 55 project on the island of Sylt in the late 19th century. Germany may have instigated World War 1 twenty years earlier with disastrous consequences for our Royal Navy.

History is not history until it is written and until then it can only be "mystery" and so I intend to write about Richards' adventures on board the "William Thrift" and make public the part he played in thwarting von Bismarck's and the

Reich Clubs' plans. Then it will be a real history. After more than one hundred and thirty years of maintaining his secret Captain Richard Raines's story, "**A Master Mariner's Tale"**, will at last be told."

THE END

ACKNOWLEDGEMENTS

My thanks and appreciation are extended to David Angus and Seaham Family History Group for some excellent photographs and illustrations from their collections of the town of Seaham and also to the family and descendants of Richard Raine who provided invaluable information and family photographs that have provided a personal insight into the main character of this book. In particular: -

Sue Roberts, Great, great granddaughter of Richard Raine
David Gray, Great grandson of Richard Raine
Pat Maycroft, Ancestor of Henry Raine (Richard's youngest brother)
Rene Powell, Ancestor of Henry Raine (Richard's youngest brother)

Fred Cooper BSc ACMA CGMA

OTHER BOOKS BY THE AUTHOR

Please visit your favourite eBook retailer to discover

other books by Fred Cooper:

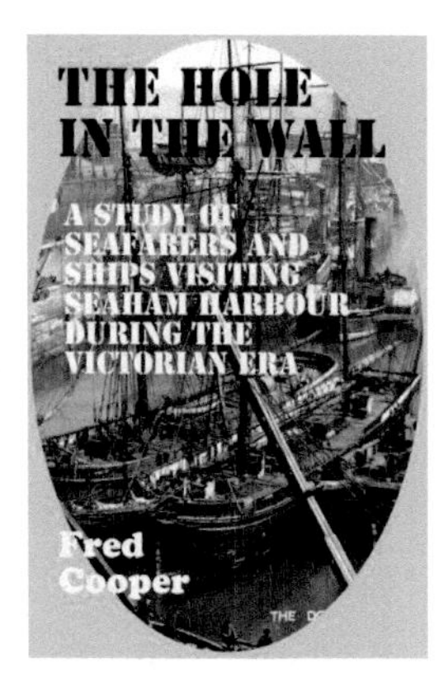

THE HOLE-IN-THE-WALL:

This book is a social history study of a maritime town on the north-east coast of England during the 19th century. The mariners and the sailing ships entering harbour on each census day from 1831 to 1911 are analysed and the results present a clear picture of the lives of mariners in Victorian times.

SHIPBUILDING AT SEAHAM HARBOUR:

The town of Seaham stands proud on the Durham coast in the north-east of England. Seaham once built ships. Not large ships. Not iron ships - with one exception - but fine and sturdy wooden sailing ships. The shipyards are now gone; the patent slipways, pontoons, dry docks, workshops are all gone and no trace remains to remind Seaham of this once flourishing industry. The ships built at Seaham Harbour are here no longer. They either sank or were sent to the breakers yard many years ago. This book documents the fine history of shipbuilding at Seaham Harbour between 1832 and 1899.

HISTORY OF THE SEAHAM INFIRMARY

The 18th and 19th century was a torrid time for the sick, elderly and maimed in the United Kingdom. Care for the sick, injured, mentally ill and aged were provided from a variety of sources none of which was centrally planned or co-ordinated. The population of Seaham Harbour was rapidly expanding in the 1830's and 1840's with many new industrial and commercial ventures starting up and a rapidly expanding township. The time was right for some form of medical, surgical and nursing provision at Seaham Harbour. This is the definitive history of the Seaham Infirmary from 1844 to 1969.

A HISTORY OF THE LONDONDERRY LITERARY INSTITUTE, SEAHAM HARBOUR:

This book documents the definitive history of The Londonderry Institute at Seaham from it's opening in 1855. Built to serve the town as a Literary Institute it evolved into a focal point for public and social groups that bound the fabric of the community together. As it approached its centenary year it appeared to have reached the end of its useful life but the town would not let it be demolished.

SPORTING PASTIMES AT SEAHAM HARBOUR

The development of sport as a social pastime began to grow from the mid-19th century when working people began to enjoy the concept of the "weekend" when they did not work. This exploration of sporting pastimes at Seaham Harbour covers the period from 1835 through to the mid-20th century when sport and recreational activities were woven into the very social fabric of every-day life in the town.

A HISTORY OF THE CHURCHES AT SEAHAM

Churches are, for some, central to their spiritual existence and an important part of their day-to-day life. To some people visiting churches is a hobby. To others, churches are places they wander into whilst on holiday to look around, to sit and meditate in the quiet and to absorb the tranquillity of the occasion. Often the visitor's book is signed with comments such as beautiful, lovely or fascinating but do people really know anything about the building they have looked around? Do they know who built the church; why it was built; why it was erected in that location and at that time; what difficulties were encountered; where did the funding come from and what events or unique features set it apart from other churches? This book provides the answers to all of these questions about the twenty-four churches, past and present that were built in Seaham.

THE 2nd DURHAM (SEAHAM) ARTILLERY VOLUNTEERS

The 2nd Durham (Seaham) Artillery Volunteers were raised in 1860 at Seaham Harbour. More than 7,000 men from the colliery districts of Seaham, Silksworth, Rainton and Durham enrolled as members of the Corps. For three generations these men had a distinguished record amongst the Volunteer Artillery Brigades of Britain. This book is a record of the history and past service of the Old 2nd Durham's. Their descendants have a right to be proud of their record and achievement.

ONE YEAR OF HELL

The author spent much of his childhood living in the pit village and community of Seaham Colliery. The pit yard at the bottom of the street was his playground during the day and at night he fell asleep with the sounds of the busy colliery ringing in his ears. He knew about the tragic 1880 Seaham Colliery Disaster that killed 164 men and boys – everyone did – but during the research for this book he was totally unprepared to learn about the unbearable pain and heartache suffered by the pit community. This book chronicles the grief and hardship of the widows and children of the victims that perished in the horrific explosion. This is the story of "One Year of Hell" in the history of Seaham.

THE BOER WAR VOLUNTEERS FROM SEAHAM

This book provides the reader with the details of events to explain the progress of the Boer War from 1899 until its conclusion in 1902. However, the main purpose of the book is to record the contributions made by, and the real-life experiences, of men from Seaham during the conflict. The people of Seaham need to remember the courage, bravery and exploits of the Volunteers from their town who fought and died when their country called them to arms.

If you enjoy these books please take a moment to leave a review for the book with your favourite eBook retailer. Why not visit my website at https://seahampast.co.uk and read more remarkable stories about Seaham.

Thank you

NOTES

The Georgian North Dock under conversion to a Marina in 2012